As the
Red Carnation
Fades

Feyza Hepçilingirler

Translated by Mark David Wyers

Milet Publishing
Smallfields Cottage, Cox Green
Rudgwick, Horsham, West Sussex
RH12 3DE England
info@milet.com
www.milet.com
www.milet.co.uk

First English edition published by Milet Publishing in 2015

Copyright © Milet Publishing, 2015

ISBN 978 1 84059 938 1

First published in Turkish as *Kırmızı Karanfil Ne Renk Solar?* in 1998

Funded by the Turkish Ministry of Culture and Tourism TEDA Project

Printed and bound in Turkey by Ertem Matbaası

Feyza Hepçilingirler was born in 1948 in Ayvalık, Turkey. After she finished high school in Izmir, she studied in the Department of Turkish Language and Literature at Istanbul University and then began working as a lecturer in Izmir. Following the military coup of 1980, which resulted in martial law and the widespread persecution of leftists, Feyza Hepçilingirler was banned from teaching in the Aegean region. In 1983, she was reassigned to Karadeniz University in the city of Trabzon, whereupon she resigned in protest and moved back to Izmir, where she worked at various private preparatory schools. *As the Red Carnation Fades*, a groundbreaking feminist novel in Turkish literature, draws upon her experiences in those turbulent times. She later moved to Istanbul, where she is currently a lecturer at Yıldız Technical University and a columnist for the newspaper *Cumhuriyet*. Her short stories and novels and have received a number of awards, including the Sait Faik Short Story Award and the Sedat Simavi Literary Award, and they have been translated into several languages.

Mark David Wyers was born in Los Angeles, California, and received his BA in literature from the University of Tampa in Florida. In 2008, he completed his MA in Turkish studies at the University of Arizona. His book *"Wicked" Istanbul: The Regulation of Prostitution in the Early Turkish Republic*, a historical study of gender and the politics of urban space in Turkey, was published in 2012. Numerous short stories he has translated have appeared in journals and anthologies, including *Istanbul in Women's Short Stories, Europe in Women's Short Stories from Turkey* and *Aeolian Visions/Versions: Modern Classics and New Writing from Turkey*, all published by Milet. His translation of Selim Ileri's novel *Boundless Solitude*, also published by Milet, was released in 2014.

Editorial Notes

Throughout this novel, we have retained the Turkish for several types of terms, including personal names, honorifics, place names and foods, among others. We have used the English spelling of Istanbul, rather than its Turkish spelling, İstanbul, because the English version is so commonly known. For the Turkish terms, we have used italics in their first instance and then normal text for subsequent instances. We have not italicized the Turkish honorifics that form part of a name, such as Bey and Hanım, to avoid splitting the name visually with a style change. A list of the Turkish honorifics that appear in the book follows.

Turkish Honorifics

Abi (Colloquial of Ağabey): Older brother, also used as an honorific for men.

Abla: Older sister, also used as an honorific for women.

Bey: A respectful term of address used after a man's first name.

Hanım: A respectful term of address used after a woman's first name.

Hoca: A respectful way of addressing a teacher.

Hoca'nım: A combination of hoca and hanım; a respectful way of addressing a female teacher.

Hanım ablacığım: A kind form of address for a woman who is older than the speaker.

Teyze: Aunt, also used to express respect when addressing a woman.

Guide to Turkish Pronunciation

Turkish letters that appear in the novel and which may be unfamiliar are shown below, with a guide to their pronunciation

c   as *j* in *just*

ç   as *ch* in *child*

ğ   silent letter that lengthens the preceding vowel

ı   as *a* in *along*

ö   as German *ö* in *Köln*, or French *œ* in *œuf*

ş   as *sh* in *ship*

ü   as German *ü* in *fünf*, or French *u* in *tu*

^   accent over vowel that lengthens the vowel

Dedicated to the youth

1

We approach the darkness
Because we cannot turn away from it.
—Gülten Akın

Alright, he says; but this "alright" means: hurry up, aren't you ready yet? I can't get ready as quickly as he wants. When he tells me to hurry, I become even more flustered, and whatever I do takes twice as long.

As I fumble around trying to find socks for my daughter and tell my son to change his shirt, I realize that I forgot to put on lipstick.

Not that shirt, don't you see the stain on the sleeve? Here, wear this one with a red sweater. You've put your socks on inside out, put them on again. Now, don't pout, you can't go around with your socks on inside out.

I never lose a button. But in this house, whenever a button falls off, it's gone forever.

Where am I going to find a matching button for my shirt cuff? You won't; I'll look for one. The lost button is a disaster; he paces impatiently, shoes on and coat draped over his arm, each step implying "hurry, hurry." The tragedy of a typical family faced with the calamity of a missing button. You shuffle through drawers and overturn every box in search of a button.

Sibel Hanım, you can put on your lipstick later, right now you should help your husband with that button.

Son, brush your hair and untuck your collar. Look in the mirror and make yourself look decent! Haluk, will this button be okay? It's the same size, but the color is a little different.

No, of course that won't do. Keep looking. I turn to my daughter:

Now brush off your shoes, but don't wait for me to help you put them on. Son, your pant cuff is caught in your sock, pull it out. Haluk, I can't find the same button, but I found this. It's a little bigger than the other one . . .

Okay fine, just forget about it, I'll wear a different jacket.

If you're going to wear something else, why did you have me spend the last hour looking for a button? In that case, I'll put on my lipstick.

Are we ready? Yes, we're ready. Let's go. Just a minute, kids, I haven't brushed my hair yet. Call the elevator, I'll be there in a minute.

My gaze lingers on the yellow blouse I'd placed on the bed earlier that day. It's too late. I'll have to go out in what I'm wearing, though I've never liked this dress. The few times I've worn it, I've found myself filled with dread, as if at any moment bad news will come my way. I have just enough time to glance at myself in the mirror, and I tug my dress down around my waist. The children call out from the front door: Come on, Mom! I know that I'll never be a good housewife. How adept housewives must be! And look at me: unable to start an evening on time, always making someone upset. How will I manage to get through the night? That will be clear soon enough, at Hülya's place.

Out of breath, I dash into the elevator. As always, when I look at myself for the last time, scrutinizing myself through the eyes of a housewife going for a night out with her family, the woman in the mirror howls back at me, mocking me for all the faults and failures I hadn't noticed: I hadn't put on any earrings, I wasn't wearing a single ring except for my wedding band, and yet again I had forgotten to put on perfume. In the end, my failure as a woman, as a housewife, overwhelms me. Was it possible *not* to think of Birsen? If she'd been in my place, she would've started getting ready in the morning, and with a fastidiousness that testifies to her womanhood, made sure that everyone was just as ready as herself well before it was time to go out. And now, as she was taking her last steps toward the elevator, with easy grace she would look over the perfection of her preparations one last time; she would be ready to bask in the nods of approval lavished on her by the hosts of the evening, the woman of the house and her husband, as she glanced at the other guests with the air of a successful housewife. Of course she would've put on accessories that perfectly matched her outfit, and sprayed a dash of perfume behind her ear and just a little on the roots of her hair—the scent lingers longer that way—and unlike me, she wouldn't have been out of breath as she strode in her high-heeled shoes, always the first to get in the elevator and the car, the first to be welcomed through the doorway, always commanding respect. Despair clutches at my heart. I know that I could never compete with Birsen—why was I even thinking about her?—and as I step into the elevator, I realize that Haluk has just been complaining about me; I can see it in the faces of our children. I'm angry with Haluk because he talked about me behind my back and didn't let me stand up in my own defense. But at the same time, I know that I can't blame him. And he knows that I know this about myself: I'll never be a good housewife. Maybe he hasn't seen it as clearly as I have. Naturally, I am much more aware of this fact than him. At least he hasn't yet said to me, "My mother isn't at home with us, that's why everything's a mess." Don't drag it out, Sibel Hanım, it's obvious that you're inept! Why are you getting upset with Haluk? But why shouldn't I get upset? If I have the right to get angry with myself, I have the right to be irritated with Haluk for not saying to my face what he dared say behind my back.

My expression sullen and tense, I pucker my lips, rubbing in a daub of lipstick. I rub a little of the red onto my cheeks; there, that's better. My daughter is standing on tiptoe, trying to look at herself in the mirror. If I don't break the tension, I know that it will hang over us all night long. Yes, we need to relax and at least look like a normal family going out for the night. There is still some lipstick on the end of my finger; I rub it on the tip of my daughter's nose. Everyone laughs, but it's my son who laughs the most, giggling hysterically— meaning he's angry that his father complained about me.

How's school? I ask Hülya. Well, you know, she says; but I sense that soon enough she'll launch into a tirade, speaking of rumors I've heard already. Hülya complains incessantly about everything: the difficulty of preparing her courses, the fact that she doesn't even have time to read a newspaper and hasn't even started grading her midterm exams. Then she shows me some new paintings she bought. I don't like the colors in this one, she says, so I'm going to give it to my husband for his office. Here, I could ask a pointed question to reveal her lack of knowledge on the subject of art; but I have no desire to get involved in that discussion. She might tell me that she was rather good at drawing in middle school and that her art teacher had lavished praise on her work, or she might launch into a more intellectual diatribe, and say something like: Oh no, dear, it's nothing like that . . . And then she'll vaunt her "knowledge" of art that she's picked up here and there. But tonight I don't have the energy for either option.

On the other side of the room, the men are engaged in "male" discussions. Inflation is on the rise; they are concerned about the high interest rates. While I haven't been expressly forbidden from joining the conversation, I know that right isn't firmly in my grasp; that's why I don't show any interest in taking part. At first they will listen with rapt attention, as if what I said is the most fascinating thing in the world, and then they'll just pick up where they left off. No, that's not how it is; I'm doing them an injustice. Am I trying to suggest that, as the enlightened men of our nation, they don't let women voice their opinions? No, let's not be unfair to these gentlemen, because later they won't take my side. This is me not joining the conversation because I don't find these "eternal issues" sufficiently interesting. Of course, the gentlemen would be fascinated to hear my profound thoughts on the topic, but because I find Hülya's complaints more entertaining, I decide to keep my insights to myself.

Patiently I wait for Hülya to start talking about the university. It's just a matter of time before, in the course of her complaints, she brings up her favorite topic.

How have you been? Yalçın asks. Apparently they hit upon a solution to the interest rate problem. Playing along, I offer a wry reply. I enjoy mocking myself. At the beginning of each month I go to the university to pick up my salary. After that, there's no need for me to go back for the rest of the month. We've made an agreement. They don't like seeing me around, and I don't like seeing them either. We put up with it, annoying as it may be; but we've learned to tolerate each other for that one day. Of course, I'm lying to Yalçın. I don't tell him that every other day, or at least every other two days, I stroll about under the linden trees on campus. Nor do I say how much this exasperates the dean. Hoca'nım, you really don't need to come all this way. Why not relax and enjoy the comfort of your home? We can even pass your salary along to your husband if you want . . . Listening to Yalçın, I try to drive the dean's repulsive face from my thoughts.

Listen, he says, I'm serious. How can they pay you if they don't give you work? I mean, if they're not giving you courses to teach?

I'm not complaining, I say. I've gotten used to getting paid for nothing. Just think, what if they tried to make me work now! Look at Hülya's situation. Grading papers, researching, preparing courses . . . She doesn't even have time to read the newspaper. And me? Not a care in the world. I've got so much time on my hands that I'm thinking of taking up bridge.

Stop being flippant, Yalçın says. You've got a right to sue them. Why don't you take them to court? Put the dean in the witness stand.

Look, I say, I'd like nothing more than that, but I really doubt that they're going to put him on the stand because of me. So it's you, they'll say, insinuating that I was guilty of something. Haluk is listening. Hülya goes to the kitchen to make coffee. In my mind's eye, I see myself standing in front of my students. I'm not afraid of anyone, I tell them. One of your classmates filed a complaint against me. But in this country of ours, we have justice. They can't sentence anybody unjustly (I swallow—even if I don't believe what I'm saying, I have to appear strong. But still, when I continue speaking, I can't prevent a certain weakness from creeping into my voice).

During the class break, a student approached me, holding out a book that I'd once said I liked. It's a gift, he said. On the first page he'd written: In praise of your strength in seeking out the truth. But I don't see anything worthy of praise in what I've done. Is it because everyone else scuttled off in fear that I was left exposed? Why is it that my words aroused so much admiration and astonishment? It was nothing new; everyone knows it, or at least could easily learn more about it. A scientific approach, a class that encourages debate, a free atmosphere. I didn't invent those things. Is the university not open to free thinking, or is it because I'm a new faculty member who isn't afraid of speaking her mind?

I thanked my student without revealing that the gift of the book, and what was written inside, heartened me. Naim is a well-read, intelligent young man, and even he is in awe of my courage, is that so? Sibel, stay strong! This voice I hear speaking in my thoughts— whose is it? I know that it's not my father's, but all the same, I ascribe it to him and, seeing myself becoming stronger little by little, I continue. That is, until I come crashing up against a wall that's harder than I'd ever imagined. And now, up against that wall that stopped me in my tracks, I ponder over what I should do.

I can't take them to court, I tell Yalçın. I know that they're waiting for me to make a mistake. Suing them would do nothing but drive me into their trap. I have no other choice but to wait. How long will they keep me in limbo like this, and what explanations will they come up with? Yalçın, displeased with my decision, merely grumbles in response.

So long as everyone bows down before them, they'll be free to do as they please. Haluk agrees with me. And Hülya says exactly what I thought she'd say:

You can't fight back against people like that, my dear. They'll just drag you into more trouble . . . No, no, there's nothing to be done with people like them.

Drinking gin and tonic is the latest fashion. For some reason, tonight the gin is going to my head more quickly than usual.

You don't want to know what's been happening at the university, Hülya says. As if I hadn't asked her a while ago, and she hadn't said, Well, you know.

So, what happened?

You remember Huriye Hanım, Gürcan Bey, Sevim and the other one, the bald guy who is a bit overweight. I think he was the chair of the Department of Sciences when we started working there. What was his name?

Cemal Bey, I say.

Yes, Cemal Bey. Well, they're all under investigation. If you heard why, you'd just die of laughter!

What is it? I ask. Politics, like me?

Nothing political at all. The men have been accused of having relationships with their female colleagues and students, while the women have been accused of doing the same with the men at the school. They're calling it something like "emotional liaisons."

No, I'm not dying of laughter. On the contrary, I'm fuming. They've completely lost it, I hiss. In fact, that's not really what I wanted to say, but I couldn't think of anything else. Have they really started investigating people's emotional relationships? Such things can't even be proven. Are they really trying to find out if there have been student-teacher affairs? Just what's that supposed to mean, "emotional liaisons" between faculty members and students?

Aren't Sevim Hanım and Gürcan Bey married? Haluk asks.

Of course they're married, Hülya titters. It's not about their love for each other. Rather, it's about their "illegitimate" relations with members of the opposite sex.

It grates on my nerves that Hülya is gossiping about her friends as we sip our gin and tonic. Yalçın chimes in:

Are they really doing that?

Yalçın, not you too! I say. We're talking about levelheaded people here. Our friends!

With my response, I destroyed any chance that the topic could turn into pleasant banter. It was clear what those conspirators wanted to achieve with their slander. But didn't they know that they'd never be able to disgrace well-respected people like them? Their goal was to raise suspicions and create tension; afterward, they'd sift through the ruins. Don't we all know what our dear dean did as soon as our program was recognized by the Board of Higher Education? Going against all the laws, weren't those militant faculty members being re-hired to fill the ranks of the school despite the injunction that they were "not to be employed as instructors"? And to achieve their ends, they were willing to sully the names of these respected teachers and make the atmosphere so tense that, unable to bear this repulsive state of affairs, they would leave, one by one . . . I understand this tactic of attrition; but preventing it, even describing it, is difficult, practically impossible.

Just forget about it, the men say in the end, as if they hadn't been speaking as vehemently as us. Isn't there anything else we can talk about, they say, another topic of conversation? Fine, but that won't drive those nightmarish thoughts about the school from my mind. Huriye Hanım comes to mind. Never having married, Huriye Hanım dedicated all of her time and energy to the school, and she addressed fresh recruits from high school as equals, treating them like teachers with years of experience. So what would she, Huriye Hanım, understand when they said she was having "emotional relationships" with her male students? Yes, they are very dear to me, both the men and the women, she'd say. You said emotional, right? Most certainly; aside from them, I have no one else in my life. No mother, no father, no children. They're all I have. And what if she said to them: What of it?

And then took "emotional relationships" to mean what she wanted it to mean, not how they were trying to describe it? Is that what it is? "An emotional relationship with a member of the opposite sex"? Huriye Hanım should lash back with one of those quips of hers that make people burst into laughter. They'll think she's just leading them on, but let them. You believe in it, that's what matters. Say it just like you did to us, with plain honesty: Dear sir, teachers hold the future in the palms of their hands; think on that when you say the word "teacher." Did Ataturk place his faith in teachers for nothing, was his reliance on them in vain? They should always be at the forefront of society, as they have been for thirty years, forty years, fifty years. If they don't lead the way, who will hold the torch on the paths to science, art and civilization?

The image of Huriye Hanım lingers in my mind's eye. Before the school was turned into a college, when it was still the School of Education, Huriye Hoca gave the "first lesson" at the opening sessions. Composed, adept in her work, she is among the last of a generation of teachers who are on the verge of disappearing forever. So stubborn that even when she feels that everyone is mocking her rhetoric for being outdated, she doesn't retreat a single inch; she's a woman who doesn't hold back and strikes with the truths she believes in, like a slap across the face.

Hülya brings me another gin and tonic; I hadn't even noticed that I'd finished the first one. There is more gin than tonic, and I find myself fascinated with the lemon seeds floating aimlessly in the glass. Look, I think about saying, sharing my observations with them, now it's going to rise to the surface, and then float back down to the bottom. But of course they'd think I was being preposterous, and they would be right; no matter, I don't feel like talking anyway. Not saying a word, I fix my gaze on the lemon seed teetering at the bottom of the glass. No one would ever guess what I'm waiting to see. I'm afraid that Hülya might think there's something wrong and try to change my glass. For a moment, the sharp end of the seed turns up, as if it will rise upwards, but then it sinks to the bottom again. Countless comparisons are running through my mind, and after I've had a few drinks, I'm powerless against the absurd wanderings of my imagination. The head rises up, and when its face hits the surface with a smack, it plunges downwards again. Like me? No, not at all. Till now, I've never turned back from anything. I've never seen such a versatile seed in all my life; it's ready to become everything. Now it has become Haluk, shouting at me, roaring louder and louder. Then he apologizes: Please forgive me, dear, I'm so tired today. I don't even know who to be angry with. Now it's the dean of our school. Hoca'nım, please try to understand, this is far beyond me. Believe me, there's nothing I can do. Rubbing his hands together, he says: I don't have any authority on the matter. And then he drops down, down, all the way down, striking his head on the bottom, without once looking up.

Haluk suddenly asks: What's in your glass? Why are you staring at your glass like that? Like a child caught red-handed, I try to protect my toy, cupping my hand around the glass to conceal the lemon seed.

Nothing, I say. Nothing at all.

Yalçın says: We were just talking about going somewhere this weekend. What do you think?

I'd say that every day is the weekend for me. What should I say?

A clipped warning from Haluk: Don't start on that again. Now he'll turn and complain that I'm overly sensitive. But in fact, I'm not. I'm none of those things he thinks about me. If he thinks that I'm emotional, I'm not, and if he thinks that I'm logical, then I'm not that either. I'm just me, trying to succeed in being myself. Someone who attaches no importance to being, or appearing to be, something other than what I am.

Where shall we go?

Let's go somewhere outside the city. There are some nice fish restaurants along the coast, we could go to one of those.

We could. It doesn't matter to me. Özlem is getting tired and wants to sleep in my lap. Even though I know Haluk will be angry, I let her. At least she'll get some rest before he notices.

Sibel dear, what's there to be so upset about? Hülya asks. I wish I could be in your position. How wonderful, you're at home and get to spend time with your children, and you're still getting your salary. Her attitude irritates me; I may have mocked my situation, but that doesn't give her the right to do the same.

No, Hülya, it's not as easy as you think, I say, and the smirk falls from her lips; I derive a sly pleasure from this. I continue: I had a lifestyle that I was used to, an order in my life that I created, that I loved and cherished. Everything I built up is in ruins now, don't you understand that? I know she doesn't understand.

You're right, she says. Of course it's difficult. But I don't go on about why it's difficult for the simple reason that I don't want to put her in an even more awkward position. Indeed, what is the difficulty? That I'm unused to sitting at home every day being a housewife, or that I suddenly found myself wrenched away, for reasons I couldn't fathom, from my students who listened so eagerly to my lectures? Is it that I feel like I'm speaking in footnotes, but am overcome by a desire to discuss things at length? Is that my frustration? Or is it that I'm getting paid without doing any work, but wish that I could teach even if I were paid but a pittance? Hülya Hanım, what is it that I find so difficult?

I've lost interest in the lemon seed. These absurd notions settle into my thoughts and then I can't let them go. How stupid of me!

I'm angry with myself because these people wouldn't hesitate to mock me and I practically led them to these trite remarks. Just then, Haluk notices that Özlem is asleep in my lap.

Is she asleep? he asks. Without waiting for my reply, he adds: How are we going to take her home? Why did you let her fall asleep? Couldn't she have stayed awake for another half hour? With my usual obstinacy, I bite back the urge to say: I'll carry her myself. No, I shouldn't upset Haluk. He's my friend, my husband, not my enemy. Suddenly I realize that I'm a complete stranger in this setting. A refrain runs through my mind like the incessant pounding of a doorknocker: I'm not one of these people. People like this, accustomed to looking down on others, couldn't be my friends. Soon enough, however, this voice finds its counterpart: And just who are you? Indeed, you're one of them, so enough of this desire to look down on others from this pedestal you've created for yourself.

Grasping the broom, Sibel tries to sweep in rapid strokes; aware of her grandmother's piercing gaze, however, she can't sweep as vigorously as she wants and keeps sweeping again and again the same tiny patch of ground. Her strength is sapped by the storm she knows is about to break out. She knows her grandmother's glare; it speaks of silent shrieks, gathering together, building up, and soon it will glow and the coals will be whipped aflame and spew forth. When she looks at her like that, she can't sweep, she can't do anything. She could offer to bring some water, or ask if there is anything her grandmother needs from the corner shop . . . No, that wouldn't do. She'd know that Sibel was trying to sneak off. That would just fan the flames of the eruption: My, my, you're a clever little girl, aren't you? The sweeping is done, and now you're going to fetch some water! And after that, run down to the shop! Doesn't she just do everything? What a girl! What a girl she is, by God!

Not looking up in the direction of her grandmother, who stands there glowering at her, Sibel sweeps with all her strength; but the harder she tries, the heavier the broom feels. She can barely lift it. What if she stopped for a moment and shook the pain out of her wrists or straightened up and blew on her palms . . . No, she knows what will happen next: Is the little lady all worn out? Ah, what a pity, a terrible pity!

Then the pandemonium breaks loose: Do you call that sweeping? You're not sweeping, you're petting the ground! Quit messing around and hold the broom tightly with two hands; put a little muscle into it! Are you playing around! Girl, you've got no heart for work. It's just like they say: If you try to force someone to work, they'll bungle it. You're just stalling, waiting for me to take the broom and tell you: This is how it's done! That's why you're just loafing around, isn't it?! What a little twerp you are! It's a good thing I still have my health. If I had to rely on you for anything, I'd die of filth first! Leave it! Off with you, wherever you're going. Get out of my sight!

Sibel backs away, not saying a word, placing the broom on the ground. Her grandmother snatches it up and begins sweeping furiously. Just like she instructed Sibel, she scrapes the bristles across the ground in fierce snaps. Sibel marvels at the strength in those frail wrists, wondering why she doesn't have the same. Eyes wide she watches: How powerfully she sweeps, look at all the dust she churns up! And she wonders if she'll be as strong as that when she grows up. Her wrists are thin, and her fingers don't even reach around the handle of the broom. If she grasps it at the base, her fingers hardly reach a quarter of the way around, and if she holds it at the end, where her fingers can actually curl around the handle, the broom is little better than a fan and threatens to fly out of her grip at any moment. When she gets older, she'll learn, when her fingers have grown a little longer. But will they ever grow? Her grandma's are thin, bony and blue with veins; but will hers be strong like that?

She is rooted to the spot, watching, and then her grandmother snaps: Why are you standing there? You're getting covered in dust, go somewhere else. Sibel backs away, unsure where she should go or what she should do. If she goes out into the street, her grandma will get angry; if she reads something, her grandma will complain; if she tries to play with her dolls, her grandma will snatch them out of her hands and toss them away, maybe even try to tear them to pieces. When will she play with her dolls? When she gets older? She knows what her grandma wants; thrusting fabric and thread into Sibel's hands, she says: Take this, do some embroidery. She hides the bundle of cloth again and again, but her grandma always finds it, shoving it into her hands. One day when you get married, she says, this is what you'll need, not books. I'm not going to get married, Sibel says. Her grandma's answer is always at the ready: We'll see about that. I've heard plenty of girls say the same. And they're always the first ones to get hitched.

She becomes furious when her grandmother speaks like that. Get hitched! All those long years of studies before her! A husband is the last thing on her mind. She's going to study so she can be a teacher and make her own money. No one's going to make her carry bundles of food in torn net bags. She'll send money so that her grandma can look after her younger brother. Maybe she'll help her uncle get married. While she may not like Zümrüt, she loves her uncle. Let him have that Zümrüt!

Hiding her book in her coat, she takes the fabric and thread from where she hid it last time. I'm going to visit Birsen, we're going to do some sewing. I have the fabric, she says. That's embroidery, not sewing, her grandma snaps. That means she can go. And off she goes. Before sliding down the balustrade, she glances around for her grandma; good, she's not looking.

But somehow she knows that you slid down. How does that woman know everything? You're going to break the balustrade! You won't be happy till you break it to pieces. You and your brother . . .

She closes the door on her grandma's voice. Why is she bringing her brother into it now? Orhan hasn't done anything wrong. He's not even

15

at home! Whatever the case, it's always the same: The two of you! You and your brother!

Is Birsen at home by any chance? What's she doing? Sibel knocks on the door.

Your parents aren't home?

No, they went out. Let's go upstairs.

Without asking why, Sibel follows her upstairs and hands the embroidery to Birsen. Here, do some stitching. You like it. And then she takes out her book.

For a while, Birsen embroiders in silence. Sibel knows that she'll never be able to embroider that well; does her grandma really believe that Sibel did that overstitch and backstitch? When she gets home, her grandma will ask for the fabric: Now let me see what the two of you have done. That's what she says: The two of you. Meaning that she knows, or if she doesn't know for sure, she can sense that Birsen did it. And that's fine; it's better when her grandma doesn't say anything.

After a while, Birsen asks: Aren't we going to talk?

I'm reading.

Did you come here to read?

My grandma won't let me read at home.

Birsen suddenly begins to cry.

What's wrong? Are you mad that I'm reading? Okay, I'll stop. Don't cry, please!

If you show me that you love me, I won't cry.

Okay, but how?

Touch me. Kiss me.

Kiss you? What, like a boy?

It's not just boys who kiss girls. You can kiss me too.

No, I can't.

Yes, you can. Like this.

I know how to kiss, but I don't want to.

What's gotten into her, Sibel wonders, to make her act this way? She was just trying to get away from her grandma . . . My God! Birsen has never been like this before.

Why? Don't you love me?

Of course I do. But I can't kiss you. It wouldn't be right.

You're a coward! Can you show me yours?

What of mine?

Let me show you. Look, like this! If you're not afraid, show me yours.

But why?

I'm just curious to see if yours is fuzzy or not.

Aren't you afraid your mother will come home?

They won't be back till tonight. They went somewhere far away.

Birsen, stop, you're hurting me.

Stupid, it doesn't hurt! I'm not doing anything bad. I'm just touching you.

Stop it. I don't want to be touched.

Get out of here then!

Fine, I was leaving anyway.

She straightens out her panties and gets up. What if her grandma somehow senses that they did something bad? She knows everything. Just as she's walking out the door, she realizes that she forgot her book and fabric. I'll get it later, she thinks. But I can't come back. He mother will be here, and when she looks at my face she'll understand that we did something bad. I can't ever come back. When she goes upstairs, she finds Birsen stroking and squeezing her breasts, which are little bigger than plums. If you tell anyone, I'll kill you. I won't tell anyone. Not a soul.

On her way home, she thinks: How could I tell anyone? Birsen touched me down there, and then later was squeezing her breasts. How could I tell anyone that?

What happened? You're back early, her grandma asks. I'm tired. I'm going to take a nap. Under her grandma's questioning gaze, she takes a blanket from the closet and pulls it up over herself, thinking about Birsen. Why, how, for what? But there was no answer.

Look, Haluk, I say, I can't go on living like this, do you understand? We need to work this out as soon as we can. What am I now? An instructor, or a housewife? I have to know. Getting paid for being an instructor while living as a housewife is killing my pride. It's like I'm taking money that I don't deserve, and what's worse, I feel like I'm stealing. Why don't they just fire me? If they don't want me there, why don't they get rid of me? Why are they dragging it out like this?

I know that Haluk won't give me a satisfactory answer. Who could?

Do what you always do and just laugh it off, he says.

Laugh what off? The only person I'm scorning here is myself, don't you see that?

I know that it's just temporary. And I despise things that are temporary. When will it end? For a long while now I've been hung up on the idea of not how but when it's going to end. Isn't this what they're really after? To demoralize you, drag you away from yourself? It's easier, it takes less effort.

Haluk takes me in his arms and tries to pull me to bed. I don't want to. Tonight I really don't want to. All's well in his life, no one meddles with him. His work hasn't been put on hold and he has no fear of being reduced to a housewife. Did I study for all those years just to stay at home? Over and over that sentence echoes in my mind. And if I don't say it out loud, I'll lose my mind. And I say it, as Haluk trails his lips over the curve of my leg:

Did I study for all those years just to be a housewife?

Raising his head, he looks at me in surprise. No matter what I say, his faith in me is unshakable, and he pulls away.

Okay, I can see that you don't want to make love, he says. Overjoyed at the liberating effect of the words falling from my lips, I get out of bed. I'm going to smoke a cigarette in the living room, and fume at "them." And that means including Haluk along with them; out of sheer obstinacy I'll smoke. And maybe have a drink too, why not? To hell with them all.

I remember the first time I entered the classroom. Like high school students, they were all ready to size me up. Let's have a look, what kind of teacher will she be? They thought that I was a little young. The first impression wasn't very positive. Why you? one student mystifyingly asked. Our teacher was good, there was no reason for her to leave. Well, I said, they had to assign me a course to teach, and here I am. They laughed. Another student wanted me to tell them about myself. Where did I graduate from, where have I worked, what experience do I have? I told them. But I remained silent on the fact that I didn't get the job because of my political views, nor did I tell that that I had the highest score on the exam administered by the ministry; I didn't want them to think I was boasting. I talked about the other schools where I'd worked and how long I worked there, and little by little that first impression began to fade away. I wasn't as inexperienced as they thought. They were on the verge of being won over. Then I heard a girl's voice, emotional and slightly childish: We really liked our old teacher. Her classmates laughed. And you'll like me too, I bantered. Thank God for hope.

For months I taught that class of students. Slowly, I was trying to bring about a higher level of acculturation. I livened up the classes with debates. Not everyone responded in the same way to the tearing down of the truths to which they held. Some became rapt and said: How could that be? Others fell silent and accepted it. None of them had ever learned to think on their own; they clung tenaciously to the most accessible positions they could find and balked at the slightest breeze that threatened to set them aflutter, because if those beliefs were to fall in ruins, there was nothing to take their place. And when they tried with all their might to maintain a certain position and found it crumbling around them, they would hold a grudge against me, as though I'd rent their homes asunder and left them in the open. You do it, you find the answer, I told them, and they became agitated. They were accustomed to being given prefabricated walls. And then, thinking that they had made those walls themselves, they set them up as if the walls were there to serve their beliefs and couldn't possibly be arranged any other way. Afterwards, they saw the resulting structure as their own creation. But it was little more than a cardboard model folded along the creases. That's not how it is, I told them. Even if you wanted, you couldn't have come up with anything different. I'm giving you bricks so that you can build up your own walls. Some thought that the perspectives they believed in were based on claims made by Ziya Gökalp; but when I had them study the works of Gökalp and offered my insights, their models of thought fell to pieces. This is Gökalp, I'd say; he never said what you claimed he did. Isn't it time now for you to reappraise your beliefs? When they would take up a certain view of Mehmet Akif, for example, I would read them some of his poems that say the exact opposite. You may not believe it, I'd say, but Akif wrote those lines too. How could that be? He has more foresight than you, doesn't he?

The truths that I left lying in shambles in their minds took their toll. They filed complaints left and right, and then one day, after midnight, I find myself smoking cigarettes and thinking about them. My hands are tied. They didn't even tell me, You're dangerous, that's why we're not letting you teach.

* * *

The dean didn't personally summon me to his office, but he dispatched an order concerning preparations for a ceremony. Dropping hints, he suggested that some cleaning up needed to be done at the school. He said he had plausible reasons. Some objectionable personages are still being discussed in the classroom, he said. I have eyes and ears everywhere. Meaning: I've got my eye on you. A threat of sorts. At a later meeting, when the dean said, My antennae are far-reaching, it came as no surprise. He reeled off the names of some of those "objectionable" figures. Nâzım Hikmet, Sabahattin Ali . . . Can we still talk about people like that? he asked. Can we even say their names? Why, yes, I said, smiling. You just said them yourself, meaning that, if need be, they can be said aloud. He looked at me incredulously; all that remained in his mind was his objection to the fact that I'd said that those people can indeed be discussed. And I made no effort to explain away my comment. The thought crossed my mind: Why are such ignorant people appointed as deans?

Later, he discussed in minute detail his thoughts about a ceremony that he would ultimately cancel, and because he began at a point furthest from what he really wanted to say, the conversation dragged on for hours; regularly I had to step in and help him explain what his intentions really were. For example, he brought up the poems that were to be selected, saying that there were a few issues he wanted to discuss with me. One of them, I said, is probably by one of those objectionable personages. Yes, he said, impressed with my insightfulness. Indeed, we must be very careful on that point, he said. Then there is the problem of the content of the poems. Some important people are coming to the ceremony, like the presidents and vice presidents of universities and deans from other faculties, so we must place particular importance on ensuring that the poems don't contain any words that could upset them. Doubting that I understood the first time, he started to explain it all over again. I follow you, I said, knowing that if I didn't cut in, he would go on and on. I couldn't tell that tedious, nagging old man about the preparations that were underway for the performance at the ceremony. I knew that he'd want to see the script of the play we'd written. But he wouldn't bother looking over the text himself, so he'd have someone else read it, and of course the play would be found objectionable, and I'd be subjected to a speech propounding the need for another round of injunctions and greater caution. I passed over that. A play within a play. I decided that after the rehearsals, it should be presented as a fait accompli. I wrote it together with Faik, and it didn't contain any objectionable names. By that time, the roles had all been assigned and the rehearsals were nearly complete. The students really enjoyed acting like they were drunk and playing the roles of various shop owners and a pompous doctor, shy lawyer and prattling banker. This isn't high school, I thought; everything should be done properly. If this is a school for the training of teachers, then on Teacher's Day the dean must ensure that students have the freedom to do what they want; but it's not that exactly, it's something different: the right to entertainment. Cancelling our simple "performance piece" would be an act of repugnance, as if it were something political.

I listened to all of his injunctions and, as I left, I expected him to say: The teacher that I mentioned is, in fact, you. But he didn't; on the contrary, he said that I'd impressed everyone with my hard work and teaching. And then he smiled and confessed his own admiration, whereupon I said to myself: What a hypocritical thing you are, little madcap mouse. He was pleased, thinking that my smile meant that I was touched by his compliments. Mickey mickey mouse, madcap mouse. As I descended the stairs I twisted his words into a children's song. I had just spent a few hours with a man who seemed to become more childish the older he got; what a waste of time! I could've gone over my yearly expenditures for reimbursement and prepared my class notes. What a pity. Mickey mickey mouse, madcap mouse.

Two days before the ceremony, I was summoned yet again to the dean's office. His majesty the dean informed me that he was distressed to say that he had to pass along some unfortunate news. We no longer need to prepare for the ceremony, he said. You may have been making some preparations, but now you can stop. We've been invited to a ceremony to be hosted by the president's office, and that's where we'll commemorate this happy day.

But I've finished all the preparations, I protested. Tomorrow we're having the final rehearsal, and the music and backdrops are all ready. Nevertheless, he said, it would be disgraceful not to attend the president's ceremony. And what about us? I asked. Are we to commemorate this day, on which you said we are so "happy," without a ceremony? His answer was formulaic: We must attend the president's ceremony. But, sir, this is Teacher's Day, it's about us. It has nothing to do with the schools of law, economics or medicine. It's the president's ceremony, he started to say, but I cut him short: We're the only school that has thousands of students who are being trained to be teachers; how are we supposed to take them all to the office of the president? Now, now, he said, they'll only come if they want to. He seemed to be suggesting that I wasn't yet aware of the fact that we were training teacher candidates, not teachers themselves. The dean was at ease; in all likelihood he felt assured that no one would be upset with him if that day passed without a ceremony. Somewhat woefully, he explained that he'd spent two days struggling to write his own speech, but in the end had to sacrifice it. As I was leaving the room, in awe of that mind that struggled for two days to write a speech—a mere opening speech, three or four minutes long at best—he said: There's one more thing. (Somehow, he's always careful to keep the most important matters for last). There was a student who came to my office yesterday to complain about you, but I kicked him out.

My dear dean, when there are so many things to complain about at the school, why did they complain about me? Didn't they complain about the way they were separated into two groups: "with us" and "against us"? And wasn't it true that they talked about how the "in" group was tasked with tipping off the others and how you tried to intimidate them through disciplinary measures and the threat of being failed in class? Even the janitors who weren't "with you" were sent off to other schools. Didn't they ask why, despite the regulations, you hired people who were fired from the school for taking part in "political and ideological activities" and appointed them as chairs of departments?

But I didn't say that. He said: I did what I had to; I just wanted to let you know. Indulging such people is pointless. If only you heard what he said about you, sheer impudence! Allegedly you speak against religion in class, are an atheist, hold all religions and prophets as equal, even see them as pointless. He went too far! Sibel Hanım is a valued teacher of ours, I said, and I don't want to hear her slandered! Then I threw him out. Don't bother yourself with people like that.

How do you expect me to ignore them? In that case, we should've ignored the increasing number of girls who started wearing headscarves and long coats, draped all in black, and by the same token, we should've ignored those trusted men of yours who protect them. And in the end, let's just disregard you, I thought: You forbade cameras on campus so that photographs of those students wouldn't be published by the press, and you had rooms set up at the entrance of the school that are watched over by guards, and there the female students change their clothes and turn their loose-fitting headscarves into the *türban* style of religious conservatives, and then you proceeded to issue a statement to the effect of, "They're just regular headscarves."

In fact, I didn't know if anyone really complained about me or not. Nonetheless, the dean's "sensitive antennae" began picking up a signal. And if students did complain, they must have said much more than what you just told me. I can't remember very well in which class the subject came up, who broached the topic, or what I said exactly, but it was more than what that student said. So, you're asking my opinion? I asked the students. I don't know why it would interest you, but I will say that it's none of my business what someone believes in or why they believe it. To be honest, I don't see a fundamental difference between people's religious beliefs. In my opinion, what matters most is believing in God and not believing. Belief brings along with it a system of support upon which you can lean; not believing, on the other hand, gives you the strength to stand on your own two feet. Okay then, but don't you think it is necessary to respect people who are believers? the students asked, just as I expected. No, I said, on the contrary. I think that people who don't believe should be respected more. Because believers create a sort of solidarity among themselves, and it's the nonbelievers who tend to be lonelier, don't they? In addition, whatever their beliefs, believers have something upon which they can rely. If you ask me, people who don't feel a need to believe are deserving of a more genuine form of respect.

I don't know in what terms they may have been conveyed, but my sentiments may indeed have been passed along to my dean of the long antennae. If that's the case, I thought, then I must give him his due.

In his own way, he seemed to have a sense of honesty. I suppose he felt a need to warn me of the troubles that would befall me through his contrivance: If you're unaware of what you're doing—look, just for your information—I know everything that's going on; think first, and watch your step. Thank you, sweet, long-nosed mouse with the antennae.

My mouth feels like it's been poisoned by the cigarettes I've been smoking one after the other. Tomorrow, I think to myself, how about if I go and see if there have been any developments? Dawn will be coming soon, meaning that it already is tomorrow.

How are you going to wake up tomorrow? her grandmother asks. It's so hard to wake you up in the morning. Couldn't you just go to bed on time and wake up on time? Put out the lamp. Don't you know that gas is burning, that money is burning up?

In order to see her grandmother's sullen face in the crack of the door, Sibel pulls the blanket down just a little and nudges the lamp back. She sits up slightly, summoning all her cuteness: It's almost over, Grandma, I'm right at the end of the book. Just a little more and then I'll go to sleep.

One day you're going to catch the house on fire and send us all up in flames. I've told you, don't read in bed. Sibel thinks to herself: But I'm cold. But again, it's as though her grandmother read her thoughts: Put on something warm. Put on your jacket and your coat, and read like that. Read sitting down, not in bed. If you fall asleep when you're reading and turn over in your sleep, you might knock over the lamp . . . Sibel thinks of a fairy tale her grandmother once told her. The girl in the fairy tale weeps, thinking: If one day I get married and have a child, and if that child goes down into the basement and doesn't see the well down there, and then falls into the well, what will I do then!

Just look at her, her grandma says. She's laughing!

Sibel doesn't say to her grandmother: I was thinking of the fairy tale you once told me. She doesn't say: That's why I'm laughing. No, she wants her grandmother to remember the story on her own. Let her find out why Sibel is laughing.

Now blow out the lamp and go to sleep, her grandmother says. Your father doesn't pay for the gas here.

When I become a teacher, I'm going to look after all of you, Sibel says. Her grandmother slams the door, and Sibel looks at the shadow that lingers behind it. I won't let anyone pay for the gas, I'll do it myself.

I place the burning end of my cigarette on the plastic wrapper of the new pack I opened. Fascinated, I watch as the plastic smolders, curling and shrinking into itself. As if it's inflicting pain on itself. I make it writhe in the throes of death. Who? The administrators. If not death, they too deserve to wince in pain.

At the same time, however, I feel indebted to them because they made it possible for me to sit up at this hour of the night. If I had to work, I would have been in bed hours ago. Truly, thank you so much, gentlemen! You may not know this, but I'm quite fond of sitting up past midnight. If you'd known that, I bet you wouldn't have done me this good turn. My mood lightens as I think about it; if I want, I can sit up all night long. You are so gracious, so kind! I really like sleeping in, you know that, right? Of course you do, you know how much I enjoy late morning breakfasts. If you come for a visit around ten o'clock, I'll even offer you a cup of coffee. I'm sure that you're wondering if I do disruptive activities at home too, so, please, take a look. I'm telling you just so you can keep it in mind; at my home there are heaps of evidence waiting for you to come and gather up.

A man stands waiting in a corner of the neighborhood shop, holding an old string bag that is unraveling at one end. The bag is stuffed with potatoes, onions and bundles wrapped in paper, and is topped with green vegetables. Recep, the owner's son and assistant, walks toward an old Greek house nearby and calls out:

Sibel! Your father is waiting.

The man, whose cheeks and chin are darkened by the stubble he let grow out over the weekend, stands holding the bag, chatting with the owner of the shop, who is from Crete. His eyes are on the bay window of the Greek house; he knows that the blond curly-haired head of a girl will appear in the window at any moment, only to disappear in a flash as she bounds down the stairs or slides down the balustrade.

Sibel does just as she is expected.

Grandma, Daddy's here!

First Sibel's cries of joy, and then her grandmother's grumbling voice:

He just picks through whatever junk he can find and brings it. It'd be better if he did something useful! We have to take whatever slop he brings. Well, go on, see what rubbish he's brought this time.

Then an earsplitting shout:

Use the stairs!

In a few moments Sibel appears on the street, wearing a pair of old shoes far too large for her which she'd slipped on in a hurry, the kind her grandmother called "papsa." "Don't wear those, one day you'll fall and break your neck!" As Sibel flounders down the road, one of the shoes flies off her foot; she turns and puts it back on, but when she starts running again, the other flips off and lands upside down. Rushing ahead, Sibel hops on one foot toward her father. He hugs his daughter without putting down the bag, which traces an arc through the air around her, stopping only when it thuds into her back. She is jolted by the blow of the bag, but pays it no heed.

Daddy!

My beautiful girl, he says, but nothing more.

The shop owner says: Come, sit down, Kemal Bey. Sibel, you come inside too, there's plenty of room. Pull up a chair and rest for a minute.

Even though he notices that Kemal Bey isn't listening, the shop owner continues the conversation they'd been having:

She's a bit crotchety. She's old, what do you expect? Old and grumpy. And in a way, she's got every right to be. Times are tough, Kemal Bey. Even if you help out, it's not easy looking after two little ones. People can't even look after their own children. But she's taking good care of Sibel. Nothing to worry about.

Daddy, should I go get dressed? Are you going to take me out? You promised me, can we do it today? Can we go to the park? Are you going to take me to the beach? You told me you would, remember?

I can't today, sweetheart. I've got work to do. Another time.

Okay, Daddy, we'll go another day. But we will go, won't we?

Sure we'll go. Now take these to your grandma. If there's anything else she needs, ask her to tell me and I'll bring it next week.

Did you bring me some walnuts?

Walnuts? No, but I brought some flour. Maybe she'll make you and your brother some börek. And there's tea and sugar. Do you like tea?

I love tea! But her voice catches in her throat. I should go. Grandma will get worried. She takes the bag from her father, practically snatching it from his hand, and starts dragging it away.

The way she walks is reminiscent of a poor housewife returning from the market.

Gönül Abla is going to visit a friend today. But Hayriye Hanım doesn't care much for that friend of Gönül's. And I knew that my dear Sibel would be at home, so I thought I'd just drop in for a visit. Isn't it nice? she asks, entering the house. Now we can see you whenever we want. From the very start, she's been counting the blessings that made it possible for me to stay at home and trying to convince me that this "lucky" state of affairs is something I have long "needed." Now, she tells me, I can look after our children to my heart's content and Haluk can get his work done on time. I have, it seems, been given the chance to take care of (with special emphasis on those words, "take care of") our household. But what's really important here, of utmost importance, is that my friends can see me whenever they want. (In this case, Hayriye Hanım is my number one friend, and now it is possible for her to check on her daughter-in-law as often as she likes. So, has Sibel Hanım been taking good care of my dear boy Haluk?) I can't argue the point concerning who this has been good for. Hayriye Hanım's thoughts are even clearer to me than they are to her, because "we all know" that educated women don't make good brides; but Sibel's not really a bad girl. Of course she grew up an orphan and isn't accustomed to housework, and after all those years of studying and working, she doesn't know much else. If she wasn't looking after her home because she didn't have time, well, now there aren't any more excuses. It's time for her to show what she can do; she'll bring this home to an epic level of cleanliness and order. And save my son from working in the kitchen. Above all, that last point. As if her son has spent his entire life toiling in the kitchen!

She thinks that this turn of events will bring me to my senses and that I'll no longer strive to work my heart out "like a man." No, not after I've become used to the comforts of staying at home! And won't her dear son look after me? She worked hard to raise him and now he's a manager; but her son wouldn't turn me into a household slave. Now, she starts counting off names of women. I don't know who they are, but like them, my fingers will be bedecked with jewels. I'll idle around, and the grass will always be greener on my side of the hill. All I have to do is make her son happy.

And he deserves to be made happy! He's a man of scruples.

Does he treat you badly? He treats me like a queen. Of course he does, who raised him? This time she doesn't bring up the fact that he'd never raise a hand against anyone. Normally, she never forgets to say that. My son isn't that kind of man, she'd say.

Just stay at home! What business do you have going out? Rather than chasing after this or that caprice, be the woman of the house. (What she means to say is: Look after my son's caprices. But for some reason, she's unable to bring herself to say it.)

At this point, she is kind enough to do some thinking on my behalf and starts telling me about Fitnat Hanım's daughter-in-law. Hoping to dispel any concerns I might have about all my studies turning out to be useless in the end, she offers the following anecdote:

Fitnat Hanım's daughter-in-law was also educated; but not once did she think of working, and she never talked about it with her husband or father-in-law. (On the question of how disrespectful I am, this means that she'll leave the decision to me. I will make an evaluation and decide: if Fitnat Hanım's daughter-in-law hadn't even wanted to work, how could you, as Hayriye Hanım's daughter-in-law, dare let a thought like that cross your mind? Heedless woman, don't you know what your daughter-in-law has been through?)

Today, Hayriye Hanım came well-prepared. She had ready answers for the questions that might come to my mind.

My pleasant afternoon vanished before my eyes. Sit now with Hayriye Hanım and pick apart the daughters-in-law of so and so. If I pick up a book and start to read, she'll be offended; I don't dare write a letter, and reading the newspaper would be an affront. Were you waiting for me to come? Do whatever you'd like. The only place I can go is the kitchen to make some börek or a cake, because that means currying favor with Hayriye Hanım.

In the afternoon I dropped by to visit our dear Sibel, she tells Haluk during dinner. She insisted that I stay, and I thought it would be nice to see you and the children. So I thought, why not stay the night? But I must say, the two of you are rather ungracious. If I didn't call, you'd never ask after me.

She missed the children; as soon as they got home, she pinched their cheeks and gasped, My God, how much you've grown! Then she gave me an order: Give the children their dinner and put them to bed so they're not making a racket when Haluk gets home. They ate their dinner, but when it came to going to sleep, they made a fuss. Ozan: I need to do my homework; Özlem: But I'm not sleepy yet. Eventually, though, they had no choice but to be ushered off to bed under the kindly orders of their grandmother.

Haluk could restrain himself no longer: I hope my sister won't be worried about you.

Son, would we ever do a thing like that? We called and told her. You know how devoted she is to me; if I hadn't called her to tell her what I was doing, she would've panicked already and started calling hospitals. She seemed a little upset when I told her I was going to stay the night. Isn't that right, Sibel? She seemed a little antsy.

The word "antsy" didn't befit her as a dignified lady. But what was I supposed to say? I don't know, Mother (I still struggled to call her "Mother"); no, that wouldn't be right. I had no idea how I was supposed to know whether the person she spoke to on the phone was "antsy" or not, so I decided to say what was expected of me:

Yes, she was probably upset. She just can't get along without you.

That dear child, she'd be lost without me. If I move out one day, she won't know what to do with herself.

Haluk and I laugh together, recalling how Gönül Abla complains about their mother, sighing: If only she wouldn't meddle in everything!

This is my true home, of course, here with my son. Mothers weigh heavy on the hearts of sons-in-law. And that's how it should be: A mother's place is in her own son's home. It's the sons who look after their mothers.

I know perfectly well what my mother-in-law means. In a few moments she'll say: And dear Sibel and I will become the best of friends.

First, however, she'll talk about Gönül Abla's culinary skills, and go on to lavish praise on how fastidiously clean and tidy she keeps her home, insinuating that Sibel is not that adept yet but will learn over time. If she lived with them, Haluk's mother will say, she'd teach Sibel everything she knew, and soon enough turn her into a housewife of incomparable merit. For thirteen years she's been ranting on about the same subject. And now it will start all over again.

I don't understand why it's like this. No matter what I am in the outside world, when Hayriye Hanım comes to our home I'm transformed into nothing more than a young bride arriving at her husband's house with her bundle. She's woven me into such a tight shroud that I can't seem to tear my way out of it. In the first years of our marriage, I thought I would be able to create within myself what she wanted to see and put an end to this game; I would transform myself without fail into whatever she imagined a daughter-in-law should be, leaving her with nothing to say . . . I think back on everything I did to get in her favor. But it was a struggle in vain. I did everything possible to outdo anyone she told me about, no matter what the talent, whether it was someone's impeccable knitting or someone else's talent in sewing; I shuffled through magazines and guides, trying to outdo them. While Hayriye Hanım liked others' cooking, she never liked mine: from rolled breast of lamb to sultan's delight, Circassian chicken to meat pudding, she was never satisfied with the results of my efforts. I put myself through the most rigorous of trials, cooking the most difficult dishes possible. I compiled a collection of books on nutrition and cooking large enough to fill a bookcase, and it went so far that even her friends who were culinary experts began asking me for recipes. And those masters of knitting and sewing began asking me for samples of my work. I labored to make sure I wouldn't fall short in her eyes, and the outcome was inevitable: the same words uttered when we first got married: "My dear, it would have been different if you'd had a mother!" Was she saying that my grandmother, as an old woman and for whatever reason not a "real" mother, had left gaps in my training to become a woman, or was it that I'd just received "poor" training? It is beyond my comprehension.

I try to swallow the words on the tip of my tongue but they lump in my throat; all afternoon she's been droning on, and I feel like I'm suffocating. She's so accustomed to my silence that I wonder if she's this overbearing on purpose, trying to find my breaking point: when will I explode, what will I say if I'm brought to the brink of rage? And I have to ask myself: why do I sit like a guilty child across from her, holding in all the frustration building up inside me? How long am I going to wait? So long as I sit here in silence, she's going to go on like this. Somehow, I need to put an end to it. Perhaps one way to stop the food from lodging in my throat would be to directly ask what she really meant just a minute ago:

If my mother had raised me, not my grandmother, what would have been so "different"?

My dear, is there anyone like a mother?

I should have known that she would feign misunderstanding.

Is there anyone like a mother? No. And as I get to know her, I understand all the more that there is truly no one else like a mother and never will be. When she says, I could be a mother to you, it is clear as day that it's a hollow statement; no one could teach me better than her that a woman can only be a mother to her own daughter and no one else, and her obsession with picking out the faults of other women's daughters will never end. But that's not what I'd asked, I meant something else altogether. I put my question more succinctly:

No, that's not what I'm asking. Of the faults you see in me, which of them, in your opinion, were brought about by the fact that I didn't have a mother?

As soon as Haluk realizes that the tension in the room is rising, he shoots me a warning glance: Stop, don't drag it out! But why? Won't it be better if we come to a conclusion? Let's figure out what the faults are so that we can set them right. Bringing Haluk's secretive signals out into the open, I say:

I'm not dragging anything out. I just really want to know. What flaws does your mother see in me?

My dear, I'm not saying that you have any flaws. But of course if you'd had a mother, it would have been different.

What would have been different? That's what I want to know.

Enough! Haluk shouts, not content with giving me a sharp glance.

Why is it always like this? Whenever Hayriye Hanım comes, a squabble like this breaks out. When I sense that the food stuck in my throat is actually a scream welling up within me, a scream that threatens to turn into tears, I have no choice but to leave the table. That way, mother and son can pick me apart without me being there. But still, as if I needed to explain my departure, I say:

I'll go check on the children to make sure they're asleep.

If I hole myself up in a room and let the tears flow out to my heart's content, I'll feel better. But if I hadn't heard Haluk apologize for me as I was leaving, if I hadn't felt the hopelessness of not being able to take back that apology made in my name . . .

Mother, I'm sorry. She's under a lot of stress these days. You know the trouble she's been having at work . . .

And then comes her housewife speech, which by this point I've memorized:

What is it that makes her drive herself to ruin just for work? She should stay at home for a while. Be the woman of the house.

I shouldn't turn around and ask: And what's that supposed to mean? I'm the woman of this house, aren't I? What do you understand about being the woman of the house? I don't cook, I let my children go hungry, is that it? You cannot imagine being the woman of the house in any other terms. But why? Why do you think like that?

The torment it causes me to call her "Mother" just isn't worth it.

One time we were getting ready for bed and Haluk started to say something. Gönül Abla, her husband and mother had left, and after doing the dishes and tidying up the kitchen, I was exhausted, and I wanted nothing more than to stretch out in bed. And then Haluk began his complaint, suggesting that I was doing everything in my power to not call her "Mother." Why are you making a fuss about it? Just let yourself go, it shouldn't be so hard.

You know that, do you? I said. It was unsettling that someone who I thought knew me so well could be so distant, a mere bystander, a stranger. It "shouldn't be so hard," you say, is that right?

You're right, I said. It should be quite easy for me. Why hadn't I thought of that before? But he didn't even notice the stabbing sarcasm in my voice.

Please, dear, do it for me. From now on, call her "Mother."

Yes, sir, if that's what the two of you want, I will follow orders.

Fine, I'll try, I said, and I took that not just as a promise to Haluk, but also to myself. My words were barely audible, but when he noticed the faintness in my voice, I managed to speak up, little more than a whisper at first but then my voice rose to a shout. Each time I said that, it was like I could hear the sound of pink rosebuds being crushed in a fist, and I imagined breathing in their scent.

Haluk was probably still mumbling something to calm me down. But Hayriye Hanım's voice seeped through the walls and doors into the bedroom: I should be here at this home! I need to be here, to show you how things are done.

She thought I was too kind to Aslı, and said I needed to be stricter, more authoritarian. Pressing the pillow down over my ears, I tried to shut out the sound of her voice.

She thought that Aslı was the house servant, but even more, her own personal servant. Maybe when her husband was alive, she dreamt of ruling over her own sultanate, and now, through Aslı, she hoped to make that dream come true by having her own servant to order around and do as she, the woman of the house, the female sultan, wished. Was Aslı here when the sultan came today? Yes, she was. And, naturally, Hayriye Hanım had flaunted her own longings for a personal servant: Now, why don't you go make some evening coffee for us, she said to Aslı. I'll make the coffee, I interjected, she actually needs to go because she's late getting home. Maybe that's why Hayriye Hanım became irritated and complained. She insinuated that I didn't know how to properly treat a "servant," and she warned that if I spoiled Aslı, letting her get the better of me, she'd never show me the proper respect.

But Aslı isn't a servant. She's just a girl. Does that mean you have the right to make her work like a slave?

One day, a smallish woman had come to our door, holding a girl by the hand. This is my daughter, Aslı. I understand that you're a teacher and that you have to go to work every day, so if you want, she could come here after school to look after your children and change their diapers. I know she looks a little fragile but, believe me, she gets a lot of work done. She does all of our housework, and when I was bedridden once, she cooked for the whole family too.

I knew the woman. We often saw each other on the stairs and elevator. Every time we ran into each other, she was all questions, asking how I was doing, and she would introduce herself each time: You may not remember me, but I work at the doctor's office upstairs. Yes, I know, I remember you, I'd say. With a sharp glance, she'd say: I haven't seen you around very much, and you haven't joined in the apartment building meetings. As though asking forgiveness, all I could think of was: Well, I've been busy, that's why I haven't been around. Ah, I see, she'd sigh sympathetically. Maybe later then, once your children have gotten a little older, you can join us. I used to think that she secretly pitied me, that, in her eyes, I forced upon myself the image of a housewife who never knew how she should behave. But why would a woman living in an apartment building like ours need to work?

It was disconcerting that even though she knew that I worked, she often said: I heard that you're a teacher, that you have a job somewhere. Maybe she was trying to remind me that I had good reason to find her offer acceptable: Since you work, who's going to look after your children?

Without a moment of hesitation I accepted her offer. In those days, before Özlem started school, the suffering I endured because of Hayriye Hanım remained fresh in my thoughts. I hadn't forgotten the ultimatum she gave before Özlem was born: If she's thinking that I'm going to look after her child, think again; I didn't even look after Gönül's children. I just don't have the strength for it. I need to take care of myself.

Though the school had given me time off and I only had to work in the afternoon, Hayriye Hanım used to complain: The first four years after Ozan was born, before he started school, were terribly difficult times, and I swear that I'd even forgotten my own friends' faces! In those days, not once did I hear her say: A mother's place is beside her son. On the contrary: You've imprisoned me in this home, making me slave away like a babysitter! When Haluk would try to soothe her, saying, Mother, it's just three afternoons a week, she'd turn it around and make him feel that, even though this would have been normal for someone else, it was not befitting Hayriye Hanım.

And now it isn't difficult to understand why she's so set on helping us. I'm not working anymore, so I'm at home all the time, and Aslı still comes around; she's grown up a lot since she first started working for us and is more than capable of taking care of things. Hayriye Hanım's intentions are obvious. She plans on moving in so that she can be the lady of the house, lording over Aslı and me. She knows everything and will make sure that we two poor creatures (she says that I'm an orphan and Aslı is more or less the same) learn everything we can from her.

The first day that Aslı was brought to us she didn't say a word; she didn't even look up at us.

Fine, I said, she can start right away. Then we talked about the payment, and her mother bargained with me like a stubborn peddler. She may not look like it but she's a hard worker; let her start and you'll see just what she can do. Her price was high, but it pained me to see her peddling off her own daughter, so I gave in. Haluk gave me a fine berating later, one of those that starts off: Just who do you think you are?

I didn't know who I thought I was; but I knew what I thought of Aslı.

Don't be so timid, I thought to myself. If only I could take her by the chin and raise her face up so she would look me in the eye. There's nothing to be shy about. They're just people; do you think they won't understand what you're going through?

But they don't. I can hear Hayriye Hanım ranting in the other room:

You can't make a servant girl work by being nice. You have to give her orders, that's what it's all about. Bring me this. Do that.

* * *

Although I wanted to, I wasn't able to cry when I left the kitchen. And I still can't. I feel like my right to weep has been taken away, as with my right to speak up. No what matter what I do, there's always someone trying to silence me and stop me from crying. Perhaps I didn't know that the frustration would grow inside me like a tumor, or maybe I didn't care; but now there's no denying it. Those feelings build up inside you, and because you never pause to tend them, a wound opens up and the bleeding never stops.

The same happened when my mother died. Don't cry, you're a big girl, they told me; and since I'd sworn to never do things that didn't suit me, I didn't cry. But now I know the tumor left over from those days is still growing somewhere inside me. Crying is a sign of weakness. As the oldest child, you have to act like a man. Don't reveal your weakness to others, because that is something people never forgive. You might be weak; but so long as you don't show it, no one will ever know. Just stay silent and wait for it to pass. Then you'll see that there really is no need to wail and cry. Who told me that? No one. Everyone. Their attitude made it clear, which is more painful than words.

I could've said something like, I've been your daughter-in-law for thirteen years. I could've said, Now look here, woman. Who's stopping me from saying that, from calling her "woman"? No one ever forbid it. Except, perhaps, my grandmother. She was always forbidding things. But on this particular subject she never said anything. So who was it, and why? It would've been a relief, saying it straight to her face: What's the problem, woman? (In particular, my suppressed sob and scream.) But something makes me hesitate. Would it really be a relief? Would I be able to forgive myself for shouting the word "woman" like I were spitting in her face?

It's too late. There's nothing for me to do but go to sleep. Have the children gotten out of bed or are they still asleep? Özlem is sleeping. But Ozan might have heard what happened, and from this day on, it's impossible to know what a single sob from his mother could stir in him.

* * *

They don't let the girl go into the room. There's a mattress on the floor and on the mattress there's an old man in the throes of death. All the women from the neighborhood are at the house. The girl is looking for her younger brother. She looked in all the rooms except for that one but she couldn't find him, so she stands at the forbidden door and begins to cry. The women pull her away.

May Azrael, the angel of death, lose his way. Did someone say something like that? Wouldn't it be better if Azrael lost his way and went to a different house? But he can't go to another house. He'll come here and take the soul of someone whose time hasn't come. What if it were Orhan? Please, no. What if he took the soul of one those women at the house who talk all the time? No, that's not possible. Of all the people in the house . . .

What if he takes the soul of your grandmother?

God forbid! Who would look after you? Such an ungrateful child! Look at the things she's thinking about her grandmother.

Where's my uncle?

Would you be quiet! My father's dying.

I'm afraid of death. Please don't die!

Is that what she says? Regardless, someone slaps her hard across the face and she starts wailing.

One of those talkative women from the neighborhood says: She loves her grandpa very much.

She's not crying for her grandpa! She's crying for her mother, because she couldn't cry when she died.

If my mother were alive, she would take me to the park. And she'd buy me nice, round roasted chickpeas, not the crumbly ones you buy.

You've got everything, what else do you want? Come on, get moving. Go get your brother, it's time for dinner. Stupid boy, he'd play outside all night if you let him. And look at you, sitting there doing homework so you don't have to do anything around here. Put away your books and set the table. Your uncle will be here any minute.

But what about my homework? Sibel wants to say. Later, when her grandmother is doing the dishes, she works on her homework some more. Her uncle never gets angry when she studies. And if he does, she can always study when he goes out to the cafe in the evening, or when her grandmother is preparing the beds or doing her prayers. She'd finished her homework anyway; all she needed to do was look over the readings.

She imagines that her teacher will pat her head again, saying to the other students: You should all try to be more like Sibel. The thought fills her with joy, and in a flash she sets the table, snatching the plates and silverware from her grandmother's hands.

As Orhan is washing his hands, their grandmother continues grumbling, and then their uncle arrives:

Hey, what are you rascals up to? Hey there, wrestler, you up for a match? And, Sibel, you little slacker, did you fall asleep again with your nose in a book?

We all sit down to dinner. Tonight there aren't any arguments about meat, because there is none. Pasta along with celery root in olive oil. After eating two heaping servings, Sibel's uncle turns and says:

Now, where were we? Mom, this girl isn't helping you out, is she?

But this time her grandmother takes her side:

She is. She set the table.

Well, at least you did something. You're going to grow up to be a decent person. I won't be there to see it, but that's what you're going to do. Mom, when are we going to visit Zümrüt's parents and talk about marriage?

Let's just save up a little money and that's the first thing we'll do, she says, avoiding the issue as always.

You're just toying with me. You're not going to let me get married.

And as he walks out the door, he taunts her some more:

I should just look after myself. My mother's not doing me any good!

She calls out:

Don't stay out late!

I'm not coming back home until you promise that I'm getting married! he laughs, and then closes the door before she can answer.

By the time her grandmother starts preparing Orhan's bed, he's already fallen asleep. As Sibel settles into bed, she has the same daydream as always: she walks into a classroom filled with students who are the same age she is now. She's holding a ruler. Even though no one is talking, she says: No talking in class. Silence, everyone. Or else you'll get a beating. Then she calls Birsen up to the front of the class: Now tell me, why haven't you been *doing your homework? Why aren't you more like Sibel? Does she ever slack off in class? Never. Then she looks for Sibel to point her out as an example. But she's not there. Of course, she thinks, Sibel's a teacher now.*

Look, Faik's coming up to the door, Haluk says. And it is Faik. I don't know if I should be happy or upset.

Come in, I say. But I think: Why are you the last one? Didn't you know? Hadn't you heard? I can't believe you didn't hear.

Haluk is with the kids in their room. What am I supposed to say to Faik now? Do I have the right to be angry because he came later than everyone else? Aren't you my friend? You heard about it. You knew. So why didn't you call? And you know everyone . . .

Haluk comes into the living room, followed by the kids. Özlem clambers into Faik's lap as usual. Ozan waits his turn, so he can ask all those questions that no one else has answered to his satisfaction.

Faik, how's it going? Is everything okay? I hope there's no chance that the same thing will happen to you? Good, good. Yes, we've found ourselves in a bit of trouble. How are we going to get out of it? Sibel, make us some coffee. You'll have some coffee, won't you, Faik? We also have *rakı*, if you'd like something stronger.

No, thanks, Faik says. I just wanted to stop by to see you and Sibel. To see if you need anything.

He's stammering, obviously nervous. Can he sense that I'm upset with him? But if he knew that, wouldn't he be a little more circumspect? It's impossible to know. I could tell that Faik wasn't going to ask for a glass of rakı, and it put me on the offensive:

Faik likes rakı. I've never seen him turn down a glass. I say that to Haluk. Then I turn to Faik:

Isn't that true? Are you sure you wouldn't like a glass of rakı rather than coffee? Faik is stunned, and just sits there smiling. Haluk steps in and answers for him, obviously irritated that I was prodding him:

Yes, let's have coffee. Faik doesn't want rakı.

That means he'll leave soon. Fine. Let him leave. It occurs to me that I'm disappointed in Faik. He's acting just like everyone else, keeping a distance out of fear that I could bring him trouble.

I hand Faik a cup of coffee, a symbol of the fact that he won't stay long.

On his first day at the school, he was the same: timid, bashful.

Faik Bey, from Karadeniz University, was appointed to our school. Have you met? This is Sibel Hanım, she teaches contemporary Turkish literature and some courses on theater and other subjects.

I was in good humor that day, and I quipped: This place is like a village school where you have the same teacher for every single grade. Because of Faik's reaction, everyone's smiles froze. His expression was cold, as if at that moment he was deciding that he'd keep a distance from us.

Very well, I decided, I won't make any more jokes. That was the first decision I made regarding Faik. He never spoke except when he had to. I wondered: Why is he like that? So that he doesn't show his true colors?

Those were inauspicious times in which to be appointed. I thought: I'd like to call your attention, gentlemen, to the fact that he moved to Izmir from the town of Trabzon. His appointment should be seen as more of a promotion. What had he done to be rewarded in this way?

Just when the seeds of doubt about him began taking root, some common friends stepped into the fray. Ah, you mean our Faik? How come you don't know him? Faik Bayral. Haven't you read his poetry? I didn't know the poet Faik Bayral; but I kept my silence. Is "our"

Faik that Faik? He was a closed book. How well he concealed the fact that he's Faik Bayral! Is he really a poet? Maybe you'll hear him read his poetry one day.

I can't recall what happened next. We heard him talking, but not in his usual way of merely answering questions. Leyla Hanım and I laughed: He actually talks!

One day, as I was handing him some papers, or maybe he was handing them to me, something happened; did our hands touch? Did we look into each other's eyes? Whatever happened, I felt the distance between us suddenly vanish. From that day on, the Faik that I knew was kind and good-humored, but composed and cautious as always. No longer could I comfortably laugh about him behind his back, and when others made jokes about him, I didn't shy from showing my disapproval. Little by little, the frontlines began to fade and Faik became one of us. We started going out together for coffee and lunch. We even wrote a play together. A play that the dean would never let us perform. Our friendship grew, until that day . . .

In the end, his careful demeanor and timidity were his undoing. Just as some people fall victim to their own courage, others are the victims of their reserve. By hesitating to show the same amount of concern as the others and trying to keep a distance from anything that could lead him into trouble, Faik sealed his fate; he may not have been aware of it, but he fell from grace as the possible hero of my impossible dreams.

And now, before even experiencing the beauty of a beginning, just as we were drawing near that point, everything was coming to an end. Glass breaks like that, shattering into a thousand pieces, but if you don't know that something has broken, you don't hear it. Soon enough, I'd have to shout at Faik, because the man I saw sitting there was deaf to the sound of breaking glass. Leave, move on to safer ports. I hope no one saw you when you came here. If someone did see you and told others of your visit, it won't bode well for you.

Hülya told me about it. At department meetings, the dean said: I've heard that some people among you are still in contact with those faculty members whose presence at the university we find objectionable. (It's the old story: We have eyes and ears everywhere.) Is there really any need for me to say that you must refrain from doing things that you might regret later?

Hülya asked me point-blank: You won't mind if we don't see each other for a while, will you?

Just visiting me was like being a lamb lead to the slaughter, as the dean was openly threatening people.

I didn't tell Hülya that she was acting like a sheep. You're right, I say. I try to conceal the sound as glass shatters: Visiting me is unacceptable . . .

Maybe he wasn't talking about Sibel, Yalçın says. Could the only "objectionable" faculty member be Sibel? Maybe he made that warning in reference to someone else.

Of course he was referring to Sibel. He warned every single one of her friends. Don't be in contact with her, he said.

Why didn't Faik show the same courage as Hülya? He hadn't even come to apologize and say that he wouldn't be stopping by for a while. He just faded away into silence and disappeared. Why?

You don't talk much anymore, Haluk said.

Have I really stopped talking to him? Is it Faik's crooked smile, his sham refinement, and those things that I'd carefully avoided before that are plunging me into thought? I probably hadn't even been aware of the fact that I was stoking the silent anger I felt for Faik. If he hadn't come over, most likely I wouldn't have realized it. But it was

good that I'd come to that realization. I'd been on the verge of toppling over a precipice; I saved myself from the storm into which I was
about to hurl myself. Who was Faik? I should be able to tell myself
that I don't have any other friends like him, so thank you, Faik, you
made that possible. I should be able to say that as well.

I'm looking at my husband. His expression is understanding and
warm. He'll never know what I've been through and neither will Faik.
He doesn't know anything, and he never will! I'd like to love you,
Haluk, I think to myself. But I'm unable to. The notion of love strikes
me as empty and meaningless. What is love? Something that binds
you ever more tightly, chipping away at your freedom . . . And as
time goes on, it just makes it all the easier for people to be exploited.
Revolting! If I love you, I'm actually opening the way for you to use
me however you want; so be smart and take whatever you can. Take,
plunder, scatter, wear everything thin; the act of loving must not go
unpunished.

You're probably not going to stay long, I say as I pick up his empty
coffee cup, and he gets up, muttering apologies for having to leave so
soon. Fool! He gently seats Özlem on the armchair and looks sadly
at Ozan; it seems like he's apologizing for not answering all the boy's
questions. Then he hands me a piece of paper on which are written
some addresses in the town of Trabzon. If you ever get in trouble,
he says, you'll be safe with these friends of mine. Haluk looks at me,
his eyes wide with surprise; I can see that he thinks Faik's gesture is
rude and senseless, inappropriate for someone like me: What are you
doing? It's scandalous. I know. I wish he would leave; I don't want
to see his face. I don't want to see anyone. If I'm going to be angry
with myself, if I'm going to confront myself, well that's just what I'll
have to do.

I don't want to leave any regrets behind.

After the door closes behind Faik, I take the children to their room so that I won't have to be alone, so that I won't have to look Haluk in the eye.

Let's clean up a little, I say.

When I bend down to pick up some toys, Özlem puts her arms around my neck, and as I stand up, she hangs there like a necklace. In the meantime, Ozan throws his arms around my legs. I want Ozan to see my Özlem necklace, I want him to laugh. But I can't. I can't bring myself to say: Look, isn't this silly? I know what you're trying to say. Please, children, don't act like this. But, no, I can't bring myself to say anything. I just don't have the strength. I fall to the ground, and Özlem is still clutching my neck. I pull Ozan toward me, and as I hug them, I start crying, giving myself over to the rush of emotions within me.

How I've missed crying; it's been building up for so long.

Haluk comes into the room and sees this bundle of tears. I'm sorry, Haluk, I shouldn't have shown my weakness, but I don't think I can help it. Is that what crying is always like? I don't know. They couldn't have done anything to stop me. No matter what we did, we couldn't have stopped it. When Özlem and Ozan see their father, they realize that the secret is out and they start crying. And I let myself break down in sobs. Our bundle of tears pulls more tightly together, rapt on that cusp between crying and laughter. This is all we can do: hold on to each other tightly and weep out loud.

2

You were there
Standing at the edge of a precipice
—Hüseyin Yurttaş

I know what comes after the question: Are you married? They always think the same thing: If that's the case, what are you doing here? Why have you come all the way to this remote town, especially by yourself? Have you lost your mind?

There's no answer. What's it to you? I am what I am. Do you expect me to sit down and explain why I've come and tell you how crazy I must be?

If they found themselves in the same situation, they would never move to a town so far away, especially if their husbands had a steady income. That's what everyone keeps saying.

I wish darkness wouldn't fall . . . But it does; no matter what I do, night falls. Not long ago, I greeted a woman who lives here. Being a woman is reason enough to say hello. It happens so rarely, especially at the guesthouse which is full of single men. At night, does she feel the same despair as me? It would be much easier if she hadn't left a man behind, a man who could warm her feet when the weather turns cold (feet and hearts mustn't feel a chill). Maybe she lives with a friend. No, I wouldn't want that; I couldn't bear a woman who complained all the time and made me take out the garbage and file away her documents. I prefer the torments that night brings and my loneliness, not knowing if I feel that way because of those slovenly women at the Istanbul School of Higher Education or because I can't shrug off my thoughts of Hayriye Hanım.

To save myself from the hawk-like shadow that Hayriye Hanım cast over me, I try to focus my thoughts on the length of the trip from the bus to the guesthouse; how many feet is it, how many steps? But my inability to estimate distance works in Hayriye Hanım's favor; I am enveloped in that shadow.

She stands at the bathroom door, hands on her waist, eyeing me as I do the laundry. Are you putting in the whites too? Okay, good. What's that you're holding? Make sure that my underpants are washed separately so they don't get mixed in with yours. I feel like saying: But, Mother! After washing the whites, I'll wash the darks. Well then, wash mine by hand, since they're not very dirty. I don't ask: If they're not dirty, why are you making me wash them? I mutter: While washing the whites I'll . . . The punishment for my muttering is a long explanation: The children may be growing up, but they may still be putting their underwear in with the other clothes. Hayriye Hanım does her ablutions and prayers, and her clothes must always be spotless. I try to explain that I washed the underwear by hand before putting them in the machine, but it's in vain. Just a few minutes ago you saw me put the towels in the washer, and you didn't say anything. But not the underpants of the lady of the house! They're a rare work of art, not laundry; so you can't just wash them in the machine. And they mustn't be washed together with our ordinary clothes. No, they must be washed by hand with gentle movements, like you're caressing them. Exquisite underpants!

As I was walking today, I tried to concentrate on the sounds I heard, in an attempt to shrug off Hayriye Hanım's hawkish shadow that looms over me. I thought about which letters could be used to spell those sounds, and came to the conclusion that we don't have enough letters for all the sounds that exist in the world. Cheep, cheep, cheep . . . No, it was softer, more like: Galoo, galoo, goo . . . No, that's not right either. The sound grew louder as I approached, and I thought: What kind of bird could that be? But it wasn't a bird. The sound was coming from a stream filled with frogs. Wanting to take a closer look, I climbed up a knoll that looks over the stream, and my teacherly side, which missed the taste of victory, enjoyed a brief moment of satisfaction: All the frogs fell silent. When one of them began croaking again, I said firmly: Silence! And it stopped. When that stern teacher enters the classroom, all the students stop talking, stop breathing even. And if one of them pipes up, they'll get what's coming to them! If anyone in the surrounding hills had been looking at me, they wouldn't have believed their eyes: A woman was talking to frogs. A frog teacher! I waited for a while, but none of the frogs dared make a sound. The class was so tame! I continued on my way.

My students were monsters compared to them. Especially when I egged them on, saying that you can never be civilized unless you object and take an opposing stance. And I played games to prove my point. When I was giving a serious lecture, I'd slip an absurdity in once in a while and wait as they took notes. Then I'd ask if they'd written everything down. You have? Good. Now please read what you've written. Preposterous, isn't it? Of course! If you're so ready to memorize everything that you hear, you might want to reconsider becoming a teacher.

Then I gave a speech that was typical of me: When you teach, you have to know much more than what you're actually teaching at the moment. You must know the subject through and through. Don't get stuck in paradigms. I've said it again and again: No matter how comforting they may be, don't let yourself get stuck in paradigms! Why did I get so angry with my students? Because I couldn't break free of my own paradigms? It's possible.

Am I seeking out a new paradigm because my old one was destroyed, or at least cracked, in Izmir? What am I doing here now? Trying to weave together a new paradigm that more or less resembles my old one? I'm longing for the chance to somehow become another person, to be who I'd been in the past. I miss those days when I'd meet people on trains and buses and pretend to be someone else. But I never quite succeeded. Who am I? I'm not a teacher. Being a teacher is never anyone's destiny. I'm the most contrary person I know. I work at a night club. My boss asked me to go to Adana. We're going to do some business there for a few months. Before heading there I have a few days off so I'm going to visit my sister in Trabzon. She's nothing like me. She lives an honorable life with her husband and two children. They're perfect angels, and she's like a budding rose. You know that people like us never have kids. And who would I have kids with? Those guys come and try to sweep you off your feet, but the next day they forget you. Have I had a lover? Sure I have. Just like in the movies, they tried to save me from this life. But there's no point! Stay away from men like that. They may be passionate but hardly any of them can succeed in what they start. And what if they do save you? Won't you carry that stigma for the rest of your life? And do I even want to be saved? No one even bothers to ask. And there's something else that people never talk about: all the trouble I've had in life started with those guys who said they wanted to save me. No one ever asks me anything; they just try to force people like me to be saved. As I speak, I imagine that the woman gets suspicious. I try to keep up my story: I'm happy with the work I do, *hanım ablacığım*. I've got a good job. Where else could I work? What would the woman sitting next to me on the bus say if I said things like that? Would she mutter an apology and turn away, or would she be curious and want to know more about this life that was so different from her own? And in fact, aren't women actually more interested in such topics than men? They would just fall over themselves wanting to know more about the life of a "woman of the night" as I spun my tale. But the best thing to do is to say that you're a teacher. At the very least, there's nothing shameful in being a teacher (although it does raise suspicions).

I suppose that ninety percent of the people I meet while travelling ask questions like that: What do you do? Do you have a job? Or: Are you a teacher? And my right to make things up is suddenly taken from me.

I am a teacher. But I'm not the kind of teacher you think I am. Do you know what I teach? At that point, do I launch into another scenario? Forget about it, stop making up stories. People know that you're a working woman. From my appearance, they jump to the conclusion that I'm a teacher. They'll see my swollen eyes and immediately understand that I'm a teacher "who abandoned her children" to come here.

Today when I was returning home after making a phone call, the sun was setting. I was so enchanted that I began walking toward the sunset. It was stunning. The horizon was bright red, and there were stars and the sea, and a crescent moon that looked like the dark, puffy face of a mother waiting for her children. Who says that the most beautiful sunsets happen in the south, in the west (like in Izmir)? That northern sun was about to vanish, setting the backdrop for the sea and ships. As my feet carried me forward to a point beyond the line of trees where I could get a better view of the sunset, I saw a watchman. He was trying to read something in the pale light of a lamp, which offered little more of a glow than the setting sun. I turned back, but my heart wasn't about to let the watchman be the only person in the presence of that magnificent view. I slipped behind the building beside me and continued watching the sunset, stunned by its beauty. But a bolt of fear ran through me. There I was, a woman hiding behind a building, secretly watching a sunset! They would find it odd. Why am I doing this? I thought. Why do I always question myself about what others might think? Perhaps because I am new in this town. But even that didn't convince me. Did I behave any differently in that garbage heap of my old life? Don't I always keep myself so strictly under control, as if there is something vile in me that I'm afraid will come out into the open? Do I have a dark side like that? I don't know. But I decided that I would examine one by one all those aspects of my character that have never been seen in the light of day. All my dark sides . . .

As darkness falls, I go back to my room. Womenfolk should always be home after the sun goes down. Who said that? My mother-in-law; but before her, our forefathers had said the same. That meant that mothers-in-law and forefathers were joining up on matters of correctness. They wouldn't have said it if they were wrong, would they? And does this room count as my home? The hallway is dark. I grope for the lock, and insert the key; the door swings open without incident, but once I'm inside, the lock isn't as well-behaved. I try again and again, but I can't get it to lock. The key just won't turn. As my heart thuds and I break out in a cold sweat, I try to keep calm. From the outside it works fine, but not on the inside. What if I can't get it to lock? At that hour, who can I ask to help me? Aside from the fat balding man who was at the front desk when I checked in, I don't know anyone in the entire city. And he's probably left already, gone home to his wife and children. Please, God, let me lock this door. I won't be able to sleep otherwise. Why? I don't know, but how can I be sure that some random person, like the watchman I saw, won't try to break down the door? No one knows me here. Images flash through my mind: scenes of a screaming woman, newspaper headlines . . . A woman thought to be a newly-appointed lecturer at a university. Who is she? There's that old saying, "A wagging tail is a sign of an easy woman." Did watching the sunset alone in a secluded spot mean the same as a wagging tail? I need to know. Finally I realize what's wrong; the doorknob is loose, and that's why I can't lock the door. I close the door gingerly without touching the knob—and the key turns in the lock. At last! But then a thought occurs to me: What if I can't unlock it? Before my mind fills with another wave of scenarios, I manage to unlock it.

I need to prepare something to eat. Cooking just for myself feels odd; I don't have to worry if anyone else will like it. I recall my old worries: Will the children like what I've made? What if Haluk was thinking of having something else? What if Hayriye Hanım comes over, and then whispers to Gönül Abla that her son is doing all the kitchen work? It's just not right, Gönül, the poor man comes home tired from work and then he's put to work in the kitchen! There are ways that things should be done and ways they shouldn't.

I'd brought some boiled eggs and börek from Izmir. Will they spoil? I wonder. They wouldn't have gone bad at home. For now, it should be fine; but when the weather warms up, this lack of a refrigerator is going to be a problem. Would they let me use the refrigerator at the university's clubhouse? Even if so, I would have to eat there before coming to my room; maybe there's a cafeteria at the university, or a restaurant? But I'm not sure if I could handle going alone. How would I endure the looks and stares of the men there? Before that, however, there are other problems I need to solve. Above all, the cold. Last night I shivered for hours, despite the fact that I'd pulled two blankets over me. My feet were on the verge of freezing, but I had the bright idea of wrapping them in my wool coat. Earlier today, I went out and bought a pair of wool socks; they were embroidered in red and blue, the local colors. Tonight I'll have no fear of the cold, I think to myself when I return to my room, and then notice that the central heating has been turned on. If only they'd turned it on last night, I would've been spared the cost of buying those socks. I wish I'd brought my sheepskin slippers, but the thought never occurred to me. There were so many things I hadn't thought of. That evening I was going to cook up some sausage, but I forgot to buy bread. At our home, I wasn't the one who bought bread; that's why it didn't occur to me, because we always had some at home.

I ate a few pieces of börek, dipping them in the pan where I'd cooked the sausage, and in place of a salad, I had a boiled egg. Afterwards, I made some coffee on the electric stove (that was the only one I had). What a life of luxury! All I needed to do now was cut down on smoking. Anyway, in that tiny room I would choke on the smoke and run the risk of bringing my voice to wrack and ruin; all that I'd suffered would be in vain if I couldn't teach anymore because my voice was little more than a wheeze.

Since the rest of the tenants in the guesthouse were research assistants, I was the oldest person staying there. Even taking into account the laziness that afflicts us now and then, I would've been an assistant professor by now if I'd done a doctorate. I would've gloated over all those poor people dealing with problems like mine. What a shame, they're not even faculty members! They're just lecturers, aren't they?

Today when I walked from the main road to the guesthouse, I counted my steps and realized that every day I was actually getting a lot of exercise, like I'd done before in the past. Exactly one thousand three hundred and seven steps. How many inches is a single step? I'd thought that it was only three or four hundred steps, but it was far more. I visited my frog students, but only that mischievous one was croaking and I couldn't get it to stop. The teaching fiasco of the day! But no one from the university witnessed my failure. If they had, I knew what they'd say: How can we entrust our youth to this woman who can't even silence a few frogs? Is it so obvious? And isn't the sole reason that I am here in exile the fact that I didn't silence the students, that I didn't impose over them the suffocating discipline of an author-itarian teacher? My dear disciplinarily-challenged teacher! When a class starts, you can say, "Silence! No talking." Or you can say, "Why don't you talk. What do you think?" Which will it be? Will you wait patiently for them to spew their sophistry and then, with the same patience, point out the flaws of every one of their arguments? Isn't it inevitable that a clamor will break out? Is it the same thing as telling those frogs to be quiet? You draw a breath in Diyarbakır, in Erzincan or in Van, the farthest reaches of the country, and rest assured, they'll arrange for you to be sent to the most distant place of all.

Come now, don't be ungrateful. It's not just about prestige. Even the driver of the bus going to Trabzon had been taken aback when I said that I was going to be working at the university.

Because the bus was making more rest stops than I expected, I'd become worried that when we arrived in Trabzon the office at the guesthouse would be closed. So during the rest stop in Giresun, I went into a restaurant and asked the kind-looking man at the register if I could make a call. I wrote down the number for him, and he said that it might be difficult to get a call through but he'd try. At that moment, the bus driver walked in and overheard our conversation.

Because he seemed to be taking an interest in the matter, I asked: Excuse me, when will we arrive in Trabzon? With the air of a commander who has no doubt that he will savor the taste of victory, he replied: God willing, we'll been there in two hours. That meant we would be there at 4:30 in the afternoon. Taking into consideration the fact that even the greatest commanders can be wrong, I wanted to persevere in my attempt to make a phone call, which most certainly was going to prolong the rest stop; but the other passengers started grumbling, so I had no choice but to give up.

I had a bowl of soup and a tea, but when I tried to pay my bill, the kind-looking man at the counter said that it had already been paid. I glanced at the driver; he was looking at me with a dapper smile, hoping I would accept his act of generosity. What could I do? I flashed him a blank smile. Then the charade of haggling began, in which I tried to pay him back.

As the bus veered around dangerous curves, the driver never took his eyes off the rearview mirror. Like the other passengers, I was terrified. The sun shone down mercilessly through the window, so I moved over to the empty seat next to me, but that it made it all the easier for the driver to ogle me in the mirror, and I had to resign myself to baking in the sun.

When we arrived in Trabzon, the driver took it upon himself to ensure that I made my phone call. Without paying a dime, I managed to get through, but when I asked to speak with the department chair, the driver's expression crumpled and he abandoned his efforts to help me with my luggage and find a taxi. Transferring my care to a man by the name of Mustafa, he refused my thanks with a wry twist of his lips. There are practical advantages to working at a university. The word itself is enough to make people like the driver think you are inaccessible. Of course I didn't tell the driver that I wasn't exactly university staff at the moment. What need was there to blow my cover?

But that very same affiliation with the university aroused not only gruffness in the driver of the university shuttle bus, which I expected, but also outright disdain. When I said that I wanted to go to the School of Education and asked, ever so timidly, if I could take the shuttle, he practically berated me. Eyes narrowed, he scowled at me and muttered, Fine, but just this time. What was the big deal? But I knew that once you learn to play by the rules of the game, everything gets easier. You observe the necessary airs, and it's a simple matter of imitating them. After a few days of long walks and transferring between buses, I examined all the subtleties of the matter and decided to try my luck again. I was halfway down the frog road when I saw the shuttle coming. While he was picking up the others from the guesthouse, I continued walking slowly down the road, and when he came back by, I acted like I was professor on a morning stroll out of sheer love of nature, and then I flagged down the shuttle. The driver stopped, and with the same swagger, I got on. I saw no need to even look him in the face; indeed, wasn't I a lecturer whose mind was positively brimming with questions of the highest order?

Out of fear that my culinary creation might turn out badly, I put some more butter and pepper into the small pan that was boiling away on the electric stove. I'd gone to the butcher and asked for some lamb. I only have hogget, he said. What's hogget? I asked. Sensing my hesitation, he explained: It's the same as lamb, but the sheep's just a little older. And then he launched into an oratory on the lineage of sheep; I learned all there was to know about their past and future, but he could say nothing about whether or not I'd like it. I had no choice but to buy it. And I'd walked so far trying to find a butcher that I'd gotten a blister on my foot. What was I going to do? Say no to the hogget and try to find another butcher? And it was possible that all they had in Trabzon was that mysterious thing known as "hogget."

I went to countless shops trying to find a bottle of something to drink. I was hoping it would be as simple as seeing it on a shelf and asking for it, but no. As I went around the shops trying to look like I'd forgotten what I was going to buy, I picked up some things, most of which I didn't even need; but I couldn't find a single bottle. I was all the more heroic for getting through those dark days, the loneliest of my life, without the small support afforded by a drink. The weekend is coming up, I thought, and it would be perfect if I could somehow find a bottle of brandy, because my children are going to be at home and that's when they think about me the most. Wails and tears won't accompany my son's thoughts; but my daughter could sob loudly enough for me to hear her. A mere bottle of cognac. Is that too much to ask?

I decided to ask someone at the school, well aware that it would compound their doubts about me. There just had to be a place that sold some booze. In that entire city, didn't anyone drink? And they say that people from Trabzon can hold their liquor! If that were the case, where were they getting their alcohol? Yes, the next day I would call and ask. Because my children . . . My children would be drawn ever so slightly closer.

Faik, you once told me that they drink like crazy here, till the break of day. I could join them, I thought. And if I tell them all that I heard about them from Faik, they will open up to me. But no, I don't want to think about him. I should keep my anger from cooling.

If I only ate part of the meat, I decided, I could cook the rest the next day with some vegetables. And maybe some zucchini; I'd seen some at the market. I also thought of gathering some fennel from the garden, if the watchman wasn't around. Abla, why are you picking those? he'd ask. Are you going to feed them to an animal? I asked the others at the school once: Don't you eat wild plants like that? They were stunned into silence. The thought occurred to me, so I asked, nothing more; but I wasn't expecting them to be so surprised. They weren't sure if it was an insult or a joke. People in Trabzon probably don't eat plants, I repeated. What do you mean? one of them asked. Someone stepped in, and I surmised that they were trying to take my side: I think she means vegetables. No, I insisted. I mean plants. The debate lasted a long while, but finally I got them to understand that I meant the edible plants that grow in the wild. They started seeing me in different way: But she looks so normal! One of the professors had done his military service in Izmir. He said that people there ate tomatoes and fresh peppers for breakfast. Someone else explained that people from Izmir are fond of arugula, "some kind of weed." In this way, it all became clear: The fact that she likes to eat weeds is odd, but let's try to be understanding. My expectations exceeded that, however, and I found myself hopelessly trying to explain what fennel is. It's like dill, I said, and it has thin stems and smells like anise. That's not fennel, they said. I had no choice but to pick a sprig of fennel during my morning walk and bring it to the office. That single sprig of fennel which I brought to the office as if it were a precious flower knew nothing of its fate. Passed from hand to hand, it shriveled up and went limp. What a bizarre plant! They pinched and then sniffed the stem: It smells like rakı! Isn't that what I'd said before? Yes, but they'd never seen it, which was obvious. It was grow-ing untouched in the yard and on both sides of the road that I walked down every day; and because it was untouched, it thrived, thrusting up in thick clusters. It goes well with everything: in börek and with roasted meat, and even boiled on its own. Why shouldn't we take advantage of a blessing offered up by nature? Our thing is anchovies, they said, and then went on to eulogize about just how "incredibly" healthy they are to eat. In fact, they boasted, around Trabzon, which is the anchovy capital, some illnesses don't even exist because people eat their anchovies! Fine, eat your fish, I've got nothing against them. I'm just saying that some boiled fennel would go well with a helping of anchovies!

I explained that my intimate knowledge of wild plants could be traced to a Greek tradition: my father was born in Crete, and my mother's side of the family had migrated from Lesbos. They looked at me pityingly: So you might have some Greek blood! they said. Sure, it's possible, I replied, what's wrong with that? It's unthinkable! one of them said. My God, what are you saying? Ahmet Bey, a historian, had traced his family tree back to Mehmed the Conqueror, but was unable to go any further back. Full of disbelief, I asked: You've traced your family tree back five hundred years, all the way to the fifteenth century? But of course, he replied, people should know their lineage. Well, I know mine, I said; we came from the Greek islands. As they flashed each other knowing glances, it was clear that they were displeased with my claim, thinking: Maybe that's why she's been sent into exile.

In fact, they differed little from me. They were all instructors at the school before it was incorporated into the Board of Higher Education, and some of them had been there before it was transformed into an institute for the training of teachers. But none of them were academicians in the true sense of the word, and that's why my current situation (exile) piqued their interest. With trepidation they awaited the month of June. The previous year, as happened with us, they were reassigned to high schools; but then the decision was rescinded and their contracts were extended for another year. So June loomed ominously on the horizon, whispering of the exile that I represented for them. In the beginning I wondered why they were so afraid of being reassigned. But of course, I thought, the prospect of being sent off to Diyarbakır or Van would strike fear into their hearts. I told them that I had friends who'd been assigned to such places. But in all truth, ever since my arrival they'd been hanging on my every word, hoping to garner clues about what awaited them. The similarity between their school and mine was horrific: the same interrogations, the same intimidation, the same threats. I told them everything, warning them about what had befallen us. I had the advantage of experience and wanted to share it with them; my openness, however, was rewarded with warnings. I wondered if I should tell them that I'd read that some of the more courageous people in prison had been sentenced to death. In any case, I was in exile; what else did I have to fear? Later I would find out that they'd been warned to keep a distance from me. Just like in Izmir. The admonitions that drove Faik and Hülya away from me threatened to drive me into loneliness yet again. The thought of it was terrifying! How did the powers that be manage to make everyone so suspicious of each other?

For the upcoming weekend, I've resigned myself to the fact that I'll cook some fennel that I'll pick in the yard and eat it alone. Thinking about home, about my children, is forbidden. And above all, don't think about Faik. Look around you: this is your home now (your room). There's your desk and your bed, and in the back is your bathroom; your single pot is boiling away on the electric stove on the floor, and your clothes are hanging out to dry on the balcony.

I hadn't brought a washtub with me, so I got one in Trabzon. But because I had to take a bus to bring it home, I bought a rather small one, which made it difficult to wash my sheets. Even though

I changed the water five times, stomping down to get the dirt out, I had my doubts that I'd really gotten them clean; still it was enough that they no longer smelled like a dorm room. Before going to school in the morning, I strung up my clothesline and hung everything out to dry, but when I came back in the evening the sheets and pillowcases were still damp. I have no choice but to sleep in the other bed that smells of sour bread. Like a women's dormitory . . .

After walking through the dormitory to make sure everyone was asleep, the teacher on duty goes to her own room. Everyone waits for what seems a proper amount of time, pretending to be asleep; some of the girls even snore convincingly. One of them snores even more loudly, and you can hear the sound of stifled laughter. The creak of a bunk bed sounds the signal and everyone throws off their covers. Someone turns on the lights as they pull sweaters over their nightgowns, and the revelry begins.

Come on, I have a biology exam tomorrow, one of the girls whines; she is silenced with a few blows of a pillow.

Shut your mouth and go to sleep, someone says. And while you're at it, shut your nose and ears too.

The poor girl will die if you plug her nose, someone titters.

No, plug it up. She's memorized so many formulas that they'll fly away if they find an escape route.

They take out pieces of bread that they pilfered from the cafeteria, spreading them on a newspaper on one of the beds, along with whatever they have left in their lockers: tomato paste, a head of garlic, a few lumps of cheese, black olives that stain the newspaper with oil . . .

I've got cumin, Sibel says. That's all she had in her locker. Everyone goes after the cumin like it is the most precious thing in the feast. It brings a taste like never before to the stale bread, becoming a main course for the first time in history.

After the meal, the girls take out cigarettes they'd hidden among their stacks of clothes and light them.

If you're going to smoke, do it in the bathroom, Sibel snaps. She hasn't started smoking yet. Don't stink up the place. Are we going to breathe in your filthy smoke all night?

Okay fine, they say, we'll air out the room.

But some of the others, emboldened by Sibel's complaint, send the girls who are smoking off to the bathroom.

As everyone gets back into bed, content that they'll now sleep with full bellies, the girl in the next bed asks: Are you going away for the holidays? Sibel answers:

I'm going to stay here and work on my literature homework. I can't get any work done at home because of my grandma. She won't let me study. Sibel doesn't say that her father had written to her, saying there was no need to spend so much money just for a short visit home and that he would send her the money she would've otherwise spent to make the trip.

What about you? Sibel asks.

If you're going to stay, I'll stay too, Yeşim replies. And you can help me with my physics homework.

But the truth of the matter is that they don't have to say anything; they already know. As Sibel thinks about the fact that they'll have to find some homework to do during the semester break in February, she knows that Yeşim is wondering if Sibel believed what she'd said about her physics homework. What does it matter? They'll stay because they have homework to do. If they didn't, they'd rush home like the other girls whose families miss them so very much.

I'd like to be able to say to myself: It doesn't matter if they don't call. But I can't. What will I do if they don't call? Everyone's fine. I listened to the voices of my son and daughter. No, their voices weren't trembling. I shouldn't make up sorrowful stories like that. We're fine, they said. Don't worry about us, just take care of yourself. I felt like my home was so near. Like I could just step outside and rush home. I even caught the scent of meat and potatoes simmering in the oven. That's what Aslı cooked today. I could tell that Ozan and Özlem had fought over the phone, and I spoke to Aslı just for a few seconds. Are you taking care of my cactuses? I asked. I reminded Ozan that I'd put him in charge of looking after them. He was also in charge of getting the new volumes of the encyclopedia I'd started collecting. I told Dad, and he said he's going to get them, he said. Don't worry. Okay, I replied. Don't do anything to upset your father and Aslı Abla.

Haluk and I spoke but briefly. I know that he's a good person. I see now that he doesn't do any of the things that other men do. When I ranted about my job and my pride, he was understanding. He didn't try to dissuade me from coming over six hundred miles in pursuit of the dignity of my profession. What could he say? Submit your resignation and stay at home . . . Didn't you always respect independent women? Here's your opportunity! How could you be more independent than this? Now you can be as free as you want without getting entangled in the games other people play and struggling against those worthless men. Ah, Haluk! Why do we see independence in such different ways? Don't you see that I won't be independent if I resign? That I'll have to rely on you and your mother? The home visits, the recipes, Fitnat Hanım's daughter-in-law . . .

I'm going to continue resisting. I won't let them get away with this. They struck out at my most vulnerable point: my motherhood. Didn't they realize that my children are young and that I wouldn't want to be separated from them? It won't be as simple as forcing me to retire so the authorities can be free of me.

I wasn't surprised in the least to see the same thing happening in

Trabzon. It's a big game and I'm just a small part of it, a pawn that will be defeated by a rook. But they're not going to win because I back out of the game. I refuse to be like those men's dainty wives. I'll stand my ground, no matter how shocking it is for them or how they try to heap shame on me: What kind of woman is she, leaving her home and children behind, how bizarre! It's a source of pride for me that they don't understand who I am. It wasn't easy for me to become a career woman, and I'm not about to back down, so don't get your hopes up.

Sibel's teacher came today, her grandmother said. They'd just eaten dinner, and her uncle, who was changing his socks before going out to the cafe, paused.

What do you mean? Here?

Her teacher wanted to talk to us and to her father. Sibel wanted her teacher to do this, because she was afraid we wouldn't give her permission.

What are we going to give her permission for? her uncle snapped.

Her grandmother tried to evade the issue: Nothing important. She's just going to take an exam or something.

Call Sibel down, her uncle said. He wanted to hear it from her. But Sibel wasn't upstairs; she was behind the door. Her grandmother found her standing there, abashed at having been caught eavesdropping. Her grandma dragged her into the room. Even though she knew that Sibel had heard everything, she told her that she had to talk to her uncle. Her grandmother closed the door.

Sibel stood helplessly in the middle of the room.

What's this I've been hearing about an exam? Your teacher came here today to talk to us. Why? Did you ask her to?

Sibel stood there pale and silent, like a whitewashed wall. Her uncle asked again:

What exam is this?

The entrance exam for the teacher's school.

Teacher's school? We've talked about this before. First you need to get through primary school. And if you can manage that, then you can go to middle school. Otherwise you'll stay at home and help your grandmother.

I know, but my teacher said that I will pass the exam if I take it. And the state will pay for it all. You won't have to pay for anything.

I've already talked to your father about your schooling. He says that he'll help you study for as long as you want. Isn't he paying for your school? And aren't we doing everything we can for you? And now you go off making your own decisions. Why didn't you tell us before you told your teacher that you would take the exam?

Her uncle continued berating her. When she noticed that his anger was subsiding, a tremor of joy ran through her. As her uncle was leaving, he said: Do whatever you want.

That was good! At least he didn't say that he'd tear that exam to shreds.

Sibel didn't mention that she'd already taken the exam and that her teacher had said it would be better if they talked about it before the results were announced. She also didn't say that she and her teacher were partners in this crime; her teacher had helped her prepare for the exam and even took Sibel to the testing center. She didn't say anything. Not that day, nor any other day. That's what she always does; she makes her own decisions, and only when it reaches the point of no return, she brings it up.

They are never weary of employing the same tactics again and again: the smears and calumny, the snakelike hisses, the snarls. Here they are playing their usual game. Interrogations, persecution. When I hear about what's happening, I feel like I'm watching a film that I've seen before. But you can't scare me anymore. Come and see, I'm not deterred by all this pointless tumult. I've really enjoyed being here in

Trabzon. I'd like to see Van as well. And why not Diyarbakır too? You'll pay for the trip. Sera Lake was lovely, I went there yesterday (thanks to you, gentlemen). It was a charming place, surrounded by towering mountains covered in trees. The banks of the lake, which was the color of rainwater, were lined with willows. It was created when a massive boulder plunged down from the mountainside, blocking a stream. You can still see the place where the boulder used to be. I saw women planting crops on the slopes of the mountain, which are too steep for a tractor, too steep even for a donkey or horse. Women are working there, our women. I saw them.

This cornbread is golden, like the fields of hazelnut trees and tobacco plants. Kiss them out of reverence. Fields of kale blossoming, a burst of yellow flowers. All along the length of the road, women are gathering up heaps of black cabbage to feed their animals, carrying bundles of it on their backs, laying it out to dry in the sun. Boys wearing dark-colored sneakers are walking down the road on the way to school, dreaming that a car will pass by so they can hitch a ride, their notebooks and pencils tucked into pockets sewn onto the front of their black smocks. The eyes of the girls are blue, agleam with wonder, and their pretty blond hair spills out from under their headscarves.

I would've paid extra to be able to see scenes like that. So much beauty! The laurel trees, dark shadows flitting among their leaves. (Black cabbage, black smocks, the Black Sea. Why is everything black? So unlike the people. I'd come hoping they'd be friendly and kind, and they are; that's what I believe.)

I traveled from Izmir to Trabzon. That was just three days ago, though it seems much longer. The red carnations are still on my desk and only one of them has started wilting. But why would one of them wilt before the others? They'd come from the same bouquet, all the way from Izmir, and they'd probably all been picked at the same time in the same place. So why would one of them start withering before the others?

I vow to never be the first one to wilt.

Haluk reminded me that the bus was leaving soon. My students came to see me off, even though for a year I hadn't been allowed to be their teacher. One day, they too will be teachers. They probably saw me as an example of what could happen to them. The following week they were going to start their practicums, and they already knew where they were going to start teaching after they finished. I told them what they needed to be careful about, as they were all nervous about teaching their first classes. Do you have any practical advice? Yes: Never focus on a single student and try to look at the entire class. Don't rush. Finishing a class too early is much more of a problem than not being able to finish on time. But if you do finish early, go back and repeat some of the more difficult points. Avoid showing that you're nervous.

Fatoş said quietly: Spend some time with your children before you go. She was like a spring, but you shouldn't be deceived by its gentle flow; it ran deep, so clear and pure. Being a teacher was my life, and that teacher within me replied to her:

But aren't you my children too? I don't know how much time passed after her kind admonition, but when Haluk touched my arm to remind me that it was time to go, I heard the final call for the bus to Trabzon ring out. I kissed each of my students on the cheek, and holding the red carnations they'd brought for me, I turned to say goodbye to my children. I saw how despondent they were. How long had they waited there, like chicks in a nest far from home? Quickly I kissed and hugged them, and then my husband. I thought that I'd have more time to hold my children, taking in their scent, holding it in my memory for the difficult days ahead. But I was hustled onto the bus which started leaving even before I found my seat. Haluk knocked on the window, pointing to Ozan, who was waving. I waved back. I knew that if I hadn't seen him and waved, he would have been inconsolable all night long. Just as I blew a kiss to my daughter, the bus turned, and I saw my students. I waved to them, and I saw that Neşe was crying. I knew that in their minds I had taken on mythical proportions. Neşe was weeping because her teacher had been reassigned to a faraway place, was being driven into exile, and three months later Neşe would be a teacher herself. I turned, hoping to see my children one last time, but they were gone, and the reality of it all struck me like a blunt blow: You missed your last chance to see them. Perhaps you'll never see them again, I thought, or at the very least, you won't see them for longer than ever before, and that period of time is beginning right now. It's over, and they're gone. I stood up and looked back, but the rear window was covered by a woman's shawl. It was impossible for me to hold back my tears. Everything was gone: my students, my children, my husband. Why had they disappeared from sight so quickly? If only they'd run behind the bus, I thought, I would've seen them as the bus left the station, even if just for a second. Why didn't they run? Why hadn't they tried to catch up with the bus? Don't they want me to see them one last time? Were they punishing me? My children . . . Please, don't be angry with me because I left you behind.

All I had were my carnations, and as I wept, my tears fell among their red petals. I was alone. Completely alone. My God, how much loneliness can a person bear? No one knew me on the bus; if I wanted, I could wail and weep to my heart's content. But the thought of that provided no comfort; it even terrified me. No, I shouldn't cry. But

Neşe was crying. She was crying because I was leaving. I can weep, I told myself. Just then, the woman sitting in front of me turned and looked at me.

I was crying. Think whatever you want, I thought. Pity me if you so desire. I'm going to cry as much as I want. If only I'd been able to properly wave goodbye to my son. What had my daughter been doing when I left? Had I even seen her? I tried but I couldn't remember, which meant that I hadn't looked. How shameful! A mother who doesn't even see her daughter as she's saying goodbye. You should be ashamed of yourself, I thought. You should weep out of shame.

We left Izmir behind, and I was still crying. We passed the turnoff for Kemalpaşa, and I saw some trees adorned with purple flowers. I wondered: What kind of trees are they? But the question was pointless. Hadn't I known what I was getting myself into when I decided to leave? My sobs began to subside. After letting myself lapse into that silent storm of weeping, I was beginning to calm down.

Chamomile flowers were blooming everywhere. From the side of the road all the way to the fields, they were in bloom, covering the hillsides as if a snowstorm of white blossoms had blown through. Spring was abloom in Izmir. Someone had once said: Spring goes as quickly as it comes. Who said that? It doesn't matter. It goes.

The gently undulating slopes of the hills were covered in green, interspersed with rows of poplars. In the sky, cheerful clouds reflected the purple of the mountains in the distance as we passed through small villages.

The bus slowed, and I noticed that there was a man walking alongside it. His coat had patches on the elbows and shoulders. This struck me as odd: Why would he have patches on his shoulders? Does the fabric wear out there? Shoulder pads don't wear out. The children of the village were playing ball in a grassy meadow. There was a woman standing on the side of the road; she was wearing a checkered head-scarf, and her hands were pulled into her sleeves.

The bus sped up and the landscape flashed by like the frames of a film.

There's a full week ahead of me before I start teaching, in addition to two long, empty days off. I splashed a little cognac into my coffee, and I'm thinking nonstop of Izmir; the weight of those two days is pressing down on me. How am I going to get through those days here in this room, all alone? The cognac, which had been so hard to find, won't be as helpful as I'd hoped. After leaving the school, I stopped at a few more shops, scanning the shelves. Nothing. I wondered if they keep it under the counter, or in a back room. I couldn't ask, because the shops were so close to the school; although I didn't know anyone, I wondered if someone might realize that I'm a teacher. What would they say? There's that woman who just moved here, I saw her check-ing all the shops trying to find a bottle of cognac. That just wouldn't do. And now, I see that my efforts were in vain; the cognac merely transported me halfway to Izmir. After a few drinks, I realize that it helps me neither to remember nor to forget. I'm hungry, but I can't eat anything. No matter what he's doing, Ozan will think of me. Özlem will keep asking about me and crying; the cognac doesn't taste like it does it Izmir and the music on the radio sends waves of sadness through me, through Trabzon. For some reason, I get the urge to tear up all the maps in the world. I know that my anger is keeping me on my feet, but it's not enough.

I stumbled through the rain today from the bus stop to the guest-house and got soaking wet. I had a plastic bag and put it over my head, but my shoes and jacket were soaked and my skirt grew heavy as it got wetter and wetter. My glasses were spattered with rain. I saw two young women who were gathering greens. They smiled at me, giving me the courage to approach them and start chatting as the rain poured down. I asked what they were picking. The older of the two said something I didn't understand, and when I asked again, she said: Plants. For your animals? I asked. Yes. And that was the end of the conversation. What else could I ask? Have you gotten wet? Her answer confirmed the silliness of my question: Can't you see that we're soaked?

Of course I could see it. They were much worse off than me. The older woman was wearing a long blue overskirt that was soaked and stuck to her legs. The younger one had squatted down so she could pull a sack onto her back, but she was having trouble standing up with the load. I could have helped her, but I was struck by the fact that she wasn't wearing shoes and I just stood there, staring at her. The other woman ran over and helped her just as she was about to topple over. I offered to give them my plastic bag, but they were so wet already that it didn't matter. They continued along their way, and I set off down the frog road.

The guesthouse had a clubhouse where people would get together and play cards. They referred to it as being "down the hill." I'm down the hill, the husband says to his wife on the phone. Some people are coming over for dinner. Yes, tonight. I'm cooking up some *köfte*, she says. Should I make some soup too? Two cars passed by, heading toward the clubhouse. I decided that if any cars passed, I would try to ask for a ride. But they paid no heed to this woman with a plastic bag on her head, carrying a bag that held a bottle of cognac. And it was just as well because I didn't want to have to feel gratitude for anyone. They didn't even slow down. It's possible that the poker game had already begun. There had been a flag-raising ceremony earlier, so maybe that's why they were late. The others, the swaggering professors free of fear for their jobs, had already gone to the clubhouse. Rules are always for us, the small people down below.

Our dean was a teacher before the school was turned into a university. He was a gentle, polite old man, almost endearing, and he smiled at everyone in his soft-spoken way. There were always police officers at the school and whenever there was a flag-raising ceremony they'd walk through each of the departments to see if anyone was hiding out. If they found someone, they'd drag them down to the ceremony. The students knew about it. Everyone knew, except for that gentle old man. He'd hidden out in one of the classrooms, waiting for the ceremony to end. Who could've known that old man would be made dean? At your age, you should be ashamed of yourself, the police would say. I was just going down, he stammered, I just had a little work to finish up . . . Sneaky liar!

One day, as the intensive questionings continued, the police came to the school and spoke with the chair of my department, asking him about my home life and where I'd worked before. Later, he told me about what happened and said that the dean's office was carrying out an investigation into a complaint that had been filed against me. I knew that the chair of the department kept a careful eye on me, and it must have seemed odd to him that the police had been called in to investigate a mere instructor like me who was at the school every day in plain sight of everyone. Maybe he was slightly jealous that, above and beyond his interest in what I did in the classroom, the matter had grown to such an extent that the dean's office was looking into my old employers and my family, including my distant relatives. But still, he said:

If you want, you can talk to the dean about it.

And that's just what I did.

I told him that the chair of the department had said that he'd requested assistance from the police in the investigation concerning me. I said: If there's anything you want to know about me, you can ask me yourself, and rest assured you'll get the truth. What exactly do you want to know? I can tell you much more than the police can.

What do you mean? We value you very much as an instructor at our school. I don't have a single doubt about you. Why should we get involved in an investigation?

The police came asking about me today.

I knew nothing about that. I can assure you that I never made a request for an investigation. And you should know that it troubles me greatly that the police are coming onto our campus. This is an institute of higher education and the police have no business being here. Soon enough, you'll see that they've stopped coming around.

But they came today and asked about me.

That's beyond me. If the president of the university requested an investigation, there's nothing I can do. Please believe me, we had nothing to do with this. And who could say anything bad about you? They'll have to ask us what we think about you, and you've nothing to fear on that point. I know that you're upset. I've been so upset about all this that I've started taking sedatives. Would you like one? It'll calm your nerves.

He thrust a bottle of diazepam toward me. I thought: Am I some kind of mental case? Why this sudden generosity?

I left the dean's office feeling more relaxed. Soon after, however, the chair of the department told me that the police couldn't have come on campus for an investigation unless the dean himself requested it.

An investigation about Sibel Gökşen is being carried out at the behest of the dean of the school. The main points in the investigation are as follows: Does she have any family members who have been convicted of taking part in the leftist movement? Is there any information connecting her to any divisive organizations? Is it true that she's maintained contact with acquaintances at her previous places of employment who have been involved in leftist activities? Does she have any contacts outside the country? Does she have a post office box registered in her name?

I felt like breaking down in tears, but I tried to appear as composed as I could, concealing the tremble in my voice. In the end, the police finished their interrogation; they had gotten their answers and there was nothing that could be done. No, I'd never had a post office box. While I missed my old colleagues, I hadn't seen them for months. I didn't belong to any organizations except for the teachers' association. I wasn't a member of any divisive organizations, or any unifying ones either, for that matter. I have a sibling in Germany who, if she wanted, could come to Turkey during the summer breaks, but she doesn't come.

The chair of the department said: That's more than I could've guessed. But I couldn't tell if he was satisfied with my answers.

Yesterday a football match was held among the faculty members. In Trabzon, football is like a contagious disease, and the fact that I care nothing for it exasperates people. The only thing that connects the university to the city is this passion for the sport. Occasionally they set up matches for the youth of the city. And academic rules hold true everywhere, including on the field. If a full professor wants to join a match, their poor teaching assistant gets dragged into it too. But then the teaching assistant is replaced by an assistant professor, who starts wheezing after five minutes because they chain smoke all day long. And there's seniority, of course, so they in turn are pulled out so that a professor can play. The results are exactly what you'd expect: They gave away a total of ten goals. The revenge of the oppressed! No one could've been as happy as me.

I smile as I think of what Ozan once said to me: Don't you see the girl on the road? I'm thinking of the drawings he used to do in crayon, and the stories he would tell about them. This evil man beats his poor son and as the child cries, his mother approaches them. The child tells her everything that happened and then the mother deals the father a terrifying blow that sends him toppling to the ground. In the blank space that I suppose is the ground I point to a purplish blob and ask: Is that the man? Ozan's answer is filled with the same petulance as before: Don't you see him?

In those days, I always complained that I had no time to read, that I never had a moment to myself: Please, just give me one minute alone. And now? I'm more alone than I ever wanted to be, and all I want is to be with my children. Let them whine, cry, do whatever they want, I just want to be there with them. I wonder: when I'm not there, to whom do they whine and complain? I even miss their naughtiness, the way that Özlem breaks down in tears at the slightest provocation and how Ozan knows just how far he can go with his tantrums.

I can't spend these next few days just sitting here thinking about them. The same thought keeps coming back to me: You can go home tomorrow and send your letter of resignation from Izmir. Just get up and go. You have the money; you could take the bus, even a plane. Go to your children. But if I do that, part of me will be defeated, and that is something I'll never be able to change. So don't think about your children! Drink your cognac and read your book, then sleep. And when you awake, keep reading.

* * *

Where had the bus stopped for the dinner break? It must have been in Kula.

Everyone was getting off the bus, but I decided not to. I'd cooked up some köfte for my son to take to school for lunch the next day, and I'd made myself a sandwich with them. With my red carnations in my lap, I was alone. On that half-empty bus, those carnations granted me a certain prestige, but it was time that I put them aside. There was still another day and night before we'd arrive in Trabzon, and I couldn't keep them in my lap the whole time.

That woman who'd been seen off with those carnations wasn't going to the restaurant with the others. Maybe she didn't have any money? No, prestige means money, everywhere around the world; we all know that. She may not have liked the roadside restaurants because she thought they were dirty.

It was nine in the evening. I bit into my sandwich; chunks of onion popped between my teeth. Next to the restaurant there was a gas station and a tire repair shop, and I saw that there were signs for bus companies. One of them read, "Pine Tourism." It reminded me of a song that Faik had once sung: "Pining for Lost Love." Faik, I thought, I'm going to your hometown; I wish you were with me and hadn't abandoned me. Without even knowing it, you stripped me of hope at a time when everything seemed to be shrouded in darkness, leaving me like a shriveled sprout. If it had been another time, maybe I could have forgiven you and tried to understand your fear. But now? I can't give you any more than what you deserve; that is, if you even deserve anything.

As I ate my sandwich, I murmured Faik's song: *The words of a friend tear my heart asunder.* Asunder. The lyrics couldn't be more appropriate, I thought, for what I'm dealing with now. As I mulled over the meaning of the song, I realized that I was singing out loud and pursed my lips. Had anyone heard me? I turned to see if anyone was sitting behind me, but to my relief I saw that the seat was empty. What would they have said? Look, that woman who was crying is singing songs now . . .

I began to wonder if I'd been unfair to Faik. What was he feeling? Was he thinking about me as much as I was about him? Could it be that he felt slighted and hurt? Maybe he was trying to understand and forgive me. But I couldn't have known, so I had no choice but to convince myself that the whole matter no longer concerned me. The only way I could survive this ordeal was by nursing my feelings of hatred and my desire for revenge. Lapsing into longing would only push my thoughts toward Izmir and the urge to go back home, but I knew what I truly wanted above all else: to resist. That was my only option. And I was going somewhere I'd never been before, to Faik's hometown. It might even be a pleasant distraction to try to find traces of Faik in the city, even though I'd promised myself I wouldn't think of him. But if I became close with his friends, wouldn't it help me get over my feeling of not belonging? Would I find him if I sought him out on the streets of the city, on dead-end roads where he'd left his childhood behind? Even if I didn't, the search itself could be enjoyable. And why not; surely there are traces of him somewhere, the echo of his voice.

When had I felt that first electric tingle? A flame glowed within me. I hadn't wanted to feel that for Faik, but I'd been unable to stop myself. I don't know if I've ever felt anything like that for Haluk. So much time has passed! Haluk was something completely different for me, a kind of prophet, a savior and harbinger of the glad tiding that I would be saved from life at my grandmother's home. A colorless light, but all the same, he was a light! In the final years of my studies, he illuminated my path, showing me what I needed to do.

I wondered: What are my children and husband doing now? Watching a show on television, now that the news is over? An American film about adventures of murder, escape and mad love, or maybe a tale of armies galloping over the moors of Europe. Our ties to the past and future would be unbreakable. From the far-flung regions of Asia all the way to America! What else could be better?

I finished my sandwich but was still hungry; crying, I thought, must make us hungry. I wolfed down more of the börek that Gönül Abla had prepared for me. Now I was ready for another round of tears. The woman wearing an embroidered headscarf who sat in front of me was standing outside with her husband; they must've finished their dinner. I heard another unintelligible announcement, but caught the words "Izmir" and "Trabzon." The other passengers clambered onto the bus, which backed up and set off down the road. Darkness had fallen and I couldn't see anything out the window. And I didn't want to see the scenery flashing past; I didn't want to see myself. The first thing the driver did when he got back on the bus, even before starting the engine, was turn on the radio. A woman's husky voice rang out, like an impassioned singer in a nightclub: *I will go to my love, even if he turns me away.*

After being on the bus for three hours, I spoke up for the first time; my voice sounded like it belonged to someone else: Can I have some water? The attendant brought me a bottle of water and was about to turn away but paused in surprise; rather than daintily sipping from the bottle, wiping her lips with a handkerchief after each sip, that elegant woman with a bouquet of carnations in her lap drank down the whole bottle at once. I handed him the empty bottle. It's no simple feat to eat a sandwich and then börek; you need to wash it all down. But then he was distracted by something, maybe the odd melody on the radio, and he turned around, forgetting the woman who downed a whole bottle of water. The blond woman, fair-haired woman, woman of flaxen locks. Woman.

I knew nothing about Trabzon, and except for Faik, had never met anyone from there. And so I thought of observing the people around me, the men and women, young and old, with the hope of gleaning some insights into how people from Trabzon behave. But I soon realized from their glances that they were, in fact, far more curious about me. I decided to put off my observations until I arrived in Trabzon because I was afraid that if I stared too much, those men would look at me all the way to Trabzon, twirling their mustaches.

The woman sitting in front of me took off her headscarf, folded it into a triangle and then put it back on again. Good for you, I thought, you're not afraid to show your hair in public. One more point for the women of Trabzon. The embroidery on her headscarf, which was patterned with branches and birds, was charming. The pink of the fringe was embellished with green, just as the green of the fringe was adorned in pink.

We passed through Uşak toward Afyon, and I imagined my children getting ready for bed. They would have to get up early because they had to go to school. Had they talked about me, I wondered. Were they sleepless? Were they haunted by my limp wave as the bus left the station?

The question wouldn't leave my thoughts: What am I doing on this bus when my children are back at home, possibly crying because they miss me already? I could sense that I'd begun to fall into the grips of a feeling of alienation that I'd never experienced before; I felt like I was becoming become another person. The lonely woman that I saw leaning her head against the window, which was like a black mirror, was nothing more than an amateur actress playing at being a heroine. Thoughts like that could drive me to a precipice.

The unknown darkness I saw threatened to send me into a panic. I tried to think of something else, but what was there? Thinking about Faik was forbidden. I couldn't think of Haluk, because that would only turn my thoughts to my children and memories of their ringing laughter and choked sobs. Had I hurt their feelings? What was that supposed to mean? Of course I had. If that's the case, I wondered, why was I was so afraid of being hurt myself, why was I trying so hard to protect myself?

Almost everyone on the bus had fallen asleep, and I wished sleep would come over me. But I felt desperate. The couple in front of me had leaned their seats back so far that they were practically in my lap. The driver had turned down the radio but I could still hear the mournful songs that played over and over. Had my children fallen asleep? If I could, I would whisk away the thoughts that were troubling them—thoughts of me—so they could sleep in peace.

Without disturbing my carnations, I reached up and pulled down my coat from the overhead stowage area and pulled it over me. I closed my eyes so that I wouldn't come eye to eye with that woman in the black mirror, but it was too late. That image of me stands up and walks hand in hand with a man toward a mountain. There's no bus, no exile, no children in tears because they'd been left behind; just a woman trying to live the moment. The man spreads his coat over the fresh spring grass under a pine tree, and they sit down together. The woman curls into the man's lap. She can feel the heat of the sun on her skirt as the man breathes in the scent of her hair. But who is he? Not Haluk, not Faik. He's pure, an unblighted lover whose love makes no demands. And the woman, who is me, wants like never before to feel the heat of that love on her lips. The man leans down and kisses her, and it feels like a silken caress. The woman suddenly wants more, she wants to make passionate love there on the grass. She realizes that she's been carrying within her a powerful desire to make love, and while she knows she may blush at the thought, she doesn't try to push it from her mind. Without having to close her eyes and pretend that she's enjoying it, she wants to savor the pleasure of every moment, not mentally but throughout her entire body. Whoever this man is, she loves him, and she knows that one day she'll find him and love him all the more.

The bus began to slow down and I noticed that there were lights outside. We arrived in Afyon and stopped at a rest area. More passengers boarded the bus there, and I surmised that the driver was pocketing the money they paid for their tickets because they weren't on the passenger list. An announcement was made, calling for passengers going to Ankara and Samsun. At that hour of the night, who could possibly want to travel to Samsun? Come now, it's time to go to Samsun. No, the woman replies, I'm not going without my lover.

An elderly woman accompanied by a middle-aged man boarded the bus. I decided that I should try to go back to sleep, but I noticed that the woman was looking for seat 11. Number 11? Just my luck; that was the seat next to mine. They just had to find a female passenger to seat next to me. That's the rule! I'd assumed the pair would sit together, and hoped that no one would sit next to me. But the man was just sending the woman off. I'd been sitting stretched across both seats; my feet weren't going to be thrilled with this turn of events, because if I had to sit with my feet on the floor, they'd get swollen after all those hours of sitting. The woman was having difficulty getting into her seat because the seatback in front of her was leaned so far back, so I asked a soldier who was sitting a few rows ahead to press the button so I could push it up. Eyes heavy with sleep, he helped us and then nodded off again. At last the woman settled into her seat.

Where are you going? I asked. Samsun, she replied, but offered no other details. In her lap she held an expensive-looking purse. It's just as well, I thought, I should go to sleep. Good night.

After Afyon, I drifted in and out of sleep. I listened to the music playing quietly on the radio, my thoughts circling back again and again to my children. I wondered if Haluk and Aslı would remember to take Ozan to the toilet at night; Haluk wasn't in the habit of doing it, and Aslı was a heavy sleeper. And I wasn't even sure if she'd stay the night. Don't worry, Sibel Abla, she said to me, I'll stay the night. But her mother could decide against it; I imagined her saying: What business do you have staying the night when his wife isn't at home? The possibility that she could harbor vile doubts about Haluk irritated me. How long had Aslı been with us? She was like our own daughter. When Aslı had first started helping us around the house, she was in fourth grade. And later, her mother often mentioned that she was glad that Aslı was learning so much with us. Then again, you never know. Things can change; there was a chance that she wouldn't even let her come during the day, much less stay the night. But I knew Aslı and I knew she'd stand up to her mother. Such a strong girl! Sibel Abla needs me, she'd say, she needs my help now more than ever. What would I have done without her? Thanks to her, I'd learned how to tell the difference between true friends and acquaintances. And her mere existence was more of a comfort than all my relatives put together. Without her, how would we have managed to raise Özlem?

Then there was Hayriye Hanım and all the attention she demanded, in addition to her false flattery: What would we ever do without you, she'd say to Aslı. And of course there were her complaints that always began with: I've reached that age where I'm in need of some care. Today Ozan exhausted me and Özlem was so naughty. I'm worn out!

Even though she's so frail, Aslı supported me with surprising strength. Because of her, I didn't have to owe Hayriye Hanım a debt of gratitude. My dear, sweet girl!

It was a cool night. Ozan could catch a chill. If only I could remind Haluk to take Ozan to the bathroom, but it's impossible. The darkness outside seemed to become ever more impenetrable, an empty screen onto which you could project your own dreams. Out of the corner of my eye I saw a fig tree; it was growing there, all by itself, a bad omen . . . The tree grew with terrifying speed, reaching massive proportions. Where had that fig tree come from? Was it a sign that they were trying to tear our family apart? They say that a fig tree planted by a house will destroy its foundations. No, the roots have to go deep for that to happen; I'll dig up the roots. There's no need for Haluk to be upset. This fig tree is mine and it's my job to uproot it. I know the cunning ways of fig trees, how they appear so gentle and kind at first, and then you see their true colors.

Had we arrived in Ankara? What a dark city! What time was it, maybe three or four in the morning? Sleep pulled at my eyelids. If it was Ankara, so be it. We still had a long way to go.

I drifted back toward sleep: Good night, old lady going to Samsun. And why are you going there? Why not just stay in the comfort of your own home?

Was that a headache I felt coming on? A kind of throb. Did the fact that I couldn't sleep properly the whole night long mean anything? I was weighed down by the weariness of all those days, all that suffering. A pendulum swung in my mind between everything and nothing. Thrust away by everything, I swung back the other way to nothing. I'm so tired. Please, I begged, just let me fall into a slumber as dark as the blackness of night.

After Çorum, we stopped at a rest area. Another restroom break, another tea break; but I don't need a break or tea, just let me be! Place and time no longer meant anything to me; who cares what time it is! Just let me fall asleep.

I don't know how long I slept, but when I awoke, I guessed that we were somewhere near Samsun. The sun is rising, so that direction is east, I thought. The bus stopped at yet another rest area. Why is it that just as you're about to nod off, the bus driver always stops for a break? It must've been around seven in the morning. I thought: Should I get off the bus with the woman going to Samsun and have breakfast? We could have tea with the börek that my sister-in-law made. And then I'll smoke a cigarette. It's been hours since I smoked. Does it mean anything if a woman smokes during the breaks on a bus journey? At least I won't be smoking alone. Why is everyone staring at me with reproach in their eyes?

Have some börek, I offered. She refused, but I knew that she'd like it. It's homemade, I insisted, the dough was rolled out by hand. In the end she took one, and as I'd guessed, she liked it immensely. But out of politeness, she refused to take another. Why, I asked, I thought you liked it. I did, but one piece is enough for me, thank you. Very well, I thought, and since my sister-in-law made it for me, I suppose it's my duty to finish it off. I have some boiled eggs, would you like one? Tea and börek made a perfect breakfast. Do you need to use the restroom? Okay, in that case let's take a little walk around. It was quite beautiful: everything was covered in frost. My breath came out in puffs of steam. A spring morning. The mountains were shrouded in fog, as was the road. It all looks so pretty, I thought. Just look at those geraniums beaded with dew. Or is it frost? Isn't it just wonderful that everything is covered in a delicate layer of white? Free of all coquetry, nature offers herself up to the first rays of dawn, waiting ever so patiently to be accepted. Mornings are beautiful. Everywhere I go, the mornings are beautiful. And you, Black Sea morning, you're also beautiful. So it's not so different after all, even the mornings here remind me of mornings back home.

One night had passed since I said farewell to my children. Ozan was probably getting ready for school, and I hoped that the only dampness in his bed was from the sweat on his forehead. Otherwise, he'd get embarrassed again, but Aslı wouldn't tease him about it. She was mature for her age. The thought persisted: If only I could be with him!

He'd been a beautiful baby and had thick curly hair, which irritated Hayriye Hanım: Why is he so girlish? she'd ask with a sneer, and as I ran my fingers through his hair I'd let a curl fall over his forehead. Why don't you just pull his hair into a ponytail? she snapped once. Why not? I thought. Beauty isn't just reserved for girls. And my son is beautiful. She never thought I'd have a son. All through my pregnancy she said: You're not the type of woman who'd have a boy. It's going to be a girl. My first was a boy, but he passed away when he was still a baby. Then Haluk came along.

That's the kind of woman she was; first, saying that not every woman can give birth to sons, and then saying that she'd had two sons. Later, she grew fond of Ozan, and now she loves him more than she loves Özlem. When she comes to our home, she wants to see Haluk and Ozan, even though Özlem is still young and wants attention. Aslı will look after her, just as she's done ever since Özlem was born. Hayriye Hanım's bullying is in vain; I've learned to not trust her. For that matter, I've learned to not trust anyone.

Before Haluk and I got married, we imagined that we'd have a son and a daughter, and that's exactly what happened. We've made so many memories together, I thought, but then I can't remember a single one. Why? Aren't there any moments in the past that you'd like to relive? Of course there are! And I'm indebted to Haluk for so many things. At first I thought that I was growing distant from him, but in fact I felt closer to him than ever before, precisely because we were so far apart. There was something there that didn't fade away under pressure; on the contrary, it grew stronger with each passing mile. Our marriage struck me as being somewhat peculiar. Quickly it had become a habit, and it's difficult to let go of the safety and comfort of habits. The further I was from Haluk, I began to feel closer to him, probably because I wanted to feel that he was by my side. It would come as no surprise if I saw him step out from behind that row of poplars. Please, don't go so far away from us, he'd say, we won't let them drive a wedge between you and your students. Relax. I promise that I'll do everything I can to make sure that you feel at peace. I'm waiting for you, just like our children. You shouldn't leave us. Don't leave us!

Why did I hope he'd say those words? My reply would be: Haluk, you must understand, I'm not leaving you and the children. In this ledger there's an account to settle, and I can't come back without settling it first.

* * *

The bus was heading straight toward the sun, but the fog was so thick that I could barely see its outline. Since there's no sunlight, I thought, I might as well sleep some more. The bus went up and down mountains as I slowly entered a world that was entirely new to me, a new segment in my life. And everything might be better in this new universe, I thought. Doesn't going to new places always signal the awakening of new hopes? There may not be things I want to change. Sometimes, all our itemizing and labeling is in vain. My dream of changing things had often been derailed, but perhaps in this new place there wouldn't be a need for that dream. My life, which was in tatters, could be revived. And maybe I had other hopes too?

I leaned back in my seat, feeling the heat on my eyelids. The right side of my body was baking in the heat. I had but two options: first, to somehow succeed in falling asleep, and second, to give up on sleep altogether. The second sounded more logical, so I folded up my coat, but I didn't stow it away in case the weather turned cold again and I needed to cover myself.

We entered a town called Çorum. Hadn't we already passed Çorum? Or were there two cities named Çorum on this route? There were attractive gardens, homes and parks. Everyone was in a morning rush and I saw students in their uniforms hurriedly walking to school. It seemed like every other shop specialized in roasted chickpeas. Our bus, conqueror of highways, was suddenly transformed into a puttering city bus as we stopped at red lights.

Gentlemen, I should thank you once again, I thought. Thanks to you, I've gotten to see Çorum. If it hadn't been for you, I would've spent my entire life in the same place I was born, ignorant of all the other places in my home country. Actually, I don't think I have a single friend from Çorum or Samsun (that is, if I don't count Leyla Hanım, who had the honor of being reposted to Samsun).

Then there were more roads, more mountains, hills and plains, like a repetition of all I'd seen before on that journey. As sunlight flickered through the trees, everything was bathed in a silvery glow. Steam rose up from freshly plowed fields as the frost melted away. It was a festivity of colors. There was a stream by the side of the road, flowing in the opposite direction. But weren't we going toward the sea? Why was that befuddled stream flowing the other way? The hills in the distance were obscured by smoke. Had a fire broken out? It turned out to be the steam from a locomotive bound for Amasya, which I'd never visited.

The train chugged down through the mountains, trailing puffs of smoke, the tenuous trace of its existence that would soon fade from sight. We rounded another bend in the road and I could no longer see the train. The woman next to me turned and said: I think that was the last mountain, so we must be getting close to Samsun. She started getting ready, brushing her hair, freshening her lipstick and checking her purse. She found a piece of chocolate candy in her purse and offered it to me. Thinking it would be rude if I turned it down, I accepted, wondering how long it had been there. If only I could smoke a cigarette, I thought. Maybe I should ask for another bottle of water? What time is it? Almost ten? So we'll be in Samsun around ten. But how many more hours after that?

My feet were swollen from sitting for so long, and my body ached. I prayed that she would get off soon so I could put my feet up again. Up ahead I saw a large panel over the road that read, "Welcome to Samsun." At last!

Samsun was a fairly large town, but there was no sea, at least as far as I could tell. There were shipyards, and construction was being done on the harbor; all I could see were buildings and trucks loaded with gravel and concrete. Where was the sea? Even after a day, I missed the sea! Had all the maps lied about Samsun being on the coast? The woman beside me assured me that the sea was up ahead. Samsun would bring me the sea, my first view of the Black Sea. But it seemed to be hiding. A passenger got off the bus in front of the university's School of Education. If I'd been Leyla Hanım, that would have been my final destination and my first day of work. I hoped she would be able to see the sea from the upper floors of the school building; living in Samsun without a view of the sea would be nothing short of death.

Ms. Passenger (that's what I called the woman beside me) told me that she was going to get off the bus at the station. She said that she would only stay in Samsun for a few days but didn't say why. Maybe for an inheritance? She talked about Izmir, and I discovered that we shared a common attachment to the city. Samsun has changed, she said. I was surprised at how modern the city was. Why had I expected it to be backward? All I knew about Samsun was that Ataturk landed there on May 19, 1919. Ms. Passenger told me that she'd been there once before long ago, that she'd traveled there by car (with her husband, I surmised). She pointed out some places, saying, "In the old days . . ." But how could I know what it had been like in the past? All I saw was that the water on the road glimmered just like everywhere else and that there were large stone outcroppings around the city that seemed to be wet too. I recalled a description of the town: The humidity in Samsun comes not from the sea but from the water that flows from rocky outcroppings.

When we arrived at the station, I saw that the woman sitting in front of me was getting off the bus together with her husband. She'd taken off her embroidered headscarf and tied a charming scarf over her hair. They got off the bus, lugging bulging plastic bags. Ms. Passenger and I bid each other farewell, and she wished me a pleasant journey. I looked out the window and saw the woman and her husband. She looked well-rested. She'd slept for nearly the whole trip; only rarely had I seen her awake. How had she slept so much? She walked down the sidewalk, wearing sandals and holding a pair of boots. The way she swaggered made me think of a soldier who has been on leave and was reunited with his gun. Her husband trundled along beside her, carrying a veritable mountain of luggage. I watched, entranced as if it were a silent film. Her expression was sharp, biting: What the hell are you talking about? Of course that checkered suitcase is ours! I'd seen him slip off to an empty seat in the back of the bus every chance he got. Even as she snored she berated him. I was watching them so intently that I almost didn't see Ms. Passenger get into a taxi; I waved at the last moment as the taxi pulled away. That must be nice, I mused, in just a few minutes she'll arrive at her destination. It'll be a long while before I arrive, and I won't even have a home awaiting me. But there's no need to give myself over to melancholy!

After Samsun, the landscape grew more beautiful with each passing mile.

These few days will pass, I tell myself. But I don't let myself lapse into daydreaming; today there's hot water, so I do laundry and scrub the floors with hot soapy water again, glad that I remembered to bring a washcloth. I arrive at a conclusion: even women who despise housework more than anything else like a clean home. It must be instinctual, or maybe hereditary, passed down for thousands of years. And it gives me great pleasure to see the floor gleaming like a mirror and to take in the scent of cleanliness. This room is in the heyday of its existence, I think to myself; I hope it realizes this fact! After I'm gone, it may have to wait for yet another exiled female teacher to be scrubbed from top to be bottom three times in a single day, and the day's not over yet.

I decide to reorganize the furniture in the room. First I turn the extra bed on its side and push it up against the wall, turning it into a kind of desk, and then I cover it with a bed sheet. Then I organize my books into two groups (I brought so many books! I'm sure that all the people who helped me with my luggage instantly regretted the decision): course books and those I planned on reading for pleasure. Then I organize my notebooks and files. I'm happy with the results. Tomorrow I'll buy a new set of sheets. That was another decision I made today. No matter how many times I wash them, I just can't get that dorm room smell out of the sheets. The bed-to-desk idea has worked out well, and I've saved the bed from having to bear the weight of my books and kitchenware; stepping back to take in the sight of my handiwork, I realize it's a functional, comfortable work desk. Next I plan on scrubbing the balcony with the leftover water in the laundry tub. Somehow, I need to make this place my own. This is my room, my charming new home. And I know that the sooner I can adopt it as my own, the easier everything will get. Tomorrow I'll buy a mop for the balcony.

I spoon some of the zucchini and lamb I cooked earlier into a pot and heat it up, and after my lunch I do the dishes. It strikes me as comical that "doing the dishes" consists of washing one saucepan, a glass, a fork and a spoon. My next adventure will consist of going out to buy bread. A single small loaf of bread usually lasts me two days, but since I'll be at home over the weekend, I realize that it won't be enough. So I'll have to set out on another arduous journey: 1,350 steps to the bus stop, a bus trip and then another 1,350 steps back to the guesthouse. On my way out, I decide to take out the garbage, which consists of nothing more than the peels of the oranges I'd brought from Izmir and stale bread. A single bag of garbage, nothing more.

There are some sheep on the road of 1,350 steps. It occurs to me that they could be the hogget that the butcher had talked about. They have short legs and shaggy fur. There's a newly born lamb that's irresistibly cute; slowly I approach with the hope of petting it, but it dashes off. They're going to eat all the fennel, I think to myself. But there is the consolation that at least they enjoy eating it as much as I do.

The center of town is busier than usual. I remember that I've been meaning to buy a three-way adaptor for the outlet in the kitchen. Whenever I cook, I have to unplug the radio, which is irritating because the radio drives away the silence in the room, breathing life into it, transforming it into my entire world. But after going into so many electronics shops and getting empty looks in response to my question about three-way adaptors, I realize this is going to be harder than I thought; but of course I won't be beaten down by hardship. I've stood up to martial law, the Board of Higher Education and the National Intelligence Agency. This is nothing in comparison. All the sales clerks at the shops say the same thing: You have to go to an electrician's shop. Sure, but where can I find one? I must have walked half the length of Trabzon without finding a single electrician. But finally I get an address and off I go, successful at last! Now I can buy some fruit and bread, and set off on my way home.

As I walk down that road of 1,350 steps, a man tending to his sheep calls out to me:

Can I have a piece of bread?

How did he know that I have bread in my bag? I tear off a largish piece and hand it to him. Gesturing to a young child sitting near some bushes on the side of the road, he says:

How about some more?

It's obvious that this guy has it in for my bread. What will I do now? Go back to town and buy more bread? I hand him two apples and two oranges, hoping that he'll spare my bread. But to no avail. The child—is it a boy or a girl?—approaches me, looking me in the eye. There's nothing I can do. I break off another large chunk of bread and hand it over. Now I'm back where I was: half a loaf of bread for two days, which means six meals. But wasn't I going to cut down on bread anyway?

As he turns away, the man asks: Where are you studying? I'm a teacher, I reply. Look, he says to the child, pointing to me: If you study, you can be a teacher just like her! I don't tell them that I have children of my own out of fear that if I'm too friendly, what remained of my bread would be put in danger. Going all the way back to town wasn't an attractive option. If only I hadn't thrown away the bread I had at home. But how could I have known? As I start walking away, I hear the child talking about their village teacher, but soon I lose the thread of the conversation. Even when talking face-to-face with the locals, I find myself struggling to understand, but I enjoy the sound of their dialect. I slow my steps as I walk down the hill, listening to the sound of their conversation as if it were a song. This is the true Black Sea lilt.

Smiling, I think back to the first day when I arrived in Trabzon; I'd felt like a stranger in a strange country that day as I made my way from the bus station to the school to meet the president of the university. In this town, everyone knows your language but no one speaks it. For example, I ask for directions and they understand what I say but I don't understand their replies. I ask again, and they give the exact same answer. Thanking them, I turn away, trying to unlock the puzzle of what I've just been told. It's like when you hear something in a foreign language you don't know very well: you roll the sentence around in your mind, slowing it down, trying to tease out the meaning. Eventually I found my way to the university and was struck by the politeness of the president, who wore a fastidiously tied bow-tie. In comparison, there was a president of another university who seemed to be completely fake; but which one? As I settled into the plush velvet sofa in his office, I felt like an actor onstage after the curtain has fallen; you no longer have to play your role but still feel its lingering effects. This play was about daily life in Trabzon. You step off the bus into a completely different world. There was a ticket seller, a handsome young man who had a John Travolta haircut. The kind of man worthy of a second glance: light brown hair, green eyes. Straight from a fairy tale. That is, until he spoke, sounding rough around the edges, and the carriage turned back into a pumpkin.

There are massive buses belonging to Trabzonspor, the local football team, parked in front of the guesthouse. What's going on? I wonder. Have they taken over the guesthouse? Football is everywhere. No matter where you look, people are playing football, and if they're not playing, they're talking about it. On the streets I noticed that the young men wear Trabzonspor jerseys over their shirts and sweaters. Managers put up Trabzonspor posters under the framed pictures of Ataturk in their offices. On the desks of businessmen there is always a Trabzonspor flag on a tiny flagpole next to their writing pads and pen holders. All of Trabzon is painted in the team colors: burgundy and blue.

When he sees me staring at the crowd of people near the university clubhouse, the doorman of the guesthouse says: They're holding a training camp here. On the entire Black Sea coast, was this the only place they could find for their camp? Fine, let them hold their camp; I'll have my own. Classes are going to start in a few days and I need to get in shape. It's been a long time since I've been in the classroom. For months they've forbidden me from exercising my mind, if not my body. Look, they seemed to be saying, look after your body, but not your mind! Mental gymnastics? Please, ma'am, don't be ridiculous. If you're a proper woman, you should look after yourself, train yourself in the art of makeup. Learn how to make yourself more attractive and to properly greet your husband when he comes home from work at the end of the day. Learn how to cook light meals with seafood; you already know how to make salads and cook meat, don't you? How to prepare hors d'oeuvres? I'm sure by now you can see that you're quite ignorant on so many matters.

People are standing around, watching the football players. I too could join in, but I wouldn't watch the athletes; I'd watch the people watching them. The games they play are more natural, more spontaneous. They'd never even notice that you're watching, because men are interested in watching and nothing else.

But you'd be wrong to think that I'd let my guard down. Go to your room and lock the door; you're grounded for two days. I don't want a single word from you! Nothing's going to change your situation. And if you complain, it'll just get worse. Console yourself with thoughts of how you've made your new home so nice. Think about how you felt the first day. Take joy in your freedom. Don't just stand around wasting time.

The university clubhouse is packed with people. Is that how they do camps here? I'd always thought that a training camp would be held outside. Go on in, the doorman tells me. As I look through the door, I realize that the room is abuzz with life. I am tempted to stay for a while, knowing that in my room I'll just sit there alone, with no one to talk to but myself. I stand at the door, torn by indecision. I shouldn't go in, I tell myself. I'm afraid that I'll be known as an "easy" woman; once that happens, there's no turning back. And don't I know how they'll see me? As soon as they find out that I'm from Izmir, it'll be over. I've seen it before: the winks when they talk about female students from Izmir. I remember one professor who said: I've got this student from Izmir; I've never seen such a hussy. It's a disgrace! She's not ashamed of a single thing. This is how they sum it up: She's not from around here. If you've got the courage, go ahead and ask: Am I one of you? Just as I am on the verge of turning around, something inside me resists. I, too, am from Izmir. I walk through the door.

Not all of the people are from the training camp. Everyone who goes to the clubhouse more or less knows everyone else; some people are sitting at tables playing cards, others are having heated debates, and others are enjoying an evening drink. I notice a few people glancing at me. They see me every time I come in here to use the phone, so I shouldn't be a stranger in their eyes.

There isn't a single woman in the room, so I stand out even more. I wonder if I should just withdraw to a corner . . . But ever since I was a student, haven't I always sat down with groups of men just to provoke them? Out of mere obstinacy, you should go sit down at one of those crowded tables. Tell them that you're also staying at the guesthouse. Say: I just moved here from Izmir, so I don't know the rules. Is the clubhouse just for men? Can women come here too? Would they blush in embarrassment? Perhaps they wouldn't; but afterwards, they'd most certainly give you more one-on-one attention. Their ideal woman: easy on the eyes and not too intelligent. It's as simple as that: a woman should be pretty and dumb. I can just imagine the attention they'll shower on me later. Enough to set your head spinning. Are you new here? Why have you come? Are you married?

Just what would happen if I sat down at one of those tables of men? I can hear it already: There's that new teacher, I don't think you've met her. Do you know what she did? I saw her sitting with a group of men, drinking, playing cards, hanging out, sleeping around. Where would it stop? This is madness! Be a lady of refinement and go back to your room, listen to the radio, eat dinner, drink some coffee, read, sleep, wake up and read more, then go back to sleep.

No, I'm going to sit down. There's a table over there, on the other side of the room—perfect. I sit with my back to the rest of the room. After a few minutes I'll light a cigarette, my sign to you that I don't care what you think. If I'm staying at the guesthouse, I have every right to sit here and read, enjoying a drink and a cigarette. They may judge me. Very well, let them. Trabzon is a university town and this place where you play cards and drink is a resort in the summer. So what do you do in the summer? When the men go down to the beach to swim, do the women wait on the side of the road? By the time I put out my cigarette, the waiter still hasn't come to take my order, so I start reading a magazine. But I can't focus and I read the same passage over and over, my eyes merely skimming over the words. Won't the waiter come and ask what I want? Do they think that I'll get bored and leave? I'm not going anywhere. I just might have dinner here; why not? Salad, some grilled meat, a glass of rakı . . . It would be so good! I haven't had dinner like that in a long, long time. Or fish . . . Maybe I should call over the waiter; I've been wanting a glass of rakı. If I were a man, the waiter would walk with me to the refrigerator to show me what kind of fish they have: You can pick one out yourself. But me? He'll say: I'll pick out the best fish for you, abla, even though I know you'll forget that act of kindness.

I only realize I've been thinking these thoughts when I come eye to eye with the waiter. I'd probably been staring at him for a while.

What can I get for you? he asks.

You've been ignoring my table, I say sharply.

Abla, I'm sorry. It's been really busy today.

I'm surprised by his sincerity. He's nothing like I'd thought, either in manner or speech.

Can I have a cola? I ask, my voice softening.

Of course, abla.

I light another cigarette, no longer interested in starting an argument. And why would I want to? The poor waiter is obviously overwhelmed.

After finishing my cola and cigarette, I get up to go back to my dreary room. As I walk toward the door, I can sense that a few people are looking at me. A new one, they were probably thinking, a woman exiled to Trabzon; she doesn't come around here often. Even if they'd never seen me before, likely they already knew more or less who I was. If I stayed any longer, they would probably come up and introduce themselves. I left at just the right time.

Walking into my room, I am struck by its silence. Perpetual silence; I left no sounds behind to greet me upon my return. If only I'd forgotten to turn off the radio.

I miss being among people and talking about even the simplest things. For example, those meteorological conversations: The weather's really nice these days, isn't it? We're halfway through spring and I can already hear whispers of summer. Or we could turn to articulations of place: Spring here is so pleasant, I wonder what summer is like . . .

But I have to keep two more days of silence, the price I must pay.

I must be strong.

Memories swarm through my mind and I try to drive them away. Memories of how I talked to my children: Please, my head hurts. Can't you be quiet for just a minute? Özlem, yes, that's very interesting but tell me about it later.

As if not remembering were possible! When I close my eyes, I find myself back at home.

I'd just gotten home after work, exhausted in mind, body and soul. The school was in a state of sheer chaos. We weren't allowed to leave after we finished teaching and had to be at the office from morning till evening. A new ruling had been passed by the Board of Higher Education stating that we had to do scholarly research. But where? And how? Nobody knew. Our department had just one office and all ten of us were crammed in there. Fevziye Hanım (we called her Ms. Prattle Rattle) would drone on about her culinary exploits, the "captivating" essay topics that she assigned to her students, how to "properly" write a wedding invitation, the "true significance" of the saying "men make houses but women make homes," her critiques of the latest film starring Hülya Koçyiğit . . . And then she would reminisce about how she met her "life partner," delving into memories about their past and their intimacy. Fevziye Hanım was a phenomenon all on her own. She'd studied at the two-year education institute, so even her own students had received more of an education than her; nonetheless, she was sent to represent the entire school during a meeting with Kenan Evren, the president appointed after the coup of 1980, and was introduced as "Dr. Fevziye Lokmacı." We should've understood that, in the eyes of the Board of Higher Education, she was far more important than us; but even if we had, what good would it have done us? Although some of us secretly sneered at her, the fact of the matter was that she had secured her position at the school while others, like myself, were assigned to schools in distant provinces, or just got fired. And she was fully confident that she would have the title "Dr." officially conferred on her. It was a relatively simple matter; all that was needed was the issuing of a decree. One morning, Fevziye Hanım would awake as Dr. Lokmacı.

I was in the kitchen. Aslı had left and Hayriye Hanım was complaining, saying that Aslı just did whatever she wanted regardless of what she was told. When she saw my indifference, Hayriye Hanım launched into a tirade: Do you know what she does? Instead of soaking the diapers in warm water like I tell her to do, she secretly washes them with detergent. And not only that, she always leaves early.

I knew what she was trying to do: by belittling Aslı, she was hoping to make herself look bigger. And if she couldn't succeed in that, she wanted to convince me of the hopelessness of it all. What do you want me to do? I asked. Fire her? It's clear that you're not happy with how things stand.

In times like that, out of sheer stubbornness I would emphasize the "you," knowing that she wanted me to call her "Mother." No, of course not, she said, as I expected. She enjoyed complaining about Aslı and took a certain pleasure from reproaching her; who else could Hayriye Hanım criticize? Me? She couldn't do it to my face. She'd have to wait until Haluk came home. Then she'd start complaining about her aches and pains. And the best way to get her to take a rest in the bedroom would be to counter her complaints with even more suggestions. Once she was gone, the children would take over:

Mom, guess what happened today! Ozan would say. Mom, there's something I want you to buy for me, Özlem would shout as she came into the kitchen. What I'd never been able to say to Haluk, Aslı, Hayriye Hanım or Ms. Prattle Rattle, I could say to them:

Could you please be quiet? I'm not in the mood. Please!

But now, I'd do anything to hear their voices. What happened at school today? Which is a better tale: a dump truck, or a walking, talking, singing baby? What toy do you want the most?

* * *

I completely forgot that I'd bought a plastic cup, which I was going to use as a vase. When I was unpacking my shopping, my heart leaped for joy when I saw it. Now I can use my drinking glass again. But much to my chagrin, the red carnations are beginning to wither. Every day I snip off the end of the stems in the hopes of drawing out their life. I change the water every few hours, adding half an aspirin and sprinkling the petals with water. But it's all in vain, and I must accept the fact that there's nothing I can do. Two more carnations have died, wilting and turning black, so I have no choice but to throw them away. Only four are left, and their stems are now quite short. If I snip them any more, I'll have to put them in a coffee cup.

Which one will last the longest? Maybe I should give that one an award, but what could it be? I could throw that one out last. But no, that wouldn't be an award—of course you're going to throw it out last! I could dry it out, saving it from death.

Night is falling, and I can't bear it when darkness falls. As it gets darker, I feel like something is swelling in my chest, a sea that will eventually gush forth and wash me away. But there's nothing I can do but wait out these two days. It might be easier if I think of these days as a test. When Ozan was a baby, he loved taking medicine, so when he refused to eat, I'd tell him that the food was medicine. And now, it's just the same for me. I understand that in difficult times, my dervish soul enjoys being tested, and I must swallow the difficulties of each and every day.

There were some people at the school who welcomed me with open arms and supported me in the spirit of solidarity, but only one of them, Aykut Bey, was considerate enough to realize that the weekend might be tedious for me and invited me out. Of course, I didn't accept his invitation, because I knew that if I tried to escape from my suffering once, I'd lose faith in my belief that escape isn't possible. I have to be strong, so that I can better understand how far my strength can actually go. And I must stop feeling resentful when people don't support me. And who would want to spend their weekend with a teary-eyed woman they hardly knew? No, it's better if they don't act so friendly in the beginning, if they don't say: Sibel Hanım, don't worry, we're by your side. Doesn't every word we speak have its own injunction? So why didn't anyone else think that standing by my side included weekends too? Just like the others in Izmir, they find my presence objectionable. Hadn't I seen that even the people I trusted the most disappeared in my hour of need?

What do the other faculty members here think of me? I wonder if they think: A woman like her, who left her husband and children, cannot be respectable. But, no, of course they don't think that. My imagination is getting the better of me. One of them had even said: I wish my wife had the strength to do what you've done. Who said that? Aykut Bey. Does that mean that there's only one person here who understands me and my outlook on life? That's something to think about.

So it's possible that they think I'm odd. But then there's Mustafa Bey; he graduated from the same school as me. And there's Turgut, who I haven't seen since I was a student, as well as Faik's friends. Some of them I've already called. But they won't invite me out either. Why? Is it because they don't know how unhappy I am, living in a guesthouse in the middle of nowhere? How could they? And why should people think that I might be upset? What right do I have to take offense? I'm not putting up with all this suffering so that people will like me or even look up to me. If I'm subjecting myself to self-denial, I'm doing it in my own name. Wasn't my pride what mattered the most? Isn't that why I'm fighting? To prove myself, to show that I won't be easily disheartened?

I believe that what I'm doing is right. Let people think whatever they want. What if I'd given myself over to the life of a housewife? After all those years of toil, becoming an ordinary woman who washes and irons her husband's shirts, always remaining in the background . . . Hadn't I worked for years and endured countless challenges to secure a place for myself and be independent? And just when I achieved all that, establishing myself and realizing my own strength, what was I supposed to do? Surrender?

Sweetie, what would you like me to cook for dinner? Are you going to take us out? We're bored of being at home. (Me and the children. Get used to being in the background. It's not proper to openly say that you're bored. It's not appropriate for a spouse who thinks of nothing but her devoted husband and mother. We're bored. Would it be okay if we went to the movies? That is, if you don't have any work to do. If you're not tired. Our weariness is second-class, the weariness of doing dishes and laundry. There's nothing respectable about it.) Knowing that I wouldn't be like that, for years I went to work every morning and came home in the dark of evening; it was a source of pride, and I had to shrug off the fact that Hayriye Hanım held me in lower regard than all the other housewives she knew, even though I never once doubted that I deserved every ounce of my self-respect. After getting accustomed to a life of holding my head high and being self-reliant, did they expect me to take on the role of what they considered to be a traditional wife, whose only purpose in life was to make her husband and children (and mother-in-law) happy? Could I bear morning coffee with Gönül Abla and the silent war with Hayriye Hanım night and day?

When I heard I was going to be transferred to Trabzon, the first thing we did was visit Haluk's sister and ask if she could help with the children. We still hadn't decided what we'd do, but Hayriye Hanım's attitude would shape our final decision. I'm thinking, I would say, of going, and if I do, I was wondering . . . Could you be there for them? We wouldn't say: You were thinking about moving in with us. I wouldn't remind her that she'd once mentioned that she should move in. No, I wouldn't say anything about the proverb "a mother's place is by her son's side." We'd plead, and nothing more.

We have Aslı, I said, but the children need an adult around . . .

SCENE 23:

INT. - NIGHT

Gönül Abla's home. The family council has gathered. Hayriye Hanım is sitting at the head of the table. Ozan is sitting in her lap. Gönül Abla walks into the room carrying a tray of tea.

HAYRİYE H.

Don't you have any pity for your poor children? Just at the age when they need a mother the most, how could you even think of leaving?

SİBEL

Mother, I'm not going anywhere. All I said was that I can't make up my mind.

GÖNÜL

Sibel, I think my mother meant to say that you should take the children into account when making your decision.

SİBEL
(Irritably)

Abla, of course I'm thinking of them. They're the reason I can't make up my mind.

HALUK

Now let's all calm down and talk about this rationally. Mother, Sibel has been working for years. She's used to it. I've said again and again that it's not so easy for her to quit.

HAYRİYE H.

What's so hard about it? She's worked enough. She should stay at home and be the woman of the house.

GÖNÜL
(Softening her tone)
My dear Sibel, haven't you always complained that balancing home life and work life is so difficult? Here's your opportunity. How could you think of going so far away? Send in your resignation and stay at home. Be the head of your household for a while.

Sibel sits in silence.

HALUK
Abla, Sibel doesn't like just being at home.

HAYRİYE H.
But she will, once she gives it a try! And it will be nice to see you more often, Sibel. Your friends and relatives, even your own children, miss spending time with you. And you know that housewives don't stay home all day. In the afternoon we could go out and visit our friends. Time passes so quickly, you'll see!

SİBEL
That's not what I'm worried about. I can't imagine not working. It's my life. How can I explain it? I know that I'd be miserable. I'd feel useless.

GÖNÜL
(Laughing)
So are you saying that women like me are useless?

SİBEL

Abla, absolutely not. That's not what I meant. All I'm trying to say is that—

HALUK

(Cutting her off)

And there's one more thing. Sibel contributes to our income.

HAYRİYE HANIM

What's that supposed to mean? Don't you make enough money to look after your family? You know that from the very beginning I've been bothered by the fact that Sibel works. What business do women have being out on the streets all day and coming home late at night? I'm not used to women acting like that. Women should know their place: the home.

Silence falls over the room and all that can be heard is the melody of a plaintive song.

SİBEL

Haluk, the kids are getting sleepy. I think it might be best if we take them home.

HAYRİYE H.

If you ask me, Ozan looks perfectly content. Isn't that true, my little prince?

Ozan looks at his mother but doesn't say anything. Özlem is sitting on the floor, clearly bored of playing with the toys she brought. When Sibel says that they might go home, she starts gathering her toys up.

SİBEL

I'm really tired too. It's been such a long day! My thoughts are a mess. I just want to lie down and think things over.

HAYRİYE H.

If that's what you need to do, then go right ahead.

Everyone starts getting up.

HAYRİYE H.

What we think is best might not seem that way for you. In the end, you'll have to decide.

As the children get ready to go, Hayriye Hanım keeps speaking but we can't hear what she says because of the music that starts playing. As the tempo of the music slows down, the volume also decreases and we can hear Hayriye Hanım again.

HAYRİYE H.

There's just one more thing. If you're thinking that I'll come over and look after your children if you go, you're wrong. At my age, I'm the one who needs to be looked after. You do see what I'm saying, don't you? I just don't have the energy to take care of anyone else.

The camera remains focused on Sibel's face as her expression hardens.

SİBEL

Yes, Mother. I know.

CUT TO:
SCENE 24:

EXT. SEASIDE - DAY

The scene opens with a shot of a bright blue sky. As the camera pans down, the sea comes into view, and as the camera pans left, the shore becomes visible. We see Sibel walking alone. Her expression is pensive. She has a purse slung over her shoulder, and her hands are in her coat pockets. We see her from the front and she continues walking toward the camera. Occasionally she stops and looks out over the sea. When she gets fairly close to the camera, she stops and sits on a bench. From this point forward, the scene is shot from Sibel's perspective. After panning around, the camera focuses on the sea. The water near the shore is murky, like pitch. The camera pans upward to the horizon. In contrast to the water near the shore, the distant sea is a crisp blue. The camera remains focused on the horizon. Throughout the scene, music plays in the background.

FADEOUT

This morning I had to throw out yet another carnation. There are only three left now. Day by day, the traces of Izmir are disappearing from my life.

As the carnations wilt, they remain perched on their stems. When roses wither, they droop; that's the sign that they've decided to give up, and once that happens, there's no turning back—they shrivel and fade. Carnations droop only at the very end, holding out as long as they can. Only when they can bear it no longer, when there's no other hope, they begin to fade. But they always stand proudly, never making concessions. And that's how they die, never surrendering.

I think I can tell which one is the longest lived. It looks fresher, more alive than the other two; even now it is a testament to its immortality. Be joyous, fiery carnation, bearing your crimson so proudly like a badge of honor; I grant you the right to eternal existence between the pages of my yellow notebook. Regardless of whether you were the gift of a lover, and even if there never was a lover, it is you who will live forever.

The carnations' race toward death . . . It might be better to say, a race *not* to die. What's the point of it all? While everyone else is competing with each other and with themselves, my sole concern is the race between my carnations. Who's going to be richer, who'll be more famous, who'll be able to buy new furniture every year, who's going to buy a new wardrobe first, whose husband is more handsome and whose children are smarter? Who, who, who? Hülya, I hope your ears are burning; when it comes to competing, no one can ever best you.

Let me tell you, my dear, these are the best you can find. And do you see that one over there? I bought it in Italy. But it's getting old. Just the other day I saw that a new one came out. As soon as I get the money, I'm going to buy it. Curtains, armchairs, side tables; skirts, sweaters, scarves . . . Everything gets old and there are always newer, better ones, Hülya observes with grim determination, never wearying or pausing to consider just what she is doing.

There may be many things that I don't know, but I do know why I'm not like Hülya. In every period of my life, I've learned the same lesson: we must be prudent, patient and perseverant.

* * *

Patiently she waited for her father to fall asleep, and then went to the place where her father had hidden the patent leather shoes he bought her for the upcoming holiday. She wanted to wear them the next day. (Not because the clothes she wore to school were old and worn; everyone was used to seeing her wear worn out shoes at school, and if she wore new shoes people might find it odd.) The fact is, she wanted to wear them to Birsen's birthday party. There was a dress that had once belonged to her mother (What's wrong with that? She'd never even worn it, and if her life hadn't been cut short, she would have worn it during the holidays) which her grandmother had taken in so it would fit Sibel; but she knew that Birsen would see the ruse. It didn't even look like a new dress, and she thought that every button and pleat seemed to be leering at her, betraying its age. As soon as Birsen saw the dress, she'd recognize the touch of Sibel's grandmother in how it had been re-sewn. While others may not have noticed, Birsen always did. But the shoes? They were something entirely different. A pair of shoes that Birsen didn't know about. That's what would save her. People would ask: Oh, are those new? She hadn't heard such a question in a long, long time. Yes, they're new. My father bought them the other day. Lying in bed, she squirmed in delight.

Had Sibel heard that everyone has a childhood memory of hiding their holiday shoes under their beds? Or did she just not want to seem overly zealous? Nonetheless, she didn't dare bring the shoes into her bed. After polishing the shoes with the sleeve of her wool coat and kissing her reflection in the glossy leather, she neatly arranged them at the foot of her bed. Knowing that the shoes would be there waiting for her the next day gave her a greater joy than anything else in the world.

Later, when she heard footsteps approaching, she thought of hiding the shoes, but in the end she decided it wasn't worth the risk of getting caught in the act. When her father turned on the light, she couldn't bring herself to feign sleep, so she just looked at him as though asking if something were amiss. He stood there looking around, not saying a word, and soon enough he found what he was looking for. He picked up the shoes and as he was leaving, he expected that Sibel would ask something, or at the very least start sobbing. But she did neither. So he turned around and, without looking at her, said: I bought these for the holiday. You can't wear them any other time.

Sibel looked straight into his eyes. She didn't say anything, but not once did she turn away her gaze, not even after he closed the door and the sound of his footsteps faded away.

The other day when I was coming home from the university I saw that, in addition to the Trabzonspor buses, a large number of cars were parked in the field near the guesthouse where the football team was training. Of course, they couldn't all belong to the trainers, so I knew they must've belonged to fans who'd come to watch the team practice. They sat in their cars, as if placing bets. I wondered, what's the difference between that and betting on cock fights or camel wrestling? The cocks and camels don't know they're being bet on, just like the football players. Or maybe they do know, and derive a certain pleasure from it? That seemed more thought-provoking. But what do I know about football?

Once you start a sesquipedalian line of reasoning, there's no end to it. I thought that if I went for a walk I could shake off my loneliness for a while. There was no need for me to be judgmental, but I was irritated by the thought that the football team and its fans had occupied the grounds. There are other places to go, I thought. I could go down to the shores of the Black Sea and dip my fingers into the water, feeling its current.

Dark, thick clouds had blown in, and rain seemed imminent. Getting stuck in the rain was an unattractive prospect. I'd be completely inconsolable if I were to get completely soaked. As if I had anyone to console me in the first place! No, I decided, it'll be better if I just stay at home. Have I always been afraid of the rain? I don't remember. What would be worse? Being here in this tiny room or out in the rain? I was already barricaded in by walls, fields and distances; add rain to that and it would be a disaster.

Today there are a lot of people in the common area near the guest-house. As the senior professors while away the time playing poker and bridge at the clubhouse, the junior faculty members, lacking the rank to join them, have opted to stroll the grounds, taking in the fresh air. It must be nice: a stroll in the light rain, some gossip. And wasn't that the entire point of the existence of department chairs? To be gossiped about in weather like this?

Is the sky darkening, or is it just my state of mind? The thought of spending the upcoming two days in my room, and even worse, the accompanying three nights, is terrifying. The darkness of night will give way to the light of day, only to be followed yet again by darkness; it's unbearable.

How were my weekends back at home? Were they more enjoyable? Less tedious? I must confess, they weren't. Especially Sundays. But I shouldn't be misguided by longing; here, the tediousness of Sundays is compounded only by loneliness.

My son would usually get up before us, and the racket would begin. Hounded by a sense of regret, like that inspired by the sin of lovemaking, I'd get up irritably, yet again unable to sleep in, which I'd been dreaming of doing all week long. Because it was Sunday, I'd think to myself that I should prepare a special breakfast: toast the bread as the kitchen fills with smoke, cook up some sausage, slice the salami, boil up some eggs just like they want. Özlem likes them hard-boiled, Ozan medium-boiled and Haluk soft-boiled, while his mother doesn't eat eggs because they raise her blood pressure. For her I'll have to soak some feta cheese in water to draw out the salt and then serve it up in slices. There's jam for Özlem, honey for Ozan and butter for Haluk, but I have to remember to let it sit out for half an hour because he likes it soft. Finally, breakfast is served!

Then the pleading begins for the children to finish their milk: Please, do it for me; if you don't finish it, the milk left in the glass will cry. You don't want to make it cry, do you?

For some reason, I'm always the last one to get up from the table. Then it's time to clear the dishes. Don't we all have the right to a little weekend laziness? A cigarette while reading the morning paper . . . But no! Hayriye Hanım has been looking after the children all week and is exhausted. Haluk Bey has been working so hard these days; doesn't he deserve a little rest? In fact, they both deserve a cup of coffee, light on the sugar. And you never know when you might have an unexpected guest. Laziness is not permitted. Haluk would admonish me: Come on, it's time to clear the table. There would always be a rush to be somewhere or do something. What are we late for this time? There's more cleaning to do, more ironing. Then, with my mother, visit my sisters in the afternoon. It's been so long since I've seen them. So very long! Just two nights ago we had dinner with them. Fine, don't get upset, we'll meet them somewhere closer to home; be cheerful and the rest will be easy.

Gönül Abla told me that she started wearing blouses and skirts because of me. Before I met you, she said, I hardly ever wore them and now it feels odd to go out in anything else. We've known each other since I was studying at the university. I usually wore pants or a skirt, along with a sweater in winter or a blouse in summer. I never had time to spend hours getting dressed and putting on makeup. And now it's the same. When female teachers were forbidden from wearing pants, I wore skirts. My sister-in-law was right. Sometimes she claims to be from the generation of '68; but in fact, she was of a different generation—the generation of skirts and blouses. She may not know it, but that's her true place. Like some people, if she doesn't complain, it's because she doesn't know how to relish complaining. This is a holiday outfit, that's for cooking, this is for home, that's for holiday visits, this is for going to the market, and this is a morning gown. A morning gown! If she insists that for years she didn't make a point of swishing through her home in the morning wearing a long morning gown, don't be taken in; it's a pale blue longing that she has suppressed and she will probably do so until the day she dies.

But what does "the generation of skirts and blouses" really mean? Could it be something like this: a new type of woman, always buried in work, constantly thinking about all that needs to be done and striving to surpass everyone else? A new type of female figure who critiqued women even more than men at feminist gatherings, and because they weren't the type of women who could vaunt their husbands' wealth, they hurled themselves headlong into the fray of competition among men but were never absolved of the duties expected of them at home and hence worked twice as hard, and were twice as tired and twice as exploited; that's why they're doubled over, that's why they're so combative, but mostly with themselves. You can find women like them everywhere in the world. In big cities you see them, standing proud and trying to raise their voices; but there's confusion about what they should do. These women aren't about to give up on their resistance in the streets and submit to being put back in a display case. In their struggle, it's unlikely that they'll be brought down to their knees.

And you, Sibel Hanım, you could be back in your warm home in Izmir, how nice would that be! Washing Haluk's clothes, ironing his shirts, playing the role of a happy woman who's proud of her husband. Never getting into trouble with the drivers of university shuttles or arguing with professors. Wouldn't that be great? No. Why not? My dear Sibel, you've really lost it. Being alone hasn't done you any good. You're so used to working like a horse driving a mill that the moment you stop, you're at a loss for what to do.

While I may not know why, this is actually a kind of escape for me, I know that for certain. Perhaps it is an escape from being a cog in the works. More succinctly, an escape from the self, only to later seek refuge in the self—if there still is one that can offer solace. We are so devastated by the years, by life, and we are so worn down that, in the end, we have to think for a long time to be able to discover who we really are.

Let's say that there is a meaningful reason why I'm here now. I'm involved in a struggle and the fact that it leaves you no time to think about who you are is what keeps you alive. I know why I'm here; it's simple: I cannot let myself be defeated. Who am I? Why have I struggled so much? The memorized response: To prove myself. Which self? As a mother, a wife, a teacher, a woman, choosing the best one among the given paradigms? Yet again, paradigms! Very well, but why is the best one good? Why is it good to be a good teacher, or a good woman, wife or mother? And conversely, what's bad about being a bad teacher (or woman, wife, mother, etc.)? Bad according to whom? All our lives, are we trying to be good (or bad) merely for the sake of others? Why? If we do it for ourselves, just think of what we could become! Would we be left with the same question? Do I have the strength to know what's good and bad? What does it mean to be the best and the worst? And why the very notion of best and worst? Can't we be a little good and very bad, or very good and a little bad?

Sibel Hanım, seek out and find yourself. There's no one here who can help you recognize and understand yourself. You must do it alone.

I started writing a letter to Haluk but haven't finished it yet. But is there really any need for me to write letters? We talk on the phone every day. And what I've written so far is preposterous:

The faucet in the bathroom has been dripping ever since I arrived here. I wonder, how many months has it been dipping like that? If Haluk were here, he'd fix it. My room isn't very well lit. Again if Haluk were here, he'd put in a brighter bulb. As you can see, life without Haluk isn't going very well. Without him, life consists of headaches and tedium. People better understand certain truths only from a distance . . .

What is this? If I didn't write it just to make him happy, why did I? Haluk isn't the type of man who goes around fixing faucets and changing light bulbs. He'll only do it when he gets tired of being nagged. And what "truths" had I come to understand? That I can't get by in life without him? If that really is the case, why haven't I packed up and gone back home then? Sibel Hanım, you're a liar and a hypocrite!

And what were you trying to say when you wrote:

"My dear Haluk, I can only hope that this will all come to an end in June. It may not even take that long. In the next few weeks, if I really can't bear it any longer, should I come back home? You're truly a selfless person. In this stubborn struggle of mine, who else could've been as understanding as you and shown me the gentle guidance that you have?"

I'd like to tear the letter to pieces. If I'm just acting and have enough self-respect left to be ashamed of what I've done, I should put an end to this charade. That is, if I have the courage to face myself.

Just a few minutes ago, didn't I catch myself thinking about the markets back home? My memories of them are so vivid. The roads I know so well that are bathed in a constant light, the same faces, the same conversations . . .

The kids have homework to do, Haluk says, so let's not stay too long.

Okay.

We should start getting lunch ready. (Yes, we've just finished breakfast so let's start thinking about lunch. Brilliant!)

What should I make? If only we'd gone shopping. We don't have much to eat at home.

Shopping? Now? Don't I have the right to sit and read the paper? (This is said in a male voice: stern, firm, imperious.)

(Female voice: fragile, slight, careful not to offend, soft, conciliatory): What would you like me to cook?

(Male voice): Just put something together! (Irritated) Why can't I ever just relax at home on Sunday? (He decides to adopt a softer tone.) Okay fine, you do the breakfast dishes and I'll go out and get something for lunch.

Hurry, there's shopping to do! Then unpack the groceries and prepare lunch. We're running late! You know that we're going to my sister's in the afternoon, not in the evening, right? My mother's been waiting for us since morning. Hurry up, quick! Have you finished your homework?

The bond of my (our) marriage is a spell which can be broken with a mere word or stern glance; even though we try to keep it from crumpling like a delicate flower, its petals often seem to be fluttering down around us.

Why are you getting so irritated? If you don't want to go to my sister's, then just tell me up front!

I'm not the one who's irritated!

Fine, don't drag it out. Are you finished with everything? Is lunch ready?

It'll be ready soon. Why don't you call down the children, and your mother too?

The kids aren't hungry yet.

Of course they're not, they had breakfast an hour and a half ago. But we can't wait for them to get hungry; we have to eat now. We don't want to be late going to see my sister, or Yalçın, or whoever it is we're visiting. We're always in a hurry. Every Sunday, every single day, must be a rush and bustle.

But wherever we go, whoever we talk to, the conversation is always the same. Sometimes we start at the end, sometimes at the beginning, sometimes in the middle. Ozan and Özlem's studies at school, their mischief and the woes they've caused. Let's say this litany of complaints is number one. Number two would be the litany of self-praise. Since we're talking about the children, we mustn't fail to mention that the younger one looks just like me, and he's always quick to retort. Do you know what he said the other day? There's no need to point out that these discussions of the comical things the children say mean nothing other than: at this point in the conversation, I would do well to remind you just how clever I am. In the subsequent litany, it's time to demonstrate a more intellectual level of thought by turning to issues of general culture and contemporary events. And for that business, there's a typical topic always at hand, ready to be warmed in the pot: the state of affairs in Turkey. Tsk-tsk. Let me tell you what, every ten years we go five years back.

(This is a suitable point to add some timeless observations about the trip to Europe we took a few years ago; my memories of that journey are still fresh in my mind.) We discuss the same topics, and only the words are different as we scramble for new comparisons and striking examples. Endless debates about details that will never change the main problem . . .

In the end, my fears came true, as if a secret agreement had been drawn up for that purpose. Everything is shrouded in darkness. I was always afraid of midnight suddenly appearing in the middle of the day. And that's what happened. The radio station in Trabzon seems to be in on it all and keeps playing songs of separation. Songs of sorrow and darkness, and me: a day of pitch dark. The bare bulb, which is reluctant even at night to light the room, tries with all its might to penetrate the darkness, but to no avail. The callous voice on the radio repeats the same injunction: Wishing you all a pleasant weekend. Thank you, but there is nothing pleasant about it. What else do I need? I have bread (even if just a little), and water. I've got it all!

This darkness and loneliness could drive a person to madness. Since my childhood I've always been afraid of losing my mind. The thought occurs to me: Do people who are afraid of madness succumb to it more quickly?

In saying that, I should be more cautious. Whenever I've said that I'm afraid of something, it has always come true in the blink of an eye. Please don't let it get dark, I pleaded; and the sky turned dark. Please don't let it rain, I begged; and the rain poured down. No, I'm not afraid of anything. In fact, I'm rather fond of madness; the one thing that I've always desired is to completely lose my mind. I hope that my dream will come true as soon as possible.

The rain is falling in torrents. A dull light hangs in the sky. The Black Sea has been transformed into a green mass. Far in the distance, probably where the shores of the Soviet Union dip into the sea, there's a thin blue line. And behind that there is a silhouette like the pallid shadow of a mountain. It could just be a mirage because it's vanishing as the rainfall turns into a deluge. It's gone. That pale green water becomes the sky somewhere out there near the horizon and rises up over us.

Eternity seems so tangible that you could reach out and touch it. And that same eternity leaves you feeling even lonelier. It's not about being alone in a world full of people; it's about being forgotten in the universe.

Out there in the distance is my nearest neighbor, the Soviet Union.

I wonder where those people who were strolling around in the rain went. They must've gone to a match. In this weather? It's possible. In Trabzon, the weekend is synonymous with football.

There's not much left of the zucchini stew that I've been eating for the last two days, certainly not enough for dinner. I think of going out to gather some fennel, but it's raining too hard.

Of course this would happen! There's always the chance that something can happen that you've never considered in all your fears. Everywhere in this country there's a blackout when it rains. The fact that I never foresaw this is a testament to stupidity. So what am I going to do now? There's nothing I can do but get into bed and pull the blanket up over my head. And then what? I won't be able to sleep. Am I going to think back over the trip here? There's only one part of the trip that hasn't become dulled by thinking about it: the trip from Samsun to Trabzon. But once I finish thinking about that, what will I think about when life becomes even more difficult? Will there be more challenging times in my life? For now, only the electricity is out. But I shouldn't take the situation too lightly. Because the electricity went out, the room has been plunged into silence; no longer does the radio accompany me with songs of grief. And as I sit in the dark, I can't even use the stove to make some tea. This couldn't have happened—for now, at least—at a worse time.

What if the electricity doesn't come back on by nightfall? Or even the whole night? What will I do in the pitch dark of my room? I don't have any candles, and for that matter I don't even have any matches. All I have is a lighter that's about to run out of fluid.

Then again I do have the phone number of Aykut Bey. I could call him and ask if he'd come pick me up. But at this hour? Just as evening is settling in? I could, if things become desperate. But as long as there's life, there's hope. Off to bed with you, Sibel Hanım!

The letter in the yellow envelope read: You are hereby notified that employment for you in the Aegean region of Turkey has been deemed objectionable and it has been decided that until further orders are issued, you shall not be assigned any duties. It wasn't exactly like that, but something similar, sounding magisterial. We knew all about the envelopes that were sent out in the days of martial law. An envelope bearing the number 1402 meant that you had been relieved of all your duties and there would be no questioning or disputing the matter. Many of my colleagues had suffered the same fate. Some faculty members who'd been awarded grants to do research abroad were summoned back to their universities, whereupon they were served papers stating their termination. Others were hauled off by the police as they were teaching and taken to the dean's office, where they were handed the glad tidings that they no longer needed to come to work. Still others got the surprise of a yellow envelope when they went to pick up their paychecks. It was a tragedy of yellow envelopes. That's how people who dedicated years of their lives to their universities were shown the door—with a yellow envelope. In those days, even though it hadn't been authorized, police were posted under every tree and in every corridor on campus; I wondered if the deans and other administrators were afraid that a professor they fired might try to kill them. As if they were blind to the fact that firing them without a word of warning, when those professors had carried the burden of providing for their households after years of building up their careers, wouldn't bring them to ruin.

So why had I been given a second-class envelope and informed that my presence was deemed to be "objectionable" only in the Aegean region? According to Article 2 of Martial Law No. 1402: A second-class yellow envelope confers upon its bearer second-class honor. And since I was deemed to be objectionable only in the Aegean region, this logic suggested that I'd bring no harm to the Black Sea coast of the country. A brilliant collaboration between martial law and the Board of Higher Education. While one lecturer might be roughed up and broken down by questionings, another is deemed to be questionable and sent far from her family to take the place of someone else who's been fired. Fine, but had the Black Sea region been inoculated against my presence? How could they belittle me like this? I have no choice but to settle accounts with them. I'll be even more "objectionable" than I was before. What are you going to do then? The order for my appointment to the university in Trabzon wasn't carried out under the auspices of martial law. Rather, it was stipulated per the terms of an article in the university's regulations, but it was unclear which article: was it "L," "I" or "l"? I read through all of the articles of the regulations that were indicated by "L," "I" and "l," but none provided reasonable justification for such a decision. The most relevant article I found concerned the exchange of movable goods between universities, which would suggest that an even more devious insult had been devised. Dear Esteemed Lecturer: Under the terms of the article concerning the exchange of movable goods, we have duly appointed you to another university. We hope that you have no objections. If you do, please indicate them and we will take them into consideration in light of the article concerning the transfer of live animals between institutions of higher education.

Thank you, dear sir. In fact, I am more than willing to be a movable good.

But those months of being sentenced to the life of a housewife were a torment. I'd rather not remember them! Months of uncertainty, of being kept in the dark. They know your weak spots and use them against you. For years it was the same: She can bear this load.

And then they heap more and more work on you, but what happens when they suddenly strip you of your duties, like a horse set free to graze on its own? You become uneasy, turning around and biting yourself, slowly losing your mind. That's what they tried to do. Did they think that I'd turn on my own colleagues and report them, saying that they were the guilty ones? Imbeciles. What offense have I committed? There's not a single offense you can pin on me. What did I do? Yes, I spoke of Nâzım Hikmet. And I'd do it again today. You just wait and see! It'll be the first thing I do when I start teaching in three days. Am I supposed to ignore Nâzım, whose fame you've only increased with all your rules and restrictions? I have an obligation to speak of everyone and everything to which you've brought fame by trying to vilify them.

I don't care an iota about the punishment you've meted out to me. I'd always wanted to see this part of the country. Just seeing the water droplets glistening like pearls on the needles of the pine trees would make the trip worthwhile, just like the rainbows. I've never seen things like this! I saw a rainbow from end to end, stretching across the sky in all its seven hues until a fresh raincloud drifted in and the rain began anew. No, I don't deserve this reward. Surrounded by so much beauty, what kind of punishment is this? Thank you, gentlemen, for this punishment. Wouldn't it have been a pity if I hadn't met that shepherd hungering for bread or those women toiling in the rain? If I'd wasted away my life with the nagging of my mother-in-law and the nitpicking of my husband? I owe a debt of gratitude to your existence; let me kiss your hand in gratitude! Neither the rain nor the clouds can dampen my spirits now, nor can the fear in your idiotic eyes that have rolled inward, blind to the world.

We were on the road to the town of Çarşamba.

The landscape was crisscrossed by rivers, streams and brooks, and it seemed like there were bridges around every curve and bend. The bus rattled over the bridges and I wondered if I'd see that river that seemed to be flowing stubbornly away from the sea as we approached Samsun. Was it still resisting the pull of the sea? Just think: A river that flows uphill! A paragon of stubbornness. Just like the folk song, "The Streams of Ordu." People and rivers compete for the title of obstinacy: *Even if Ordu rises up against me / I won't let you go.*

All along the road there were strings of villages. I tried to read the names of the villages on the signs along the roadway but they flashed by too quickly. In the light of day, life was thriving. Bright white clothes hung up to dry reveled in the sunlight; Monday must be laundry day, I surmised. Not content with just hanging out the laundry to dry, they brought out the elderly too, seating them on porches and patios so they could take in the sun. I saw them in front of the houses, leaning against trees, idling along bridges, giving themselves over to the embrace of light. Only later would I learn how precious a few rays of sunlight are along the coast of the Black Sea; maybe that's why it still strikes me as odd that life here is shaped by the sun.

There were herd animals, either wandering alone or watched over by women and children as they grazed along the sides of the road.

We arrived in Çarşamba.

Just like in the song, a flood could have taken the town. Wherever I looked, water seemed to be gushing forth and everything was green. The trunks of poplars vanished into water. Were those hazelnut trees? They were squat and, like everything else, bursting into leaf; their branches seemed to grow straight out of the ground.

Just outside town there was a large river flowing into the sea. Could it have been the Green River? My knowledge of geography had abandoned me. Why hadn't I brought a map? Then I truly would have been a tourist, eager to see the Black Sea coast in spring after hearing praise of its greenery, seashore and rivers.

O my Mehmet, my Mehmet,
I was never upset with you.
They were just spreading rumors,
Never once did I say those words.

On the dashboard of the bus there were fake birds, probably the work of prisoners, that had beads draped over them; as they swung on the perches in their cages, they looked at ease, even free. Someone needed to tell them that we passed a place—somewhere that might be unknown to me but that they would know, a beautiful place where they don't live in cages. But not everywhere is as nice as being in a cage! At the very least, they should have felt some unease. For the love of God, where are we being taken! Driver, could you pull over, we want to fly back to our homeland!

Just below the birds, there was a calligraphic plaque, also draped with beads: "Entrust Yourself to God." That struck me as being unnecessary. Could we entrust our souls to anyone else? We'd placed our lives in the hands of the driver, and he'd done the same to his god.

In the yards of the homes there were grass huts that reminded me of the ones made in some places in Africa. What could they have been? Almost every home had one, and some of them were built up against trees. Do they hang things in there to dry? Perhaps corn cobs and husks have to be dried so they can be kept as feed through the winter. But there was no one to ask.

Most of the homes were built up off the ground, probably because of the constant threat of floods; if one river doesn't over-flow its banks, then surely another will. Like the farmhouses in old American films, there was a set of steps leading up to a porch where the people spend most of their time during the day. But that thought gave me pause: How alienated we can be in our own countries! The only description I can come up with to describe a house on the Black Sea is an image from an American film. In a while, one of the young women living in that house will be visited by her lover. (Contraception is for people like us. Reproduction among "superior" Americans can't be held back by birth control! Every home should be brimming with children; three or four girls, and just as many boys; if not, others may take over the world. To realize the American dream, it's the duty of every citizen to reproduce and create well-raised, mature, developed individuals of superior character.) He will be a blond-haired, blue-eyed handsome cowboy riding a sleek sorrel horse. The young woman will step onto the porch with her curly blond locks and hoop skirt. Before they say a word, they'll kiss; after they talk, they'll kiss. It's the director's orders. Development is proportionate to kissing. The young man will invite the woman to the dance being held at Joe's place that night, and the woman will giggle and accept. Then the woman will leap onto the back of the horse, and the man and woman will ride off into the sunset, gazing out at the horizon of that Texas plain studded with craggy boulders, and we'll watch them get smaller and smaller as they recede into the distance.

We passed over more streams and rivers: Cüri, Akçay, Lahna . . .

Ünye is a charming town! I realized that we had crossed into the province of Ordu because the license plates all started with 52 instead of 55. Did I have any friends from Ünye? No, but a friend of mine had been reappointed to Çakmak, a nearby town, where she had to stay for three years. She must've been the one who told me about Ünye.

Çakmak! It's a noun, but also a verb, çak. Meaning to grind, to pulverize. My grandmother used it like that: First you have to çak the walnuts, then you can do your homework. She also used it to mean, "get a beating." Get over here right now, or I'll çak you over the head!

Take off what you're wearing. What a disgrace! This is your holiday outfit. You're so careless! As if you had a closet full of clothes. What are you going to wear now? Our relatives are going to come pay their respects and there you'll be in your muddy clothes. Now go upstairs and change, and change your brother's clothes too. If you knew you were going to fall down in the mud you should've told your father so he could buy you an extra outfit. Our relatives only come to visit once in a blue moon, so make sure you don't look like a beggar. You're nothing but a ragamuffin.

Sibel was still trying to hide the muddy splotches on her skirt. She didn't tell her grandmother that she'd been playing hide and seek with her friends, and she had no intention of telling her. The game was going along just fine until her brother came and told her that she had to go home. To draw out the game a little longer, she had her brother join in. While Fatma didn't say anything, Hüseyin was upset that someone younger than them was going to join the game. He waited until it was his turn to count; when he finished counting, he went straight for Orhan, chasing him down before he could run to the safe zone. Just as Orhan was passing a muddy puddle, running with all his might, Hüseyin caught up and shoved him into the mud. When Sibel ran to help Orhan, Hüseyin did the same to her. But then, with Fatma's help, Hüseyin got a dousing in the muddy puddle too. But what was done was done; just like Orhan's corduroy pants, Sibel's yellow taffeta dress was in a state that would undoubtedly incur her grandmother's wrath and a çak on the head.

Sibel knew very well what she had coming. Fatma tried to help her clean off the mud, but aside from spreading it around, their efforts were in vain. When she realized there was no hope, she took her brother by the hand and began plodding home to the inevitable çak that awaited her. Sibel's grandmother wouldn't be angry because the dress that she'd so meticulously sewed using her friend's sewing machine was as dirty as a mop; rather, it was the fact that they'd be disgraced in the presence of their wealthier relatives who only came around on the holidays. Without protesting or complaining, Sibel did what she was asked and changed her brother's clothes. Then she managed to find an old dress that had been given to her grandmother; maybe it had been given to her by one of their relatives who would never dream of wearing a dress like that or having their own children or grandchildren wear it. Without saying a word, Sibel put on the dress. She had an urge to say unspeakable things to her grandmother, who snapped: Is that all you could find to wear?

That day, Sibel greeted her relatives wearing that faded print dress.

It seems so far away when I think about it now.

Does Orhan yell at his daughter when she comes home covered in mud? Even if he tried, his voice would knot in his throat. He was taught to remain silent, to resist and endure, but not to shout.

We were such well-behaved children! Condemned to being well-behaved.

Soon, I thought, we'll arrive in Perşembe. The road wound along the coastline. Some of the tight curves seemed rather precarious, but the beauty of the undulating shore was enough to make you forget the danger. After each curve, you were confronted with a view as alluring as a painting. On the one side, there were hillsides bursting into flower in sprays of yellow, white and purple, and on the other side was the green-blue sea with frothy waves.

Ordu, with its broad streets and large apartment buildings, seemed to be a nice place to live.

Ünye, Çakmak, Perşembe, Ordu, Bulancak . . . The names of the towns stirred in my memory the lines of a poem I'd read long ago. They were so faint that I'd never be able to remember them; nonetheless, they were like flashes of scenes of stunning beauty, like the beauty of dreams that can never be named or described. Above all, Bulancak. The connotations it conjures up are more powerful than the others. I recalled a folk song: *O Bulancak, what is ever to be?* And then I thought of someone I knew from my university days. His name was Akın; he was tall with wavy, light brown hair and green eyes, and his expression was always dreamy yet intent. He was from Bulancak. Like most of the girls, I had a secret crush on him. So did Ferda. But she didn't just like him; she would talk all night long with the other girls at the dorm about how mad she was about him, to the point of swooning: Did you see the shirt he was wearing today? He looked soooo handsome! In fact, it didn't matter what he wore; everything looked good on him. She'd titter: Doesn't he have a nice body? Was he looking at me? When I was going to get tea I could swear that he looked at me. Did he really look?

Yes, I saw him looking at you, we'd all say. He just can't take his eyes off you. He's always watching you, haven't you noticed? This game would go on until Ferda would slip into bed, alone with her dreams of Akın. Then we'd try to concoct plans to get Akın interested in Ferda. Telling him straight out wouldn't work, we knew that; but we couldn't come up with a decent course of action. But I'd always sensed that he was gazing at me. It was a young woman's intuition; but I felt it, and it made me uneasy because I didn't want to be like the other girls who foolishly admired him. And then, of course, there was Ferda, who exhausted herself night after sleepless night thinking of him, ready to give anything just to see him smile at her, even just once.

In those years, Akın would have been surprised to find out that I liked him and that my nights were filled with thoughts of him.

Would he have swelled with pride? Swaggered a little? That unforgettable swagger! Trying to console Ferda, I'd imitate his walk, making the other girls in the dorm break into laughter.

What's become of his life? Is he as handsome as before? Would I recognize him if I saw him? Would he recognize me? I knew that such questions were pointless in the end. All these years after we parted ways, what difference would it make if he remembered me or not? The games that memory plays are bizarre. Sometimes it takes me days to remember a name; but why can I close my eyes now and remember his face so clearly? There he is in the cafeteria, wearing dark green; he looks distracted as always, as if he's just woken up, and he's leaning against a column near the tea counter talking with his friends. Without turning his head, he's gazing in the direction of a table. When I sense that I'm in his field of vision as I sit chatting with friends, having just told a joke that made everyone double over in laughter, I get up and leave the cafeteria. The possibility that my sudden departure might sadden his heart sends a jolt of pleasure through me.

We arrived in Giresun. Next would come Aksu, Espiye, Tirebolu and the others. Enough! Why do I see myself as deserving this punishment? It was nice; I enjoyed it. But now it's over. Whenever I think about travel, I'm overwhelmed by a desire to go back. Haven't I exhausted my observations about journeys?

As we approached Trabzon, the scenery became even more beautiful. What could I do? If it was beautiful, so be it. In the end it made no difference; I was going to Trabzon. My thoughts kept returning to the same question: When will I be able to go back home and be with my children?

I'm not even halfway through Saturday yet. If I pity myself, and out of self-pity set about cleaning the room and rearranging the furniture again and again, will these looming days pass? When I was upset at home in Izmir, I'd go into the kitchen and cook so much food that it would take us days to finish it off. In a flurry I'd cook meat dishes, desserts, vegetables, whatever came to mind. Eventually Haluk caught on to what was happening. When he saw the table set with enough food for a feast of ten, he'd start asking: What happened today? Is something bothering you? What happened, sweetie? I could try the same approach here, but certain things are missing, like a kitchen. Rather than daydreaming about full course meals, I should be a little more practical and come to the realization that there's nothing to eat for dinner. There's nothing in the world that could make me take the trip to town again, just as there's no way I'm going to eat zucchini stew again for dinner. So if I want some greens, I have no choice but to go out and pick some. And it seems like the perfect time for madness like that.

I tie a scarf over my hair and set off with a plastic bag and a knife. I can just imagine someone asking: Abla, what you are up to? Oh, I'm just off to gather dinner.

Nobody else is going to gather those plants. The ground is muddy and there are bunches of chicory, mallow, turnip sprouts, fennel and thistles. I decide on chicory. The knife is covered in mud, and so am I. For a moment I pause and look around to see if anyone is watching me. There doesn't seem to be anyone around. It takes less than ten minutes to gather all the greens I want. Actually, it seems that I've picked far more than I need. After three days of eating zucchini, am I going to eat chicory for a week? Sibel Hanım, get ahold of yourself and don't be greedy.

And now am I going to return to my room and cloister myself? My room seems more like a prison cell than a home. No, I don't want to go back to my room. I remember the first day; how I'd swelled with joy! Only three or four times in my life had I felt a joy that was so tangible. I hadn't expected that. I thought that I'd be overcome by sadness or a sudden wave of wistfulness, wounded by loneliness and sadness; but that didn't happen. The first thought that crossed my mind was: This is my place. At first it was a whisper, but it rose into a shout:

This is my place!

My room. My home.

I'd never had my own home. The first home I remember was my grandmother's. Then there was my father's home. He'd ask: Why don't you ever stay with me? And then anytime I stayed with him just to spare his feelings, he'd lock me in the house when he went out, which terrified me; I felt like I'd been imprisoned. When I'd go back to my grandmother's dilapidated home, it seemed like a palace in comparison. Shout as you will! I had friends, I could go out into the street. And the house was huge. Until now, I've never had my own home (even if it is just a room). My entire being filled with joy when I first unlocked the door and stepped inside. I began laughing, and soon the room was echoing with the sound of my laughter; I felt as if I were having a breakdown. I wondered if someone might hear me; what a disgrace! But I didn't care. Feeling like I'd signed my release and was waiting for the ink to dry, my joy built up to the breaking point and then suddenly burst free in peals of laughter. Such a wild and mad exhilaration!

Just remembering that rush of feelings changes my world now, and the gloom of the rainy day seems to fall away. I'll start preparing my chicory; what sweet pleasure! Then I'll boil it, and serve it up with the juice of fresh lemons. Keep your hands off my good mood.

But where did these ants come from? It never occurred to me that I might bring ants into the room along with the chicory. Dear ants, you simply aren't welcome in my home, which I sweep and mop five times a day. Please be understanding. There just isn't enough room for the both of us in here. I should squash them wherever I see them. They should be squashed wherever they go.

Can I say that I've survived the first week unscathed? Not particularly. I'm just now venturing forth into that first week. Tomorrow I'll go to Trabzon's market for the first time, and then after that it will be my first Monday. Only after Tuesday will my second week here begin. So let's see how Mondays are in Trabzon. That's how I'll start my first week of teaching. Tomorrow I'll be here, and then on Monday there's an exam; my students will be returning from their practicums. I'll only be working with the fourth-year students. Just as I'd done, they met their students and got to know them, and now they're returning to school. And who will they find standing before them? A victim of the state, exiled from a city on the other side of the country; a kind-faced teacher, full of love and compassion (no, that will never do if I want to win their trust!). A punished criminal. How will they react?

Am I really going to be teaching in two days? My God, it's been so long since I've been in front of a class.

One day last June, after we'd finished our final exams, the police raided the school. It seemed like there was a policeman under every tree, armed with guns and clubs. There wasn't even time to wonder what was happening before they started handing out those yellow envelopes. We were being transferred to the Ministry of National Education, as it appeared that the Board of Higher Education wanted nothing to do with us. The students were going to be in the hands of "trained experts," not teachers who'd merely made their way on experience. We were no longer an institute of higher education overseen by the ministry, but a genuine school of education. And professors teach at the schools of universities. So who are you? Look where you are now! Fine, but won't graduates of this school be hired by the ministry? And will the ministry request that the Board of Higher Education train its teachers? That seems to be the case. In addition, the ministry, unhappy with the board's training, is going to launch a new exam to choose its select candidates.

That day we were sent en masse to be reappointed at a high school. There were 124 of us, but one of our colleagues hadn't returned from abroad yet, so we argued that we shouldn't start at the new school yet. But off we were sent, 123 of us, surrounded on all sides by police. The director of the school was bewildered. What would he do with so many teachers? He may have needed a few teachers, but not 123.

Objections and complaints were filed; there were court cases and hearings. In the end, it was decided that a mistake had been made. In August, a new article was added to the existing law and all the teachers who had been transferred to the ministry were now returned to their original positions.

You might think that the Board of Education stopped there; but no, the true struggle was yet to begin. The board, having realized that it couldn't handle everything alone, would try other tactics to deal with these problematic teachers.

During the exams in September, all of the teachers were at the school but no one was given any duties. The exams were administered by people brought in from outside the school, salaried teachers and officials who weren't even instructors. We, as the school's old teaching staff, weren't allowed to enter the classrooms or even the corridors, so we milled around among the linden trees. That session of exams was colorful beyond description. The exam for the course on contemporary Turkish literature that I'd taught that year was being given by someone who'd never stepped foot in the class and was clueless about what I'd taught. Under the trees, students approached me: Can they really do that? Well, that's what they decided to do, so what can be done? The exams given at the painting and music departments were even more surprising. News from those departments resulted in bouts of frenzied laughter: The person giving the piano exam doesn't even know how to operate the fallboard of the piano. Did he really close it on his hand? And you should hear what the *solfège* teacher has done! Oh, but we have . . . It was like a war zone, and we were hearing about everything that was happening on the various fronts. At the conservatory (which was also being absorbed by the university, along with a system for getting students into the university from primary school), board officials overseeing the string quartet's recital room were foaming at the mouth: Savings, that's what I'm talking about. Savings! What do you mean, "quartet"? You complain about how small the recital room is, but you only have four people in this huge space. Bring in eight more people and have them all play together.

Around that time, I sent a telegraph to the command post of martial law. I don't know who came up with the idea, but they couldn't find anyone who could muster the courage to actually go through with it. They were afraid of getting drawn into what might be seen as "collective action" backed by the signatures of a handful of people. I'll do it, I said. In my own name, with my signature. After the rigors of passing a background check, some light interrogations at the post office and paying a steep fee based on word count, I finally sent the telegraph. In the short space I had, I recounted the injustices that the teachers had suffered when the school was transformed into a school and then taken over by the Board of Higher Education, and I asked the commander to investigate those matters and make corrective measures to ensure that further injustices weren't committed. Of course, I never heard anything back. That is, unless we count the yellow envelope I was given.

The commander probably thought that it would be easier and more cost-effective to answer me that way.

I'm counting on my fingers just how long I've been out of the classroom, and realize that it's been as long as a term of pregnancy. Nine long months of not teaching, of not being in front of a class. My nervousness, I think, is justifiable. I'm so nervous that when I think about being in a classroom full of students again, my mouth goes dry. Being in front of all those students isn't an easy thing to do. In two days, I'll meet my new students and start teaching again. It's unbelievable, and foolish too. After going through all that pain and suffering, you'd think that I'd give up on being a teacher, that I'd be fed up with working under the whims of the men pulling the strings. But I'm not worn out yet. I'll hold out as long as my strength allows. If it's a battle they want, then I'll be at the front. Since you didn't fire me but sent me into exile in Trabzon, I'll start a war here.

I feel like this is the first time I'm going to step into a classroom and teach. If I have the courage, I'll do a few practice runs in front of the mirror. And even if I don't do that, I've already imagined that first meeting with my new students again and again.

I'm taking up the only role I can play: that of being a teacher.

3

The word explains itself
And tyranny peddles its soul.
—Leyla Şahin

Just a year ago, we could look into the long, broad, dimly lit hall from the entryway. The door would be open, or at least partially so. If you wanted to go into the office, all you had to do was knock on the door, and as soon as you peered inside, you'd be welcomed in. But now that door is locked. First you have to pass under the stairway and go to an adjoining room where you have to explain to the official what you want to discuss and how long it will take. That is, of course, after you've provided proper identification and given your address. Then you have to wait, sitting on one of the uncomfortable chairs lined up along the wall, based on the principle that you cannot just walk into the offices of high-ranking officers; no, first you must wait a meaningful amount of time before you're allowed in. And you'll wait longer than you'd estimated would be necessary because your estimation, based on what you deemed a normal amount of time for a discussion, would be flawed.

A large desk occupies the farthest end of the office. The curtains are half-closed and the dim lighting makes the man sitting behind the desk appear smaller than he actually is. There is a female lecturer standing in front of the desk; she waited a week for her scheduled appointment and then waited in the adjoining room for the required amount of time. The elderly man behind the desk, which dwarfs him, is taking notes as the conversation proceeds.

Man – You said that she completed her PhD in the United States. Is that correct?

Woman – Yes, sir, that's correct.

Man – Can you please tell me the name of the university and the department, as well as the topic of her dissertation?

Woman – You noted those down just a few minutes ago, sir. And she provided that information on her application form.

Man – (Shuffling through the papers he's holding.) Ah, yes, right you are. Yes, here it is. Harvard University, Department of Physics. So, she wants to work at our university. (He puts down the papers and leans back in his chair.) Well, hoca'nım, indeed we do need esteemed professors at our school.

Woman – (Exasperation creeping into her voice.) Yes, sir, we do.

Man – As you may know, we're trying to bring this school up to international standards. You understand what I'm saying, don't you?

Woman – But of course, sir.

Man – That's what the Board of Education wants for our school. World-class education and esteemed professors. Isn't it just so worthwhile? So wonderful?

Woman – You're quite right, sir.

Man – This woman is your sister, is that correct?

Woman – Actually, no, sir. She's my brother's wife. My sister-in-law.

Man – Ah, yes, you mentioned that. (He pauses, lost in thought.) And she wants to work here?

Woman – Yes, sir. On the application form she . . .

Man – (Cutting in.) Yes, I see. Why does she want to work here?

Woman – (With measured patience.) I believe I mentioned that already, sir. There are some problems with her tenure where she's working now.

Man – (As though to himself.) I see, I see. What did you say her name is? (He picks up his pen, which he holds poised over the paper.)

Woman – Sol Demir, sir.

Man – Can you spell that for me?

Woman – (Spelling it out, letter by letter). S-O-L D-E-M . . .

Man – (Suddenly bolting up in fear, glancing at the closed windows and doors.) But you do realize that "Sol" means leftist? My God, we were about to make a huge mistake!

Woman – How so, sir?

Man – Now look here, haven't you ever noticed this before? How could you let such an important detail slip past you? Someone who didn't know better could read it as "Sol." Don't you see? (He leans over the notepad on his desk.) Come closer and take a look. S-O-L. How is that pronounced? "Sol."

Woman – No sir, it's not. The "L" has to be pronounced lightly: "SOL."

Man – Please, this is a serious matter.

Woman – I'm aware of that, sir, but this word means "Sun" in Hebrew and is pronounced with less emphasis on the final "L." Sol, Sol.

Man – But this will not do, it will not do at all! How are we going to explain that this is "Sol" and not "sol"? Even if we tried to explain it we'd find ourselves in all sorts of trouble.

Woman – (Speechless by this point.)

Man – Do you understand what I'm saying? We'd find ourselves in a very tight position indeed. All sorts of trouble.

* * *

We were summoned to the School of Economics for an interrogation. As we waited, a woman was idling about in the corridor. She was a lecturer, and seemed half mad. Eventually she went into her office, leaving the door open, and made a cup of tea, whereupon she sat down and propped her feet on her desk, sipping at her steaming mug. There were about ten of us, but no one knew what the questioning was about. One by one we were called into the office. We discovered that there was an interrogation committee consisting of three people in the office. One of them was a professor from the School of Economics and the other two were assistant professors, one of them from the School of Theology. But that's all we could find out. As they walked out of the office, our colleagues looked terror-stricken, beaten down, exhausted. This happened at the end of June, and it was a sweltering day. They called another teacher for questioning, so we went down to the cafeteria to get something to drink and send off our colleagues who'd already been questioned. Some of the topics raised during the interrogations were hilariously absurd, but no one had the strength to laugh. As we debated whether they were just toying with us or truly were that ignorant, we were driven to new heights of irritation. One of our colleagues was asked: Why did you spend your weekend at an expensive hotel? Another was asked: Why do you enjoy playing card games? Tense nerves don't uncoil like a taut spring, and we were all wound up. As Nüzhet Bey from the Department of French Language and Literature told us what happened during his interrogation, we were stunned into disbelief. This is what they'd asked him: Since works of French literature have already been translated into Turkish, why are you requiring that your students read them in French? Naturally, we asked him how he replied. He said that he merely laughed, and said: Well, gentlemen, I'll leave it up to you to find the answer for that. Leyla Hanım was called in next. As Nüzhet Bey left, we offered what words of consolation we could: That's just how they are; don't worry, nothing will come of it. Then we went back up to that dark corridor. When Leyla Hanım emerged, we were expecting yet another round of absurdities. But her interrogation took on overtones of religion. She was accused of insulting the religious beliefs of her students and inciting divisiveness. The reason: We've received reports that you've told your students that when we die, our bodies just return to the earth. How could you say a thing like that? Don't you believe in the soul, in angels, in God? What about heaven and hell?

At the time, we didn't realize that the interrogations were just a ruse for the mass expulsion of lecturers at the end of June. While we sensed what might be happening, we didn't know what was truly going on behind the scenes.

My name was called and I entered the room, trembling from rage, fear and nervousness, but above all irritation. They gestured for me to sit down and I settled into the chair. It was like a trial in court. They asked: Do you swear on your life and honor to tell the truth and nothing but the truth? It was terrifying! Yes, I do, I replied. Aside from the three inquisitors, there was a "court" recorder, an ashen woman with eyes like a dead fish, and the machine gun rattle of her typewriter. The head of the committee rose to his feet and began the proceedings.

First question – It has been claimed that you have repeatedly praised Nâzım Hikmet, although it's your duty to remind students that he was a traitor to our country and that his citizenship has been revoked. We've been informed that you've stated that he is one of the greatest poets of Turkey and a world-renowned figure. What is your defense against these allegations?

Me – I've never discussed Nâzım Hikmet as a topic of our lessons.

But if students ask me about his poetry, beliefs and character, I believe that I have an obligation to answer them and hence, yes, I have spoken about him.

Professor – (Addressing the woman at the typewriter). Mevlüde, please write the following: Sibel Gökşen has confessed that she regularly discusses Nâzım Hikmet in her classes.

Me – I'm sorry, sir, but that's not what I said.

Professor – It is what you said! If you say that you answer questions about Nâzım Hikmet and students are always asking about him, then, yes, you are constantly talking about him. Did you ever say that he is the greatest Turkish poet and a renowned figure in the world?

Me – Sir, I answered the questions that students asked me by taking into consideration his qualities as a poet. Seen in that light, he is known around the world, and to date, no other poet has written as well as he has about the Turkish War of Independence.

Professor – Type: She claims that Nâzım Hikmet is the best poet in all of Turkish literature.

The true colors of the interrogation were becoming clear. No matter what I said, he was going to report whatever he wanted. I objected, saying that he was twisting my words. And the answer was always the same: No, it's exactly the same, and no matter what you say, it changes nothing. What do you mean "it changes nothing"? I'm saying one thing and you're having her write something completely different. In reply, he opened an envelope and pulled out some yellowed exams. The next question was recorded as it was asked, unlike the previous ones which had been prepared in advance.

Question – In the academic year 1978 to 1979, you asked questions about Nâzım Hikmet and Sabahattin Ali on a midterm exam, which was administered in February of 1979, for the course you taught on contemporary Turkish literature. Do you know that those writers aren't in the curriculum? Did you insist on including them in your course with full knowledge of that fact?

This time, I thought to myself, you've truly been deceived, Mr. Professor. I would like to have been the one who asked those questions, but even for your sake, it's just not possible. Patiently I waited for the recorder to type up the question. Then I began my measured reply, speaking slowly enough so that each word could be typed down.

Me – It is not possible that I asked questions on an exam given in February of 1979. (I pause and look at them, but I realize they are confident that I will try to make something up, unaware of the error they've made. I continue on in a monotone voice as the recorder types away.) Until 1981, I had no connection whatsoever with this school, and in 1979, the year when this exam was given, I was working as a literature teacher at a high school. (Panic!) In 1981, I placed first on the exam given by the Ministry of National Education (at that point, they tried to cut me off, but I continued) and until I took up my current position, I'd never even visited this school. For that reason, it has become clear that trying to hold me responsible for exam questions given two years before I began employment here proves that there is a hidden agenda behind this interrogation.

The fish-eyed recorder immediately stopped typing when I spoke those last words. The committee proceeded to inspect the exams more closely, asking each other: Which signature is hers? Finally they brought the exams to me. Isn't this your signature here? No, sir, it can't possibly be mine. What about this one, or that one there? No,

149

I said, but if you'd looked at my class registers and yearly syllabi, you would have realized it wasn't mine.

The assistant professor of theology pulled out a piece of blank paper and suggested that I sign it so they could make a comparison. I laughed knowingly, and said: I don't trust you. I refuse to sign a blank piece of paper. They decided to remove that question from the record, crossing it out: xxxxxxxxxxxxxx, followed by the note, "Stricken from the record," accompanied by the committee members' initials. But of course the questioning didn't stop there.

Question – Reportedly you've given homework assignments on the subject of Islam and socialism. If that's true, could you explain how such an assignment has any bearing on a course taught in the Department of Turkish Language and Literature? And could you please explain why you have spoken of imperialism and other such concepts in your classes?

Me – The topic assigned to that student wasn't about Islam and socialism, but the Islamic perspective of Mehmet Akif, which we discussed in class. I only would have spoken of imperialism in class during our analyses of his poetry. It is well-known that his line "the single-toothed monster" is a reference to Western imperialism, so it would be impossible to discuss that poem without using the word "imperialism."

Dissuaded by my confidence, they moved on to another question.

Question – It has been claimed that you've discussed the leftist Kadro Movement with the aim of spreading propaganda. What is your defense against these allegations?

Me – It is impossible to discuss the life and works of Yakup Kadri without referring to the Kadro Movement and the journal *Kadro*. It is well-known that the Kadro Movement represented a turning point in Yakup Kadri's life. That's why I asked a student to analyze the journal *Kadro*, which first came out with the support of Ataturk, and to do a presentation for the class. Furthermore, the ideas in Kadri's novel *Wilderness*, which we discussed extensively in class, were formulated in close connection with the articles in *Kadro*. The only propaganda that could be spread by examining the journal would be the principles of Ataturk. And since when has it been a crime to promote his beliefs in the country he himself founded? I most certainly hope that you aren't accusing me of committing the crime of spreading Ataturk's ideas.

I thought to myself: Since we're playing a game here, gentleman, forgive me but you left me with no other choice than to play my trump card. Needless to say, the questioning was brought to a rapid conclusion. There was nothing left to say. Then came time for the signatures. There it is, dear professors! Compare it with the one on the exam to your heart's content. Before the decision to transfer us to the ministry was thrust upon us and we were removed from the school, we realized that new lecturers were being hired and filling the ranks of the departments, to the extent that there were almost as many of them as us; but we didn't understand the implications. In short, we were in no position to fully grasp what was happening. Aside from proposing solutions for the new conspiracies that arose on a daily basis, there was nothing we could do. And it was worse for the students. First, the school's staff and officers were screened and classified into two political and ideological groups, "with us" and "against us." Those who were deemed to be "against us" had already been appointed to other schools. Among that group were staff from various departments, a landscaping crew, a librarian, two drivers and the head of internal administration. For the students, just saying the words "democracy" or "freedom" was a guaranteed way to be called in for questioning or be expelled. Every day, disciplinary committees held meetings to try to prevent the almost daily disturbances, especially in the classes of the newly hired teachers.

The teaching staff knew the new arrivals. All of them had worked at the school before the coup of September 12th and been removed from their positions under martial law because of their political beliefs; some of them had been banned from teaching altogether, while others were banned from schools that trained teachers. But now, they were being hired back and appointed to their original positions. The administration was appointing people to teach part-time in the Department of Turkish Language, whether they were civil defense experts from the School of Theology, editorial staff from the dean's office, or even managers at a milk company, and they carried out their duties without skipping a beat. Their real job was to find out which students were supposedly stirring up trouble in the classroom and then try to get them expelled.

Before the coup, many of them had been fired from their positions at teacher training institutes, especially Gazi in Ankara, because they took part in violent protests. And now they were being brought in based on randomly drawn-up lists, and despite the fact that their paperwork wasn't in order, they were tasked with administering exams. Students graduated as the result of those teachers' efforts, which included turning a blind eye as entire classes copied from each other and forged exam papers, and they even went so far as to erase sections of answers and rewrite them. We'd heard about that being done in the past, and now we were face to face with it.

It won't easily be forgotten: the sacks of exams brought to the school and reviewed one by one, and the forming of boards of experts. We saw it all. But there was nothing we could do, and the sense of despair increased over time. How could we complain? Who were we going to complain to? The dean's office, the president's office? The military commanders in charge of martial law? Could they have gotten away with all that without their superiors knowing? It was impossible. The office of the prime minister, of the presidency . . . Everyone knew what everyone else was doing. No, we were the mistaken ones, the forsaken, the sacrificial victims. We, the teachers who had worked for the school for years and suffered during that turn of fortune, were so broken down that we no longer had the strength or desire to fight back; and innocents like me, hoping to renew and develop ourselves and be helpful, found ourselves at odds with the times as we pursued aims that were a challenge and seen as a luxury. Everyone had resigned themselves to awaiting what would befall them. Our efforts just never went beyond ourselves. We knew what was happening, but were powerless to do anything. All we could do was hope that it wouldn't get any worse.

What we saw on those exams was unthinkable. Without even bothering to change the style of writing, they had the audacity to alter answers and even randomly add points to the total scores; if they didn't do that, they just added the points that were needed to pass when the grade was noted down in the register. We saw it all. It was exam fraud on a massive scale, and we'd soon realize that the new teachers coming to take our places would reveal their old wiles. To get a true understanding of what it means to protect a student who holds to the same beliefs as you, you have to see to what extent they went in that endeavor. What heroes! There wasn't anything they wouldn't do for their little protégés. They let students who just started their last year of studies take the graduation exam and then pass them; they falsified documents so that a student who hadn't even taken the final exam could graduate; they prepared reports stating that their students had completed their practicums when they hadn't even started; and despite all these "kind acts," if there were any students who still hadn't graduated, their professors just issued them a temporary diploma.

After the sacks of exams were scrutinized, all of the students' rights as graduates were revoked. The diplomas that had been issued for these students who graduated through "kind acts" were cancelled and the students were required to resit the exams for classes that they'd actually failed. It was a sight to see. Some of them were furious with the professors who'd done them a "good turn" and tried to find them to make sure that they wouldn't suffer the results of their beneficence again.

It took about a week for the exams to be retaken. In the meantime, the campus had become a circus. The lecturers who knew they were on the cusp of losing their jobs were bewildered; who should they try to corner and plead with? Who should they try to threaten? But it was no laughing matter; in fact, it was tragic as the students retook the exams. Balding men with bulging bellies suddenly found themselves in rows of desks trying to answer questions on topics about which they knew nothing. Despair echoed through the corridors. One would go on about his recent marriage and all the debt he'd accrued, and when he stopped talking, another would pipe up about the payments he had to make for a refrigerator he'd recently purchased. There were middle school teachers, high school teachers, even managers. Some sat in the back hoping they'd be able to copy from someone else, and they looked at you with woeful glances. They dropped their copied notes on the floor. They got their cheat sheets mixed up with those of other classes. Look at it how you will, they were our colleagues. The fact that they had fallen to such pitiable lows was painful to see; but wouldn't pitying them mean not pitying the thousands, the hundreds of thousands, of students they would teach? But still, we overlooked a number of indiscretions to avoid embarrassing them, and when the exams were finished we marked them. The results were heartrending. They didn't have a clue about some of the most basic, commonplace concepts. And their knowledge of Turkish was deplorable. Their essays were a scrawled mess, practically incomprehensible, and their knowledge of punctuation was nil. What astounded us wasn't the fact that they'd graduated, but how they'd gotten into the program in the first place. How could they possibly teach Turkish and literature?

Those who failed the exam either tried to avoid their old teachers, who'd never actually studied education themselves, or they huddled away here and there, lamenting their troubles. Although those teachers tried to conceal the fact that they wanted to help their students, or occasionally did it openly and were subsequently warned, they no longer held the sway they once had because the school was turned into an institute of higher education and most of the old guard had been forbidden from training teachers. But as fate would have it, they were brought back and they settled back into their old positions and every department had far more instructors than needed. But who was superfluous? Certainly not the old guard who fought tooth and nail to get their old positions back. No, we were the superfluous ones; we just suddenly appeared and they were suspicious of us, wondering what we might try to do under the guise of being honest. The Board of Higher Education was informed about the situation and an order was handed down to take urgent action; but when those 124 lecturers were transferred to the Ministry of National Education, the school was occupied yet again.

Soon enough we found out who those teachers were and why

they'd come. They were students who'd been expelled from various institutes of higher education before the coup of September 12th for participating in "armed ideological activities." But now there was nothing standing in their way of becoming lecturers. The processing of our return was delayed by the ministry and before we could start teaching again, the matter of the students' exams was handled in a flash, and under the supervision and guidance of the old guard who were preparing to take our places, they graduated with the highest of honors.

Upon our return, those lecturers were sent off. But what they'd managed to do in so little time was astounding. We were infuriated, but it was in vain; even if we'd been there, there was likely nothing we could have done.

Our return was just as magnificent as our exit: 124 lecturers were back at their posts. When the ministry rejected our reappointment, the Board of Higher Education extended the contracts of the other lecturers for another year and they were brought back, but they were stunned to see us back at the school. And as we swaggered like we'd scored a victory, those informants were petrified: what if we sought revenge?

A day or two after our return, one of my old students approached me at the entrance of the school, pleading to talk to me. But I'd just arrived and was already exhausted. He was one of those well-known students who sported a mustache. He said that we needed to talk, immediately. But what was the hurry? We had plenty of time; classes were over and we hadn't started final exams yet. Now that we'd come back, we'd be seeing each other often. But he insisted that we had to talk right then and there. Fine, I thought, curious about what he might have to say. But although he was so desperate to speak, when I agreed, he was suddenly tongue-tied. Finally he summoned his courage:

There's something I want to say. I'm sure you'll understand.

Of course I would, I thought. That's our job: to be understanding in the face of all the absurdities around us.

First, I want you to know how much I admire you. You're the one and only person who I truly respect.

Let's get past that, I thought. What does he really want to say? But he kept dragging it out, laying on the compliments to the point that I could feel tears of frustration coming to my eyes. You've made your point, I thought, I can see how important I am for you. Just as I was thinking that I should give a sign that he needs to cut it short and get to the point, he got around to what he really wanted to say:

I never told you this, but for days now I haven't been able to sleep at night. I decided that there was something I needed to say to you so I could put my conscience at ease and free myself from the feeling of guilt that I've been carrying around. You see, I was the one who reported you.

I knew that already.

You might be wondering why I had to report someone who I like and respect so much.

I didn't ask, but he told me:

I was put up to doing it. I didn't want to, but I had to do it.

It was all becoming clear. I more or less knew how things stood. And I knew that he expected me to say something. But what could I say? Something like:

I can't save you from your own conscience. I hope it doesn't trouble you with too many pricks of pain. What else can I say?

Even though I already knew what he'd done, I was still touched by his confession. Why had he felt a need to confess? Was it really his conscience tormenting him, or was he worried that he'd be my student again and I might hold him to account?

Soon after that day of panicked confessions, everything came to light. When our return to the school proved to be unpreventable, initial steps were made to ensure that we'd be rendered powerless. Just as we weren't allowed to be present during the exams, we couldn't even go to our departments, so we sat under the linden trees.

Yet again we found out what happened after the fact:

"According to the tenets of Article 5, which has been temporarily appended to Law No. 2547, the employment of lecturers whose contracts have been extended shall be evaluated according to the following criteria and lecturers deemed to be superfluous shall be reappointed to their positions under the auspices of the Youth and Sports Ministry of National Education:

a) Individuals who want to return to the ministry of their own volition.

b) Graduates of two-year education institutes.

c) Individuals who were enrolled in completion programs of study which they did not finish and lecturers whose academic qualifications were deemed to be lacking.

Addendum 5, Protocol Department."

It was obvious how that protocol was going to be implemented. First of all, were there any people who wanted to "return of their own volition?" And once you thought there were enough people like that, you'd accept them as if they'd submitted a petition and immediately reappoint them as they desired.

And there were graduates from two-year programs who were so dear to you, so of course you're not going to let them slip away. Maybe it would be better if you broadened this criteria and made it a little more flexible. And did it really matter how long those instructors you want to keep at the school had studied? But we knew that the fates were sealed for those who were unwanted by the powers that be.

As for "completion programs of study," nothing like that had ever existed. Just what did that mean? Among the lecturers who were fired there were some who'd completed their master's degrees or held numerous certificates in art. Did you intend to place people at this school because they have that qualification? Step right up, gentlemen, and implement that article too.

Fine, but what was going to happen to the people who you didn't want at the school and who didn't fit the criteria? Something should be done for them as well. Was there no recourse to assistance under martial law? Of course there was, why not? The most dangerous of those—and you would report them—would be promptly removed from their positions, and plans would be drawn up for the others who were less dangerous. For example, you could send them to other provinces; so did that mean that you'd have to consider every single case? There's martial law, they said, and if we can't save you from those dangerous men—and women, it doesn't matter, there's really no difference between women and men like them—then what good is martial law?

VARIATIONS FOR A SURREAL NIGHT FILM (1)

SCENE 127:

INT. - DAY

Waiting room of the Military Supreme Court. There are well-dressed people holding files and briefcases as they sit silently. One of them stands up and approaches the officer on duty.

LAWYER
Look, I have a document here sent by the Office of the Prime Minister, and I've been waiting for two hours.

Please help me so that I can see the undersecretary as soon as possible.

Doors open and close, stirring hope among the people waiting. Shot of the broad corridor leading to the undersecretary's office.

LAWYER

Sir . . .

SECRETARY

Please, sit down.

LAWYER

With your permission, sir, I'd prefer to remain standing. I'd like to speak with my client as soon as I can, especially if I have good news. We're hoping that the sentence will be turned over and commuted to life in prison.

The lawyer hands the document to the undersecretary.

LAWYER

It's from the Office of the Prime Minister.

The secretary reads the document.

SECRETARY

"You are hereby informed that the case file that you requested concerning the retrial of the condemned has been sent to the Office of the Military Supreme Court and will be reviewed by the court on October 24, 1984."

LAWYER

Three days have passed since that date.

SECRETARY

(Gruffly)

I'm well aware of that.

The undersecretary shuffles through a cabinet and eventually pulls out a file, which he places on his desk and begins to read.

SECRETARY

Sir, the decision regarding this case has already been published in the supplement of the Official Gazette.

LAWYER

I know, but the case was sent back to the Military Supreme Court based on our request for a retrial.

SECRETARY

So?

LAWYER

Has our request been accepted or not?

SECRETARY

(Flipping through a few more pages)

Your request was denied. Look, here is the ruling. The Military Supreme Court upheld the sentence of execution.

LAWYER
Very well, sir. Thank you.

Everything was drawing to a close except for the investigation. Lawyers had long been working on the case and there seemed to be no end to the correspondence, statements and arguments of defense. First, a document was issued by the Board of Higher Education which stated: "The recommendation has been made that you be banned from the field of education." Per the terms of the Disciplinary Regulation, I had the right to "examine the investigation reports, request the testimony of witnesses, and defend my case before the disciplinary committee either personally or through a representative, orally and/or in writing." And I would do that of course, but it was made clear that I wasn't to visit the campus, and they were even trying to arrange it so my husband would collect my paycheck. Left with nothing to do, I was bored to the point of madness. I had my lawyer go to Ankara to examine the investigation file. My God, it was a fiasco! They'd included the exam that had questions about Nâzım Hikmet, the exam that was given two years before I even started working at the school. There was a statement in the file stating that I'd "incited" students to ask about Nâzım Hikmet, but there were neither signatures nor dates on the document. If they'd forged documents to that extent, I'd have no choice but to go back over the original statements and then go back to Ankara, only to find that they'd twisted my statements yet again: ". . . makes bold claims about subjects such as Western imperialism when discussing the work of Mehmet Akif, and even more troubling topics. Not likely to give a confession." What else could there be? ". . . and openly stated her admiration for Nâzım Hikmet and talked about him often in class." Then there was the complaint against me filed by the student, just that one, and the same student's petition of objection regarding his midterm exam score, in addition to an unsigned letter of denunciation (all of which I thought were inadmissible, meaning that they knew they were in a bind and were willing to stoop that low!).

From my lawyer, I found out something else: people under investigation aren't allowed to give "sworn" testimony. Shouldn't the rights granted by the Constitution be upheld? But they'd taken my "sworn" testimony and then treated it as my "defense," arguing that I no longer had the right to a defense. That was the first objection I raised. Then I requested that the school produce all of the questions that appeared on the exams I gave when I worked there, including copies bearing my signature so that they could be added to my file. Next, and most importantly, I provided a statement arguing that calling for punishment based on the complaint of a single student (the one with the mustache) in a class of forty ran counter to the code of Disciplinary Regulations. So, what about the other students? Wasn't the investigation committee or the Board of Higher Education interested in their thoughts? Weren't they curious about the notes that my students took during my classes? Perhaps I'd said even more objectionable things. The student who complained about me had friends in the class; maybe they heard something that he missed. Without a moment of hesitation I named those forty students as witnesses despite the fact that I knew those other three students who shared the same ideology as the student who complained about me would be singled out as witnesses; I hadn't discriminated or engaged in divisive acts, but you, gentlemen, go right ahead! I suggest you listen to everyone because I'm not afraid of anything coming to light. If you're going to fabricate damning evidence, do it knowing the truth.

And weren't all my students ready to do anything to help me? Weren't they constantly telling me that they didn't like feeling so helpless and wanted to do whatever they could? And hadn't they come to my home and said they'd be more than happy to testify on my behalf and if need be even rent a bus to go to Ankara? That was my chance; so yes, do whatever ever you can for me.

The prospect of taking an entire class of students to Ankara was certainly attractive, but it would be expensive. And of course I couldn't ask them to pay for it themselves; how much would it cost to rent a bus? And then we'd be there all day and would have to buy food and drinks, not to mention possibly stay the night at a hotel. And surely the Board of Higher Education wasn't going to try to squeeze the testimonies of forty students into a single day just for my sake; it could take days, even weeks, for all of the students to give their testimony. I was on trial, under threat of being banned from ever teaching again, and it seemed that they were on the verge of succeeding. With my salary, I was already struggling to get by, so naturally I couldn't put on a profligate show like that for the board. But it would be magnificent! You were taking the word of a single student, a single political informer, as sufficient evidence; and in any case, it had been planned out beforehand, isn't that so? Well, I'll bring the whole class to you! Could I really do that? Haluk and I talked about it. The thought of actually doing it gave me courage. He told me not to worry about the money, that we could borrow it if need be. Thank you, Haluk. I was finally able to send my list of forty witnesses.

After two long months I finally got a reply from the board: "Your request has been approved. On so-and-so date the testimony of your witnesses will be heard at our headquarters." That was fine but the date they gave was at the beginning of the students' final exam week and was just five days away, not even enough time for me to get in touch with all of them. They'd all sequestered themselves away, preparing for the exams. How would I find them and spread the word? Get together everyone, we're setting off . . . I wasn't even teaching them anymore. Forget about your final exams and go to Ankara to give testimony on my behalf. Could I really say that? I decided that I shouldn't push my luck, especially when I knew that it wouldn't change a thing. And I had no right to impinge on their final exams; if they didn't take them, the students would be set back an entire semester, and I couldn't do that to them. There has to be another way, I told myself, because I'm not going to give up after making the claim that I would submit a list of my students as witnesses.

My lawyer suggested a possible solution: The students could give their testimony as *istinabe*. What was that? I should've known, since I'd taught Ottoman Turkish before. Depositions. Written depositions. Maybe there was a way. Before this convoluted situation had reached a strident point, at the time when we'd only recently been transferred to the oversight of the Board of Higher Education and tactics of intimidation and disempowerment were in their nascent stages, the chair of the department sent our tenured lecturers off to teach Turkish in other departments. That was our lot; we were even given a list of books that we were to use to teach the courses. That was a heretofore untried method of punishment. And who was the chair of the department? The right-hand man of the dean. Time and time again he was driven from the school because court records indicated that was involved in a certain movement, but each and every time he managed to find his way back and, to everyone's amazement, land himself an even higher position. We all expected that he'd return as the dean if he were fired again, and from there move up to be the president of the university. Like he'd done with his other old acquaintances, he arranged for me to teach a class in another department as a way of keeping us "dangerous" lecturers at a distance. But that wasn't enough; he came up with another strategy of pressure and intimidation along these lines: You've never really liked Ottoman Turkish, have you? You know, those old texts in Arabic script? Well, here's something you can do for our historical culture. We've organized an Ottoman language course, and you're going to teach it. You're welcome, and please never forget the kindness we've done you. Of course, we're not taking away all of your courses in contemporary Turkish literature; if we did, we'd be hard pressed to get scandalous information about you. It's hard to get yourself in trouble when teaching Ottoman . . . So that was my punishment. But I've always enjoyed surprising people who think that I'm going to rise up in revolt, or even quit and save myself the trouble. So I said: I'll teach the course. Actually, I'd almost forgotten that I had been thinking of brushing up on my Ottoman, and this way I'll be able to bring it to a whole new level. And the chair of the department was crestfallen. The senior students were in for a surprise, because until then they'd only had Ottoman teachers who were hafiz, but now for the first time they had the pleasure of reading contemporary Turkish poetry in the old Ottoman script.

The lawyer realized that my failure to recognize the word "istinabe" touched a sore spot for me as a teacher of Ottoman. Don't let it bother you, he said. It's normal that you wouldn't know the word because it's a legal term. When I got home I looked it up in my Ottoman dictionary: "The deposition of a witness's statement which will then be sent to the court where the actual trial is being held." Perfect! We informed the Board of Higher Education: "Our witnesses' statements will be delivered via written deposition so they may be read at the hearing . . . "

And as I was dealing with all that, of course I didn't know that there were yellow envelopes stamped "Confidential" being sent from the Board of Higher Education to the president's office and from there to the dean; nor did I know that the flames were being stoked beneath me or that a yellow envelope had been prepared in my name and, as they always did, they'd wait until the last minute to give it to me, just two days before I was to be sent off. A new yellow envelope, new glad tidings. How many had been sent out already? "The Dean's Office has been informed of your appointment to Karadeniz University under the terms of Article 7/1 of Law 2547. Effective February 8, you will no longer be deemed a member of your department. At your earliest convenience, you are requested to obtain your travel funds from the school's accounting office." Thank you; but wasn't I already considered to be 1402? Wasn't my presence in the classroom considered "objectionable" (at least in the Aegean region)? So that meant my "objectionable nature" wouldn't accompany me to the Black Sea; but why didn't the order for my reappointment indicate that I'd already been classified as 1402? I supposed that must be a good thing. At the last minute, had they decided to protect me from a state of being objectionable? Why the sudden goodwill? Well, in that case, I thought, I should go. Shouldn't I? Wasn't it just another game? Two days later I was supposed to sever all ties; what then? I'd either have to accept the appointment or resign. In a way, resigning seemed to make more sense. At least, that's how it seemed to them. Can a life-changing decision be made so quickly? Quit your job and stay at home; that way, we'll be free of you. Is that what they thought? If that was the case, then by all means I had to go! But how? First I'd have to settle all my family matters. Who would look after the children and run the household? What would happen to our family? And how would I go? After taking care of that, there was the question of the "travel funds." The accountants at the dean's office and president's office both said the same thing: There's no such fund, and you haven't been transferred there—it's just a temporary reassignment. You'll stay on the payroll of the department here. So a travel fund hasn't been issued for you.

It was completely incomprehensible. What business did I have going to the Black Sea? For my own pleasure? The debate lasted for days. Only through the intervention of an influential friend were matters resolved; since they were sending me off, the school would cover my travel expenses. How simple!

Now that I'd found a friend with so much influence, it would be hard to let him go. The thought occurred to me: Maybe my influential friend could get me an appointment with the local military officer in command? Sure, he said, I'll set up an appointment. Why do you want to see him? I said that I wanted to explain what's been happening at the school. They think that I'm dangerous, but do they know the dangers that will come up when they replace me? In short, the incompetence of the person who will replace me? Do they know what will happen when someone who graduated from a two-year education institute teaches at a four-year program? The problems that will ensue? As I explained what was happening, his eyes widened: How could they do that? he exclaimed. How could someone who graduated from a lower program of study be appointed to a higher position? Indeed. And what I was describing was the most innocent problem. He promised that he'd set up an appointment for me. All I wanted was to explain the problems.

Two days later the reply came: negative. The commander refused my request to speak with him. I was beside myself; but why? I asked. Because, the commander said, if things are different from what was reported to me, and a kindly lecturer comes to me and convinces me that I've made the wrong decision . . . what would I do then? Stick to what I've decided even if I know it's wrong? I won't be able to do that. I'd be in a bind. That's why I can't meet with her. That's what he said. What could I do? Fine, there's nothing to be done.

In the meantime, the document we'd been awaiting from the Board of Higher Education arrived. Which problem was I supposed to deal with first? The board, or the problems brought on by martial law? Or should I have rallied against my reappointment, or the travel fund? I opened the envelope: "It has been decided that the witnesses may not submit their statements by deposition. They may, however, send them via an official notary. Their statements must be submitted within fifteen days of the date of this notification." Now, dear students, I'm off to Trabzon and you're off to the notary . . .

It turned out that there was no need for me to rush off to Trabzon; there was a statute that gave me some extra time. After that, I could use my annual leave and even get doctor's reports. Some people told me I could get through the whole semester like that. My annual leave, then a doctor's report, then annual leave again. Fine, I thought, but I miss teaching. But I couldn't really say that to anyone for fear they'd laugh at me. Of course, I said, I'll do whatever I can.

My students got in touch with each other, and I rushed around trying to get ready for my departure to Trabzon, trying to convince my husband that it was the right thing to do, asking my sister-in-law for help, pleading with Haluk's mother: When I leave, please . . .

I realized I had to leave the day before we'd planned on meeting at the notary. I knew I'd never be able to manage it all. And trying to postpone my departure with fake reports wasn't my way of doing things. I had no other choice but to leave Haluk and my lawyer in charge of making sure the students submitted their statements through the notary, and getting the texts together and ensuring they were stamped and signed. I implored them to make sure that there weren't any mishaps in the dispatch of the statements: Please make sure that they're sent to the ministry. I had my doubts that they'd be careful. All the same, I couldn't shake off the feeling that I was putting so many people to so much trouble and expense for nothing. And my lawyer struck me as being somewhat naive. He tried to convince me that we had them cornered; once all the students from the class submitted their statements via the notary, he said, there's no chance they'll hand down a negative verdict. They won't find anything incriminating in the file, he said. The students' statements will refute everything. All of the complaints were about the lessons given in that particular class. As soon as we send the statements, he said, the whole business will be over. Those guys aren't stupid; they wouldn't want to go down in history for having made a criminal mistake like that.

Go down in history? What a notion! I gazed at my lawyer; in all his enthusiasm, he actually believed in what he was saying. But I had my doubts; didn't he know who he was dealing with? Still, he'd been handling my case for months. Although I knew it was an impropriety on my behalf, I was incapable of being caught up in his enthusiasm. I said: Do you think that while we're going to so much trouble, they're just sitting there doing nothing? Who knows what they have up their sleeves. But he was insistent: There's nothing they can do, he said. Thinking that he hadn't explained things clearly enough, he launched into a more comprehensive explanation of why he thought there was nothing to worry about. He tried to convince me that they'd have to provide proof of their accusations. I knew, however, that the problem ran deeper; until that time, none of my supposed "crimes" had been based on any evidence whatsoever. In three days, I said, I'll be leaving for Trabzon. You'll be in charge of making sure the students send off their statements and dealing with all the ploys that are bound to come up.

As we said goodbye, I couldn't resist asking my lawyer: You think this business is over, don't you? You just wait and see what else is going to happen.

Yes, he said, I'm sure it's over. This is it. You'll be cleared of all the charges.

I wasn't guilty in the first place, I said. If I had to teach the class again today, I'd say the exact same things. That's not the problem. The real problem here is how far they're going to take this. They're going to add whatever they want to my file. You'll see.

He countered that I was exaggerating my suspicions. I listened in silence. If I were a betting woman, I would have put my money on the table right there and then.

I knew something new would come up. I didn't know what; but I knew it would.

You've just been through too much, my lawyer said. You're stressed. You know that we've won the case, but you don't want to believe it. Maybe subconsciously you're just trying to protect yourself from another disappointment.

If you ever find yourself not making enough money as a lawyer, I said, you should take up psychology. He could be right, I thought. As I went home, I hoped he was right.

But when I got home, my hopes withered. Haluk met me at the door, holding out a new yellow envelope sent by registered mail. It was from my inquisitor:

"As regards the correspondences numbered so-and-so on such-and-such date, you are requested to present your DEFENSE per the terms of Article 24 of the Disciplinary Regulation regarding the investigation based on a complaint that was filed against you for:

– Engaging in leftist and divisive propaganda on campus; and,

– Eulogizing Nâzım Hikmet and denigrating religion, and referring to religious individuals as 'barbaric' and 'backward.'

Per the terms of the same article, if you do not attend the hearing on Monday at 11:00 a.m. you will be considered to have accepted the accusations against you and measures will be taken concerning the information and documents in your file.

Please come to my office on the day and at the time indicated above."

The final sentence was like a personal invitation. What was that supposed to mean: "Please come to my office"? Maybe he missed me.

And he asked me to come on Monday. Which Monday? I was

supposed to leave on Friday. I'd even bought my ticket. What was I supposed to do?

You're not even going to be here, so just forget about it, Haluk said. No, I had to go; I finally had my chance to present all the documents and evidence I'd been gathering over the past few months. There was no way I could leave without standing up for myself.

So, Haluk said, you've decided not to go.

No, I replied, I'm not giving up. First I'll give my defense and then I'll go. I can call the university in Trabzon and tell them that I'm going to be a day late. They're expecting me on Monday, but I'll tell them that I'm leaving on Monday and will be there on Tuesday. They'll understand. It's not like I'm trying to put it off by giving them a fake report. I have to give my defense. And I can change my ticket; there's still time.

The next day I went straight to my lawyer with the envelope:

I don't make a habit of saying "I told you so," but I said: Look at what they've done!

My lawyer was disconcerted. That's unheard of! he said. After all this, why do they want you to give your defense! No, it is heard of. They took my statement the wrong way; didn't we say that sworn testimony can't be given? Didn't we write that I was deprived of my right to a defense? I knew something would happen, and this was it: a legal defense against the claims that were made about me. The file they had on me was being brought up again. No leaf would remain unturned. They were starting to be more careful.

My lawyer suggested that I submit my defense in writing. That would be fine; I could do it without my lawyer. I'd been gathering up documents ever since the investigation began. I had facsimiles of the issues of *Kadro* that we'd discussed in class. All my resources were at hand. But one word of warning echoed in my thoughts: I'd have to inform them that I would present my defense in writing, not in person.

I looked again at the letter: "Engaging in leftist and divisive propaganda." In particular I was irritated by that, because that wasn't the original accusation. Obviously they were trying to render the claim in concrete terms so that they could mete out their punishment. And what did they mean, "on campus"? Didn't this whole investigation start because of a complaint made by one student about a single class? Wasn't that enough? Did they feel a need to broaden it to include the whole school? And what was the deal with religion? How had they come up with that word, "backward"?

Incorrect grammar, erroneous punctuation, dangling modifiers . . . Dear inquisitor, if only I'd been able to have you in my class. You'd be able to actually write a proper text and pen a more grandiloquent statement.

I spent the next few days sitting in front of the typewriter, hardly ever getting up. I'd sit the children down to eat and head back to my study with a hastily prepared cheese sandwich. Haluk thought I'd lost my mind. But I hadn't; I knew quite well what I was doing. My defense had to be flawless. I didn't want there to be a single point of regret. In the end, my defense became an exposition far broader in scope that what I'd taught in my class. If only my inquisitor had been just a little more informed, I wouldn't have had to go into all those explanations. Was it my job to fill in the blanks of his knowledge?

It was a defense replete with footnotes, explanations and a bibliography, bolstered by encyclopedic information . . .

On Monday I took it to my lawyer. A full twelve pages. It's fantastic, he said. So poignantly written. I had no choice; what else could I do with all the poison that had built up within me? Who else could I direct it to but the poisoners themselves, who injected their venom like a snake?

At the stipulated hour, I arrived at His Excellency's office. He'd been appointed assistant dean. After all your struggles, I thought, you should have been made dean long ago. Not just dean; the Board of Higher Education has done you an injustice. Dean wasn't enough; you should've been made president of the university. Even if no one else is aware of it, I know how you've persevered and tried to vanquish the enemies of the state.

VARIATIONS FOR A SURREAL NIGHT FILM (2)

SCENE 258:

INT. - DAY

The most ostentatious room, the grandest pasha, and the grandest pasha's closest pasha pal.

1st PASHA

Do you remember Colonel Yaşar? In Salihli we used to
steal plums from Rüstem Ağa's garden with him.

Meanwhile, he's going over the documents on his desk, trying to find where he's supposed to sign them. But he doesn't look; he just traces his finger along the paper. Without looking at the photographs, names or dates of birth, he traces his finger down the page until he finds the appropriate place and then he signs his name. Then, he moves on to the next file.

2nd PASHA

His wife was rather pretty.

1st PASHA

Colonel Yaşar's wife? What do you mean, she was an absolute knockout!

Zoom in on sixteen flags of various Turkish republics toward the right. 1st Pasha pushes the stack of files aside and rings a bell.

2nd PASHA

There were photos everywhere.

1st PASHA

Well, what do you expect? She was pretty as a picture.

2nd PASHA

No, I meant it was his thing. Colonel Yaşar had a passion for pictures.

1st PASHA

He didn't know a damn thing. He was nothing more than a cuckolded fool!

The door opens. With a snap of his heels in salute, the pasha's aide enters.

1st PASHA

Here, son, take these. I've signed all the execution documents. You can send them along.

FADEOUT

With excessive courtesy he greeted me in his office, and motioned for me to take a seat. As if it were no more than a trite comment about the weather, he offered an explanation about why another round of questioning had been arranged. Apparently the Board of Higher Education had requested it, a fact which seemed to have peeved His Excellency. He went on to say: I infringed on your rights when I took a sworn statement from you.

He gazed at me as if to say: Isn't it all so illogical? I could tell that he was waiting for me to approve of his insight, waiting for me say: Well, of course it is, don't we swear on every word we say? Even if I pledged out of deference to you, what would the problem be?

He turned up the irony, trying to savor the fact of our meeting; he was openly mocking me. He said: It's as if by making you swear to tell the truth I was in fact making you lie. Whether it's sworn testimony or not, what difference does it make?

My first thought: Esteemed professor of interrogation, you seem to be trying to prod me into reacting. I was trying to keep my calm and not get irritated so that I wouldn't say something that would get me into even more trouble. But the problem was this: if I didn't say something, I'd never forgive myself. Something like: I'm no longer afraid of you. What else can you do to me? Today I'm leaving behind my children, my home, my family—in short, everything—so that I can be subjected to the punishment of exile you meted out to me. With cold resolution, I looked him in the eyes and said:

It makes a world of difference.

He spun toward me in a rage, as though my words had stung him like a searing hot needle. If he had a gun he would have shot me between the eyes. What do you mean? he sneered. I knew I had to stay calm. If I let myself get upset, the entire conversation would be derailed. My only choice was obstinacy laced with irony.

It's like this, I began. But I paused for a moment; his face seemed to be turning purplish. Or maybe I just wanted to see him that way because I thought it suited him?

I continued: If you hadn't made me swear, I wouldn't have used such expressions as, "I may not have said that" or "I may have said that."

We were alone in the room, and if he so desired, he could have strangled me on the spot.

And so? he asked. I could tell that he too was trying to be ironic; but now his face was beginning to pale.

The "and so," I said, is that because I was under oath, I had to take into account the fact that I may have forgotten something. So I had to say, "Maybe, it's possible. I may have said that." But when I did, you put down in the official record, "She confessed to doing it" and "She confesses that she said that." If I hadn't been under oath, I would've said, "I didn't say that" and "I didn't do that" and "Nothing like that ever happened"—and then you would've been forced to prove your claims. But you chose the easiest way and put words into my mouth, calling it a confession.

He snorted, and I'm sure he was cursing me in his thoughts; but he tried to keep up a pretense of staying calm. He muttered something along the lines of: Teachers are always like this. I didn't bother trying to understand what he was saying. His problem was that he couldn't hold his temper in check. He acted like he'd done me a favor, the value of which I was unaware. He paced the room, muttering to himself. After a while, he stopped and said:

Let's get on with your defense.

A secretary was called into the office, and I sat in silence, waiting. She rolled carbon copy paper into the typewriter; how many copies was she going to make? At last she was ready. Professor Inquisitor made the introductory statement. By that time, we all knew it by heart.

He began: As regards document number so-and-so which was issued on so-and-so date by the office of the president, quotation mark, the list of offences in her file has been expanded with additional items, the description "barbaric and backward" indicated in the letter of complaint which an investigation has been launched regarding Sibel Gökşen (Should I point out that this sentence is grammatically incorrect?) and because some deficient points have been identified (Ha, is that so?) in the file which must be corrected per the terms of the Board of Higher Education that have been decided (Dear professor, yet again your grammar is failing you) . . .

She's been asked to come and the offences filed against her have been restated, whereupon she shall present her defense. In capital letters at the beginning of the line, type "defense" followed by a colon.

At last, that fiasco was over.

DEFENSE:

They both turned to me. And what did I say?

Because I have doubts that my statement will be correctly transcribed, I have opted to refuse an oral defense.

The young woman at the typewriter looked at me in shock, and the professor turned beet red. He growled: Now you've gone too far!

I gestured to indicate that the secretary should write down what I said.

He turned to me: So, you're refusing to give your defense?

I won't go on until she types down what I've said.

He gestures to her, and she begins to type.

Now I'll answer your question. No, I'm not refusing to give my defense; I'm refusing to give an oral defense.

In that case, you should've brought your defense in writing.

I have.

VARIATIONS FOR A SURREAL NIGHT FILM (3)

SCENE 379:

INT. - DAY

Lawyer visitation room at a prison. The condemned runs toward the room, wearing an undershirt like a football jersey. He's sweating profusely.

LAWYER

Hıdır, what's going on here?

HIDIR

Abi, we're playing a match.

Hıdır wipes away the sweat on his face with a large towel. As if making small talk, he asks:

HIDIR

So what's happening with the case?

LAWYER

We're trying to postpone it, but it doesn't seem to be doing much good. Our request for a retrial was denied.

HIDIR

Abi, forget about it. One way or the other, in the end they're going to hang me. If you can hold them off until the end of the tournament, that'll be enough. Let me finish out these last matches, and then they can hang me like a pasha.

FADEOUT

I think that once I start teaching, most of the distress I'm feeling will fade away. Back in the classroom with my students, all new students . . . A new hope, a new excitement. The kids are probably at home today; everyone is probably at home. Maybe I should give them a call: My weekend is going splendidly, I'll tell them. You'd love it here, it's so beautiful! In the afternoon I'm going down to Trabzon to meet up with some new friends and maybe I'll do some shopping. I've got everything I need in my room. If only you could see it; it's a tiny room, but ever so cute.

What would my daughter say? Mommy, what are you going to eat today? Zucchini stew again? Do I bring it up every time I talk to them on the phone? Probably it wasn't the taste of that dish in itself but its name that stirred them to pity my situation, at least for Özlem. I'd make my voice deep and gruff like the wolf who settled into granny's bed in waiting: No, my child, I've grown so weary of zucchini. I'm going to eat you!

She'd giggle: You do that so well, Mommy! Do it again.

I won't tell her that I'm going to eat fennel. It's easy to make that transition from zucchini. Another reason to pity me! I can see her in my mind's eye. Pouting lips, a tearful voice: Mommy eats weeds every day over there, and zucchini too. I can't eat this.

I can't ask Aslı to make the food Özlem likes, it would be an imposition: fried wedges of potato, pasta, grilled meatballs . . . Just saying the words would sting my heart. It starts with fried potatoes and from there moves on to wanting to be there with you, by your side.

My dear sprout of a girl. Don't worry, we'll get through the meal somehow.

On the phone the other day, Haluk told me about Ozan. Haluk's mother and sister were visiting, and Ozan was in his room doing his homework. At one point, everyone in the living room burst out laughing, and Ozan came running out. Why are you laughing? he asked. My mom is in some faraway place and you're all sitting here laughing. You should be ashamed of yourselves! Then he went back into his room and slammed the door. Haluk talked like it was a joke: Guess what your son did today to my mother and sister? But I felt something inside me crumple in silence. Ah, my son!

First I'll take a long walk and then I'll call them. I should make sure that my voice doesn't tremble. Everything's going great, and I feel just fine! In the afternoon I'm going to go on a little outing. Of course I will, why shouldn't I? Today I'm going to call on the people Faik suggested I meet. Once I start teaching, I won't have time for anything else. But is the weekend the right time for unexpected guests? Everyone may have their own plans, but I'll come knocking on the door: Hi, I'm a friend of Faik's; he gave me your address and said I should come by for a visit. I've come all the way from Izmir and I don't know anyone here. Faik told me: They'll help you out, so don't hesitate to call on them. Can you help me? Just some conversation. I've missed the sound of human voices (that aren't metallic, rasping or rife with parasites), their tones and music. That's all I want, nothing more.

What if I felt out of place? Couldn't I just come right back? Don't I have a home, a room, here?

Just as I guessed, everyone was at home. To my relief, Aslı answered the phone. Are you there on the weekends too? I asked. Of course, Sibel Ablacığım, she said, don't you worry about a thing. We're just getting ready to have breakfast. I tried to wake up Özlem but she's still in bed. Ozan's fine, he's here with me. Haluk Abi is here too.

Then I heard Özlem's voice in the background: Are you talking to my mom? I want to talk to her! Haluk got on the phone, and I heard him say: Just wait your turn, none of us have gotten to talk to her yet.

Haluk, it's okay, I said. Give her the phone. I'll talk to her first.

Mommy, how are you? I miss you so much!

She stopped talking for a moment, so I knew the others were probably making faces at her. Why, was it forbidden for her to say that she misses me?

I've missed you too, sweetie. I've missed you very much. And as I guessed, she asked:

Mommy, are you going to eat zucchini again today?

No, sweetie, I'm fed up with zucchini. I'm going to eat something else, something very, very delicious. (What about my wolf imitation?) But she didn't ask: Then what are you going to eat? Someone took the phone from her; I suppose our zucchini conversation didn't strike them as being very meaningful.

Haluk: How are you, is everything okay there? Have you gotten settled in?

I'm fine. I've already gotten used to being here, and I feel just fine.

Something happened, and I want to tell you about it. You're going to get a laugh out of it. They've put Hülya under investigation. Our Hülya, Yalçın's wife.

My God, that's bizarre. For what?

She was talking with some of her colleagues and started telling them about her housekeeper. I don't know why, but that's why they put her under investigation. That, and the fact that she complained about her husband.

That's the reason?

Precisely that, Haluk said.

I couldn't help but think that it was somehow fitting. But it truly was preposterous, and I was glad I hadn't been faced with a situation like that. Gentlemen, I thought, be careful; you're casting a shadow of doubt over this investigation.

The phone was passed to Ozan:

My dear son, how are you? Is everything okay?

I'm okay, are you? Did you buy the Trabzonspor uniform you said you'd get for me? (My God, I'd forgotten.)

I'll get it, I said. I'll buy it today.

And I want a map of Trabzon or a book that tells about the city. Can you get that too?

Of course, I'll get that today too. Anything else? That was all he wanted. Haluk got back on the phone.

This is a long-distance call, so you'll have to pay for it. We should probably hang up soon.

There are few things I can't stand more than affected thoughtfulness. I had to muster all my strength to ask:

Isn't your mother around?

No, he replied. Didn't you know that she's been staying with my sister?

I hadn't known, but it seemed odd to me; why was that woman who, when I was there, had been so "unwillingly" staying with her daughter and always repeated proverbs (more precisely, mother-in-law maxims) about a mother's place being with her son, not there? Where was she now, why wasn't she at her "real" home with her son? Did all she say mean nothing more than: "This is where my son and I belong, so who are you?" Of course I didn't say anything to Haluk about that. Taking up his thoughtful offer from a moment ago, I replied coldly:

Fine, let's hang up.

I'm trying not to let Hayriye Hanım get under my skin. God knows why. She told me not to expect any help from her, and now she thinks that she's put me in a difficult position. Her calculations are clear: if I'm not there taking care of the children, Sibel will come back. In her own way, she's trying to make me return all the sooner. To what? To washing her and her son's clothes (replete, of course, with mandates: her underpants have to be washed separately—yours smell of urine— I'm clean and my laundry has to be washed with special care), to doing her ironing, to putting up with her whims and bowing down before her caprices?

I was thinking of my children, unable to decide if calling had been a good or a bad idea. When we talk, my thoughts become a jumble.

I thought that I'd tell them that everything was fine, all the while breathing in the air of home. I wanted them to remember how far away I am and feel that sadness, but also I was dying to hear that they love and miss me. With my entire being I wanted to feel like I was there, but I was unable to let go of the role I was playing; not once did I forget to control my voice, and I forced myself to smile, hoping it would show through. On the one hand, I was listening to myself, but at the same time I was trying to decipher from their tone of voice what they'd done, what they were wearing, trying to envision the curl of their lips and closing of their eyes.

Now that I've hung up the phone, the pain is worse. It becomes all the more poignant that I'm not there, that I'm far away. The sounds have faded away, along with the images; I'm completely alone. After we hung up, I wondered if Ozan went into the kitchen and Özlem clambered back into bed and pulled the covers up over her head. Maybe she's crying and sulking because her father took the phone away from her. Maybe she's upset with me because I didn't even ask how her classes are going. Or maybe she was going to tell me about her red ribbon or how the teacher pointed her out to the class and said: Be like Özlem.

After talking on the phone I don't feel like going back to my room. I wander around the grounds of the guesthouse, gazing at the Black Sea and looking at the trees; then I caress a cluster of flowers and look out at the sea again. It stretches out, placid and flat. There's no sign it will break out into a raging fury. But what fear it has struck into the hearts of the people here—when they speak of the sea, it's with respect, like they are describing a monster, a supernatural power, a god. In my mind's eye, I see the details of an anecdote that I was told at the school.

Once there was a man named Hamit Bey. He became wealthy and was so blinded by his riches that he forgot about the unrestrainable freedom of this sea. He had a large villa built for himself, perched on the shores of the Black Sea (nobody said anything to him about that); but that wasn't enough, so he had an ornate garden built that stretched right down to the shore. Truckloads of soil were brought in from the most fertile of plains, along with the finest of fertilizers, and then sapling trees, seedlings of fruits and vegetables, and flower seeds were planted. The garden was as elegant as could be and anyone who saw it was stunned by its beauty. But he was wary of the sea, so he had boulders brought down from the mountains which were arranged into a formidable wall as thick as a human is tall and just as high. Later, people's smiles betrayed a knowing kind of acceptance. Someone explained that people occasionally came to see that garden. Heads nod: Yes, even we went to see it. And then? Their expressions lit up with smiles that revealed that they knew what was coming next. The Black Sea let this show of ostentation go on for the summer, because it was waiting for winter. In the first months of winter, it all washed away: the saplings, sprouts and flowers were gone, and nothing remained of the garden, not even the wall. In a measured voice that hinted at a desire to be forgiven, or maybe a plea to be in the good graces of a terrifying god of nature, the teacher telling me the story came to the main point. It affected me so profoundly—I can even say it frightened me—that I can still here his words ringing in my ears:

The Black Sea forgives no one.

Was this the same sea he spoke of? Placid, unruffled, timid as a mouse. One day I'll descend the slope down to the shore and plunge my hands into its waters, watching it trickle from my palms. So, you little ruffian, is it truly you who's instilled this fear in our hearts?

But not now. There are things I need to do. Can I make one more call before I go back to my room? A local call. The operator is kind: Of course, he says, and doesn't charge me. Today I've decided that I won't stay in my room; I go through the numbers that Faik gave me, putting them in order of my interests. First I call his friend who is a poet he admires. As soon as I say my name, he realizes who I am; it seems that Faik told him I was coming and he knew I was here. I was wondering how we'd get in touch with you, he says. We've been expecting you.

And that's how easy it is! I write down the address. A friend of the telephone operator overheard our conversation and launches into a lengthy explanation about how I should go there and how much it will cost, explaining each and every stop along the way. Of course I don't tell him that they already explained all this to me and I listen to his explanations. Contrary to what I expected, he doesn't ask where I'm from or point out that I'm new to town. It's probably already obvious enough.

I watch impatiently as the fennel boils on the electric stove. Little by little, Trabzon is opening up to me. And at least now I have plans for the afternoon.

It's going to be nice; as I get used to life in this town, I'll start to build up my own history here. Over time, I'll gather up memories that I'll talk about one day: When I first arrived here . . . Today is waiting to find its place and to be lived out among those memories. Black Sea, are you ready? It's not an enemy coming, it's me.

First I decided to walk around downtown; one of the names Faik mentioned is right there, on the sign of a doctor's office. Faik had lavished praise on him, speaking of his endeavors in literature, poetry and music. I'd seen the place before, but hadn't been able to muster the courage to knock on his door. It was easier to tell myself that I knew where his office was and could visit him another time. But now, knowing that I would do the same again, I sought out new excuses, surprised at how I was criticizing myself for how I acted before. What if he has patients, waiting in pain for their turn to see the doctor? Part of me says: You'll wait then, and anyway you're just out for a walk. But another part of me rose up in revolt: Do you think it would be in good taste to wait among the other patients so you can talk about literature? Is he going to hang up his doctor's coat and sit down between two patients, one leg over the other, and say: Okay, it's your turn, so let's talk about poetry? Fine, but how do you even know if there are patients waiting in his office? Would it be so out of the ordinary if he came to his office on his day off and met up with friends? How can you know that today isn't a day he sets aside for talking about art and literature? Maybe now is the perfect time? And you don't even know if he's in his office. Perhaps he's not there. Yes, that's good; most certainly he's not even there.

I don't think that everyone is like that. At times, I feel certain that I'm actually two people. And what's more, two people who don't get along. If one of them says get up, the other refuses to budge, saying:

Stay right where you are. Or am I three people? Who's the third person trying to reconcile these two quarrelsome enemies?

I remember that I'm supposed to buy a Trabzonspor uniform for Ozan. But should I do it now? If I do, I'll have to carry it around with me all day. If the doctor has children, he may think that I've brought a gift for them (and what a pointless gift at that; what would a child from Trabzon do with a Trabzonspor uniform?) I'm going to meet some people for the first time. I'd do better to bring something like chocolates or a bouquet of flowers.

I easily found their home.

It's small, but cute and tidy, sparkling clean.

The husband and wife are both teachers, and they have a son whose name is Ozan.

Ozan? Isn't that nice! My son's name is Ozan too. Should I confess that I believe this means that there's some kind of bond between us? The fact that our sons have the same name is a good sign; it means we'll get on well. Starting with that, we already have a common culture, common likes and language. Do poets, and lovers of poetry like me, name their sons Ozan? How are expectations, longings and desires reflected in children's names? That's what we observe most often in the classroom. One semester you notice that the class is full of Ebru's and Esra's (from the age of nostalgia), and another semester they all have names about freedom, revolution and activism like Özgür, Devrim and Eylem (the age of the coup). If a cute young boy whose hair curls around his face is named Hamdi, Nuri or Abdullah, or if a blue-eyed girl is named Hacer, Zeliha or Huriye, you know that it's a reflection of a traditional family or that they'd moved to the city from the countryside. But I don't say any of these things; they're just the chattering of the swarm of voices I carry within.

They ask me what I think of Trabzon. It's a lovely place, so beautiful and green. Since I arrived here, I always give the same answer when people ask that. But the truth of the matter is that I've never thought about it; I don't know, I suppose that I like it. I recall my first impressions, but I know that if I speak openly about them, I'll fall short of their expectations of praise. That's how it always is; people want to hear about the beauty of the city in which they live. Isn't that why they ask that unchanging question?

In Izmir, many of the people who heard that I was going to Trabzon were united in their responses: You should count yourself as lucky, they said, Trabzon is the most beautiful city on the Black Sea coast. There are always people like that who try to turn misfortune into a stroke of luck. I'd prepared myself for a city of unrivalled charm. That might be why I felt the way I did. I came to Trabzon, and found myself in a grey city. Why had I thought that? Was it just that particular day? I don't know, but it appeared to me to be grey, used up, dilapidated and threadbare. After that, I don't think I ever took a close look again. I just didn't have the will. And then there's this: people don't have to like the places where they're in exile. Just because the poet known as the Fisherman of Halicarnassus liked the town of Bodrum doesn't mean that everywhere should be like that.

I know that Metin Bey was born and raised in Trabzon, so I tell them that I went to Sera Lake and was struck by its beauty, expounding on the reasons why it was "beautiful" and "green," as I'd said it was. But of course that isn't enough for Metin Bey.

You should go to Maçka, he says. And you should see Sumela Monastery too.

I promise that I will.

I was also expecting the next question that comes:

How's your life in Trabzon?

Yet again I roll off my memorized response:

My classes haven't started yet. I'm going to be teaching contemporary Turkish literature and theater. I brought my literature notes from Izmir, so I've been preparing for my classes. My students are doing their practicums now, but they'll come back next week and we'll get started.

These days I've been bored but that'll pass as soon as classes start. Yes, to be honest, I'm bored because I don't know anyone in Trabzon. It seems like the guesthouse where I'm staying is completely cut off from the city.

Well, now you have us, Metin Bey says.

Thanks, but what am I doing? Trying to make them pity me?

The place I called the guesthouse is actually the university's summer residence. The president of the university told me that. He's a very polite man, and for all appearances an aristocrat. It didn't quite sit right. Is his politeness the kind that sneers? Or was I suspicious of it because my only experience of aristocracy was through films? His appearance was refined with a red bowtie and his sentences were given whole new meanings as he traced graceful circles in the air with his small, manicured hands. I'd really like to, he said, but I can't give you a place in the university housing. As I'm sure you know, housing is always a problem at universities. Some of our faculty members have been waiting months to get into housing. For now, you can stay at the Seaside Residence. If you have any problems, please come directly to me.

The words "Seaside Residence" seemed much more charming than "housing," and I immediately accepted his offer. He made a final comment on the matter: It'll be fine, since for now you're not bringing your family. The words "for now" rang in my ears. Would Haluk join me here? That means it's possible; in other words, my family could join me. I didn't know that I had any choice in the matter. All

I could hear were the voices that judged and condemned me when I was making my decision: What will you do with the children? I was stunned to realize how I'd become used to being under someone else's control. So, I could bring my husband . . . Haluk, however, had resigned himself to my being here, confident that when my anger subsided I'd go back to him like a lamb. He's waiting for me to wear out, to break down and fall to pieces. That thought strikes me like a blow.

Why hadn't I thought of it before?

Yet again I find myself drifting away from the conversation. Metin Bey is saying that summer doesn't really come to Trabzon. If the sun is shining, he says, and you decide to go for a swim in the sea, don't be surprised if you have nothing dry to wear when you get out because rainstorms can come out of nowhere.

I catch myself feeling a small rush of pleasure at the idea that when summer comes, bringing in beach season, I won't be here. But why this pleasure? Is it the thought of going on vacation, or that, as Haluk expects and I probably believe too, I'll lose my nerve and return to Izmir long before beach season arrives?

We're drinking tea with cakes and cookies, speaking of poetry and literature. It's precisely the kind of conversation for which I've longed. The thought that I haven't had discussions like this in such a long time brings on a feeling of gloom. At home, we never have conversations like this. Haluk talks about work and money; my mother-in-law drones on about how smart and diligent her daughter's children are; if I have any incurable traumas about my work at the school, I summarize and submit them like a report. But now I'm talking about things that I'd only read about and, what's more, only discussed with myself. Metin Bey shows me a journal that recently came out in Istanbul which he said he's enjoyed reading. In the previous months, I'd been so busy that I hadn't been keeping up with new publications, and I hadn't heard of that one.

In Turkey, Istanbul is the center of the arts. Even if you were born and raised in Trabzon, there's nothing you can do; it's far from circles of culture and art. It must be difficult living here while trying to be a part of that circle, isn't it?

It's very difficult, Metin Bey says. Trying to make your voice heard and stake your own claims is truly difficult here.

Next we turn to books, and we read some poems. I know that a few books of his own poetry have been published; however, shamefully I have to admit that I've never read any of them.

But he's not taken aback in the least. I'll give you all of them, he says. And I'll even sign them for you.

That would be great! I'll read them right away. Here I have lots of time to read.

The conversation has been great, but it's getting late and I think of going home. I have a long way to go and I don't want to get caught in the dark because the roads are so steep.

But they don't let me go.

Didn't you tell us you were lonely? There, in that room by yourself? What are you going to do? You don't have to go to work tomorrow, so you'll just be just as bored as before.

In a way, since I told them about my loneliness, wasn't I forcing their hand in asking me to stay longer?

Why don't you stay the night? Tonight we'll go visit the Hıncals together.

As I recall, Hıncal is another friend that Faik had told me about, a sculptor.

They're really nice people, I'm sure you'll like them. Afterward, you can go back to your room. And wouldn't it be good to have a circle of friends in Trabzon?

But I'm torn. Part of me says: Why not? That empty room, the loneliness . . . Hadn't you been dwelling on the loneliness of the weekend? And is there anyone waiting for you back at your room? The other part of me warns that by escaping, I'll only be devising new ways of fleeing and seeking shelter. But it doesn't take long for me to decide: Sure, since you'd like me to come along with you. So long as I won't be disturbing you. But of course not, Metin Bey says, far from it.

Zehra Hanım prepares the dinner, tea, cakes and cookies, and then offers me a cigarette. But she doesn't join the conversation. She sets the table, listening as we talk, nodding in approval on occasion. When she goes into the kitchen, I get a feeling—typical of feminine sensitivity—that she won't feel it's appropriate if I sit in the living room with the man of the house and continue our conversation. So I go into the kitchen, but she refuses my offers to help. Anyway, she says, there's not much to do. The other food is ready, so all I need to make is the stuffed zucchini. My God, I think to myself, zucchini again?

It occurs to me that there really are no differences between homes, families, or life in general. The cooking and serving of meals, the offers of tea and coffee, just like in every home. And especially the man of the house. If we eliminate the fact that there's a guest in their midst, it's obvious that Metin Bey is the head of the household. When Zehra Hanım suggests that we eat, she glances at Metin Bey to make sure he's hungry. Shall we have coffee now or after dinner? Metin doesn't like coffee, she says; we don't drink coffee very often, it upsets his stomach. And it's the same for tea. He only drinks two cups of tea a day at breakfast. Today, because you're here, he joined us for tea. In the evenings I steep linden tea. Ozan has gotten used to it, and he even enjoys drinking it now.

I offer a token gesture of thoughtfulness and say: We've left Metin alone. Zehra Hanım brushes aside my concern and replies: No, he'll start working, but then she remembers Ozan. She dries her hands and rushes into the living room. If Metin is working, Ozan should be in the kitchen so that he won't disturb his father.

I have to admit that, even if just slightly, I'm jealous of the care and attention Zehra Hanım lavishes on her husband. If only someone would make sure that I could get my work done . . . I have to prepare a class for the next day and check the midterm exams; but does anyone care? First I have to make dinner and clean up. And you can't just throw something together for dinner. Why? Because guests are coming. Who? My sister and her family. Why didn't you tell me before? Well, aren't we going to eat dinner anyway? I thought that we could eat together. I ask, knowing that my dear sweet mother-in-law was behind this: Did you invite them? The answer is always the same: Yes. Why, don't you want my sister to come?

Why does Haluk do that? "Not wanting" someone to come is one thing; having work to do, and "not wanting to be disturbed" is another. Then he'll twist the issue, and open it up to generalities: You've never liked any of the people I'm close with.

As if I have others in my life! I don't have anyone. They stopped coming around years ago.

But I'm unable to stop the "other" from stepping in and speaking on behalf of Haluk: Maybe your husband also wants the same things. Haven't all men been promised that one day they'll have a wife like Zehra Hanım?

For no particular reason, the home of the Hıncals makes me think of Birsen. That could be precisely why—simply because there's no connection. Homes can be charming, modest and cozy without precious silverware, crystal glasses and expensive rugs. Maybe when you don't have all that ostentatious pomp, a home can be filled with the naturalness of having been lived in for years.

Some friends are going to be gathering at my place tomorrow, Birsen said, and I'd like you to come too so you can meet them, so don't tell me that you have to work. They're the wives of some important people. And it would be a change for you.

Every time we met up she invited me to come over, and every time I refused, so that particular time I didn't want to hurt her feelings: Sure, I'll come.

We realized rather late just how close we live to one another. We ran into each other one day on the street. I was on my way back home from the school and, as always, I was trying to file away in my thoughts everything I needed to do. I heard someone call out my name and I turned around. A well-dressed woman was approaching me, but I didn't recognize her. I don't have any friends who dress like that, I thought; she must've mistaken me for someone else. But how could she know my name? She introduced herself: I'm Birsen. Birsen? Which Birsen? For the love of God, how can you forget your best childhood friend? All I managed to say was: You've changed so much! Stammering, she asked: Do you mean that I look like I'm getting old? No, it has nothing to do with age. (But really, how could your age show through all those jewels? But of course I didn't ask that.) I don't know, you just look like you've changed! Of course people change when they grow up. We happened to be in front of my home so I invited her up for coffee.

Hayriye Hanım loved her: That's how a woman should be. She even joined in the conversation. If you can call it conversation. She said that every week she and her friends get together at one of their homes and play cards. But when I say cards, she added, I don't mean for money. Just to pass the time. Hayriye Hanım loves talk like that, and women who dress up.

So I went to her gathering, which was a mere display of her wealth that she was slowly whittling away. My dear, where did you find these, I've looked everywhere but I just couldn't seem to find them. What, those old things? They're not worth the trouble.

All the conversations were like that, with all the savor of distilled water. The "important" women were the wife of the deputy governor, a few wives of businessmen, and the wife of a colonel who was involved in running martial law. (At the time, I hadn't yet become caught up in the machinations of martial law and it never occurred to me that I ever would.) In the game of cards, about which she'd said, My dear we don't play for money, Birsen was tossing around as much money as I made in a month like it was spare change. My mother-in-law once said: You're friend is so smart. How'd she find such a rich husband? Of course I shunned her rude way of implying yet again that my stupidity was in direct proportion to her son's financial standing. All I said was: Oh, yes, she's smart alright. She doesn't take after me.

How's Faik? they asked. What's he been up to? He's doing just fine. But there wasn't much I could say about Faik. And they knew more about him than I did. Rather than talk about him, I wanted to listen to them reminisce. I tried to change the subject and turn the conversation to the time when Faik was living in Trabzon. Hıncal said that they used to drink till morning. But I already knew that. For some reason, Faik had always spoken with praise of those conversations over drinks.

Songül asked if Faik was still opposed to getting married.

I said, as if I knew: I don't think so. Then I asked: Why didn't he get married when he was living here? I wanted to turn the topic to matters of the heart, Faik's heart. And I succeeded. They asked if I met Jale, a secretary at the school. No, I replied, I haven't.

I was introduced to some of the secretaries, but I couldn't recall anyone named Jale. Which one is she? I asked. Hıncal described her one way, and Songül another. This is what I imagined: A woman with straight, light brown hair and dark green eyes. Then Songül said something that struck me: She's a very attractive woman, and after Faik left, she went to pieces. My God! We were in the presence of a powerful love.

Hıncal said that when they got together for nights of drinking, he would taunt Faik: Don't you see that she's burning for you? But how did Faik respond? That's what I really wanted to know. Hıncal did an imitation of Faik's response: A dismissive gesture, nothing more. But why, I asked; wasn't he interested in her? I don't know, he replied, and said: Faik is a strange man; even if he did love her, he'd never admit it.

And what did I know about Faik's feelings? Did he ever say anything to me? As I'd been told, he "never" said anything, not to me or anyone else. But there was something, a certain something that couldn't really be put into words: a spark, a reflection, an echo, a reverberation. A glance, maybe a smile that I imbued with meaning, or a word (perhaps). What did I do? I turned away, avoiding his eyes, and I became distant, and then changed the conversation to a trite, general topic: I'm sorry, what did you say, Leyla Hanım? Are we going to go get something to eat? Forget about that, what about the exams? I made everything so confusing. But what could I do? I was firmly closed off to any relationship that could veer toward more than friendship. The sanctity of family! But I had a desire to meet Jale. We began talking about Hıncal's latest project. He was commissioned to make a bust of the parliamentary deputy speaker, and it turned out well. Had Faik said that Hıncal's wife was a painter? I couldn't remember. They were always referred to as the "Hıncals" and he talked about their interest in painting and sculpture. So why had I always just thought of the husband? In fact, his wife was a painter and, in my opinion, her work was better than his. Was I just siding with her because she was a woman? Maybe. But I don't see anything wrong with that. It was a small favoring against the general state of injustice. A kind of partisanship. Songül was different from Zehra Hanım; she didn't withdraw into the shadows during the conversation, and she often cut in to state her opinion on the matter at hand; but it was interesting that when the topic turned to the works of art they made, she was hesitant to speak her views. Maybe it was mere conditioning, but my interpretation was this: she wanted to avoid surpassing her husband. It was as if she'd shunned that right which she'd never been accorded.

I was waiting for the conversation to revert to Faik, but it didn't. They were more interested in finding out about me, and I answered their questions with my standard replies. They wanted to know how and why I'd moved to Trabzon, and about my home and children. I wanted to satisfy their curiosity about me as quickly as possible; I'd memorized my answers thoroughly, but if they were to cut me off, there was a chance that I might make a slip: I'm married; I have two children; my husband is a good man (no one ever asked about my mother-in-law); he works for a company; his salary is decent. As for me, I'm here and, as you may have noticed, I'm an obstinate person. "Sibel the warrior." And this war gives me strength, it sustains me in life. I'm joining the race from Izmir, and I wish all my competitors the best of luck.

Naturally I didn't share all my thoughts with them; but soon enough it came to light that this was no laughing matter, and Hıncal asked: Sibel Hanım, are you really a dangerous person? That question wasn't in the program. I could have bared my fangs and claws and said: Don't you see that I am? Or, I don't know, I could have said something like: We've been together all evening, so why don't you decide for yourself. But for some reason, I took a serious tone: In fact, I'm not, but they've made such a big deal about this. I'd give anything to be the person that they claim I am.

Although I wasn't joking, they laughed when I said that. And at that moment, I knew that the time for laughter had come. I even told them about my room on the shores of the Black Sea where I crawled into bed wearing socks and a sweater. But I could only talk about those things in the presence of others who'd find the humor in it all and laugh, because otherwise I'd be drowned in the rushing waters of a flood. I'm a pearl on the shores of the Black Sea, number one in the art of gathering pity.

Songül and Hıncal insisted that I stay the night with them, not with Metin Bey and Zehra Hanım, saying: She's our guest tonight; she can stay with you another night. How nice it must be to be un-shareable! No one asked me what I wanted to do. But Metin Bey and Zehra Hanım prevailed in the end, and so it was decided that I'd stay with them. Now that's settled, they said, let's get going. Ozan is starting to get sleepy. We walked back to their place, and along the way Metin Bey pointed out mosques and tombs, telling me about the history of each. I realized that I'd heard these things before but they'd begun fading from memory, and I listened as though deeply interested. Ozan was tired and he didn't want to walk.

Dad, pick me up and carry me.

Zehra Hanım said: What an embarrassment! Sibel Teyze would laugh at us for carrying a child as old as you. But Sibel Teyze, unable to take joy in her status as "teyze," merely listened. Metin Bey continued with his historical explanations, saying that a certain building had been constructed in the time of Sultan Suleiman the Magnificent by so-and-so pasha. It's magnificent, I said; but I was tired. It had been an unexpectedly busy day, and I could think of nothing except going to their home and crawling into bed for the night.

In the beginning, everything was fine, but after I'd settled in and was just about to fall asleep in Ozan's room, my roommate started crying.

What's wrong? Is everything okay? I'm also a mother, and I have some experience in finding solutions to bouts of weeping in the night. But he didn't stop, and as expected, soon enough Zehra Hanım came. Ozan insisted, however, on seeing his father. In a hushed voice, Zehra Hanım tried to explain why that wasn't possible:

Ozan, you know that we have a guest tonight, so would it be appropriate for your father to come into this room? We don't want to disturb Sibel Teyze, do we?

But those words were like a signal that sent his howls into a crescendo, and it was impossible to get Ozan to quiet down.

Zehra Hanım, I said, call for Metin Bey to come.

Personally, I saw no problem with Metin Bey coming into the room and seeing me in bed. But maybe there was? Zehra Hanım picked up Ozan and took him into their bedroom, and then the crying stopped. If I had the energy, I would have been bothered that I upset the tranquility of their home. But now I could sleep in peace.

First, updates were given in some newspapers and on a few radio and television channels. Maybe everywhere in the world, morning was breaking for lower level bureaucrats. Tea was sent for as they lit their first cigarettes for the day, followed by the first rounds of coughs as they inhaled the smoke.

Did you listen to the prime minister last night? He talked about "order," and then about the "setting."

One day, he'll start to learn Turkish too . . .

Those last words were spoken by me. Was that a glance of warning when the chair of the department looked at me? I can feel the prickle of fear that is stirred up by my voice and the fact that I've joined the conversation. This happens each and every time. They're still not used to me. Whenever the conversation turns to politics, the economy or contemporary events, the sound of a woman's voice always has the same frightening effect: a silence, like they've suddenly remembered that there is a spy in their midst. Why didn't I sit in the other room where my female colleagues were? A struggle of logic and tradition. Logic is defeated; soon, someone picks up the conversation and it continues. That is, of course, until I wait for them to forget about my presence, at which point I speak up again . . .

Someone brought up the topic of Ataturk's speech in Erzurum: Take off your headscarves, he said. It won't be a sin if I see you.

Someone says: Did he think that he was every woman's husband?

Another retorts: Maybe he meant that he'd do them no harm. Something like, I'm an old man and I've lived out my life.

Someone cuts in: According to rumors, it wasn't like that. He was involved with singers, and stage actresses too.

They forgot about my presence again, and so I snuck in a reminder:

I think it's notable that he spoke of sin. The head of a secular state shouldn't issue fatwas on sin and good deeds like he were a sheikh of Islam.

Again, it had the same effect, like I'd heaved a boulder into the flow of their conversation. Silence.

It was different when I first arrived. They had much to learn from me. Especially because they realized that what I'd been through would soon be happening to them. We knew that the play that had been staged at the Izmir State Theater was about to be put on at the state theater in Trabzon too. Almost every morning the people around me were talking about it. In almost every era, teachers have been subjected to these kinds of investigations and legal proceedings, but they didn't tell stories like mine; they spoke in terms of articles of law:

Hoca'nım, as you know, Article 5 of Law 2880 repealed the decision regarding teachers who were reassigned to their original positions and their periods of employment have been extended for another year. Why is it that this decision hasn't been put into effect at your school?

I was set on edge by the fact that I could sense their incredulity, and discussing the "law" had an allergic effect on me.

What do you mean when you say that it hasn't been implemented? I explained it all to your colleagues. We were reassigned to our department but not to teach or administer exams; our duty was to sit beneath the trees when the exams were given.

Yes, they said, laughing. Patiently and with an open heart, I answered all their questions.

But now I'm no longer the focus of discussions. My presence no longer causes a stir, and so long as I remain silent, they even forget that I'm here; but it's not easy for me to resign myself to being forgotten. Most of the time I pull into my shell and sit and listen; but on occasion, when they least expect it, I speak up. There's no other option; they'll just have to accept me.

Last week I met some of my female colleagues from the other departments. They invited me to join them in a room in another building where they get together for tea and chat. That's how they spend the afternoons.

We'd love it if you'd join us, they said.

But I dislike such gatherings of women. I asked them why they don't join the men's conversations: Do you feel uncomfortable, or are you uninvited?

They ruled out the second possibility, and said: We just prefer being here.

Like this, making your own tea and serving it yourselves? I'm against the segregation of men and women. Forgive me, but I can't join you here in this room. Why don't you take part in their conversations? We're also teachers at this school, so they have to get used to us being around.

But they refused: There's really no problem . . . Of course . . . They're already used to us being around . . . It's just a matter of feeling more relaxed . . .

So! That's my place of work, and that's where I'm going to sit. Join me if you like. I can't bring myself to shuffle off to a corner and sit there like I'm hiding.

Did they think that I was boastful, ridiculous, or perhaps spoiled? Who knows? It was a sincere invitation, and my reaction was harsher than they expected, I know that. But on some subjects I just can't back down. A few of my younger colleagues sometimes come around. Good morning, they say, and drink a cup of tea, but that's all.

They ask: Aren't you going to come over to our room?

My reply is curt: I already told you.

I hope they understand and aren't offended. I don't want to upset anybody, but if I was going to let myself be cowed into going along with opinions with which I disagree, I would've done that in Izmir.

Even though my first two-hour class hasn't yet begun, I go early to the office, flushed with excitement because soon I'll be meeting my students. And it's easier to come with the university shuttle. Had

I been a little stubborn with the driver? Yes, it goes to the university campus. But it doesn't go into the city. That's what the driver said. At first, I meekly got onto the shuttle. When everyone except for me got off when we arrived at the campus, he glared at me, and I smiled in an attempt to win him over: I . . . As you might know, I work at the Fatih School of Education. That's why . . . But my stammering only elicited defiance: It's forbidden! he said, I'm not supposed to go there.

A few times I went along with his refusal and took the city bus down to Trabzon, but it's a tiresome journey and if I missed the bus, I would've been be late. And as if paying for the return journey weren't enough, I had to pay to get there too. It's not my fault that my school isn't located on the main campus! I never wanted to be appointed to the Fatih School of Education and interred at the Seaside Residence. If I'm an employee at this university, I should have the same rights as the others. So in the end, I had an outburst.

Abla, I'm not allowed to drive down to the city.

Don't call me "abla." Look, this is a serious issue. Who said you aren't allowed to go to the School of Education?

Those were my orders. I can only take people from the residence to the campus, and from there you have to go on your own.

Is that so? In that case, I'll talk to the president of the university about this.

Just as I expected, the driver cringed when I mentioned the president.

Okay, today I'll take you, but I can't take you every day.

You have to take me every day. I was appointed to this university; if I'd been employed at the School of Science and Literature, you would've had to take me. But you say that since I work for the School of Education, you can't take me. Do you see the point here? How can a university discriminate among the various faculties?

It's a good thing that the driver wasn't aware of the intricacies of the administration of the university and that he found my argument logical. If he'd known about the discrimination that existed not just among the schools but within them as well, and if he'd known that my appointment was actually a punishment and not an attempt to get my professorship, then he probably wouldn't have let me on the shuttle in the first place.

Before going to my first class, I wanted to look over my notes again. Just a little while ago, a lecturer from the history department came by along with two others, but I didn't know who they were or where they worked. They didn't introduce themselves, nor was I introduced to them. The chair of the department had told me to keep a distance because they were "dangerous," but it didn't really matter because apparently they don't shake hands with women. They have some kind of immunity, and the faculties are more or less under their thumbs. But I can't help eavesdropping on their conversation. They are talking about a professor who was in love with the sound of his own voice and came down with tuberculosis. It was like the myth of Narcissus. So fascinating!

Someone who joined the conversation is talking about a friend of his who became wealthy by selling religious books, and then the topic swings back to the "professor." Someone says that if you weep and plead from dusk to dawn, you'll get a child. Then they talk about an agricultural engineer from Samsun who was working at the regional directorate office. Listen carefully to that teacher, they said.

I should probably put my notes away. I can't focus on them, nor can I follow their conversation.

His uncle summons jinn. He brought my sister to ruin, and in the end she was tearing out her hair. My brother-in-law said, I'm going to kill you. You have to get sand from the place where a river empties into the sea and some hair from the tail of a goat. We went to Değirmendere and found what we needed.

Their conversation is nonsensical.

He continues: We set out to sea in a boat, and threw them into the water. The warming and cooling is good. He's a hajj and he's done good and bad magic, but there's no place for him in the afterlife.

I open up my notes again. But in vain! My mind keeps drifting to their conversation. The more I try not listen, the louder their voices get. A veritable attack on my ears . . . Why can't we make ourselves stop hearing? These men are the untouchables at the university, and they know it. They have no fears of being fired or driven out. Unlike the others, they don't listen in trepidation when I recount my experiences, nor are they caught up in uneasy anticipation. Whenever I talk, the others signal for me to stop when one of those men come into the room:

Change the topic, it could cause problems; don't talk around them. When they came into the office this morning, I was sitting here. But none of them said "Good morning" or "Hello."

The historian is talking about a fortune-teller from Tirebolu named Şakir and how he "found" his aunt's missing bracelets. They say that he always knows when Trabzonspor will lose a match. Then there is a woman named Oflu who lives off cigarettes and nothing else.

I feel like I'm in the wrong time and wrong place. What business do I have among these men?

One of them has started talking about his sister's jinn. He says that one time she made seven dishes of *muhallebi* pudding and went to sleep, but when she got up in the morning, two of them had been eaten. For all appearances, the jinn had come and eaten them in the night. But the historian can't bear it and asks about her husband and children. Maybe they ate it? The others glare at him as if he's an unbeliever: You believe in jinn, don't you?

What didn't those jinn do? They ransacked her home, breaking every single mirror.

My stomach lurches and a wave of nausea rushes over me. A bolt of pain shoots through my head. I don't have to be in this room. I don't have to work at a school where men like this are "wanted" and I'm "unwanted." When everyone else tries to ignore them, running off and leaving them at the center of everything, why should I run the risk of standing up to them? Shouldn't I? What are you talking about, why are you talking such nonsense? Do you think that talking about hair from the tail of a goat, puffs of breath and spells are what people like you (and just who are you? Intellectuals? Educated men? Faculty members? Lecturers? For God's sake, just who are you?) should be talking about? But no, I shouldn't say anything. Soon I'll be going to my first class. I should keep my cool. Admonishing them is none of my business. They're permanent, and I'm just temporary. And since I can't be like them, don't they want me to keep silent? This time, I should keep my silence, I really should.

I slam the door on my way out. I know that if I don't react somehow, I'll never forgive myself. I also know that I'll regret what I've done. What did they understand from the fact that I slammed the door? Did they even notice? Why didn't I speak my mind? So, you'll be in charge of the school. Well, that's just great; you'll enrich the university with your goat hair, puffs of breath, prayers, spells and jinn.

Why am I still being so timid? Am I becoming like Hülya? Am I on the way to becoming an "agreeable" lecturer who always nods in approval, flatters others and bows and scrapes before those in power? Is that what I'm becoming, someone who, in full view of everyone else, bites her tongue even when she's irritated to no end?

I decide to wander the halls before my class and step outside. I have to calm myself down. In my first class, I should be calm and at ease. Soon enough, that which I've dreamed of for months will become a reality. At last, the hopes I harbored under the linden trees in Izmir are coming true; I'm going to meet my new students, and do what I love: Teach!

I love my students, and I know that I can't live without them. They didn't deserve to be punished this way.

Her father brought her all the way to the door.

Ring the bell, he said; if anything goes wrong, I'll be here. Then he stepped back, waiting under the linden tree. She couldn't have come alone without her father, who was so timid that he couldn't bring himself to be there with her when she rang the bell.

Sibel rang the bell. Then once again. She turned to see if her father was still there. He was standing there, waiting.

The third time, she rang the bell longer. Then she heard the shuffle of house slippers. The door swung open.

Ah, my dear, it's so good to see you. We've been waiting for you. Come inside.

Sibel didn't have the chance to turn and look back at her father. She was taken into an embrace, and then the door closed.

Her father left. He left when he saw her go inside.

Her teacher said: This is Neşe, gesturing to a young girl who started coming down the stairs when she heard voices at the door. She's my oldest, her teacher said. She's studying chemistry. The other girl didn't wait to be introduced. She came up to Sibel and said:

I'm the younger one. Sibel didn't hear the name of the girl, who planted two kisses on Sibel's cheeks.

Everyone sat down to the breakfast table, which had been laid for Sibel.

You were late, her teacher said. We were worried that maybe they wouldn't let you come.

At one point, Sibel said: My father brought me. But no one heard her.

That day, Neşe Abla found a swimsuit for Sibel.

We're going to the sea, she said. We're going to sunbathe and sleep the day away.

Sibel overheard them talking: Just as you said, she's a very sweet girl.

She also heard her teacher tell her daughters about her grandmother, father, uncle and mother:

Her mother died giving birth to Sibel's younger brother. Sibel doesn't remember her mother very well.

Oh, my dear, they said, taking Sibel into their arms.

Sevinç Abla never left her side that day. She showed Sibel around the house, took her to the seaside and took her shopping. They made plans for the next day and the day after that.

Sibel doesn't remember how long she stayed at her teacher's house that summer. In later years, she'd say: That was a wonderful summer, so those few days must have seemed like an entire summer. She recalls that when it was time for an afternoon nap, she and Sevinç Abla rolled around on the large bed, and then there were the games they played on the beach, and after Sibel read the books her teacher gave her, she talked about them with Neşe Abla.

In the summers that followed, she was invited again to her teacher's summer house and she went there during the holidays when she was studying at the teachers college. Then her teacher's daughters grew up. Neşe Abla got married, and when her teacher retired, she moved to Istanbul with Sevinç Abla. Sibel never saw them again.

Almost all of the male students have mustaches. And here too mustaches are a political symbol, one that I need to take as a sign that I must be cautious. The student with the gentle conscience, my "informer," had a mustache just like theirs. There weren't many female students, and the few women in the class seemed meek, pallid. Maybe that was just because it was the first day.

When I walked into the classroom, I realized that I'd been harboring the hope that I'd be reunited with my old students. That feeling of despair inspired by the conversation about goat hair lingered on through the beginning of the class. Maybe that's what drove me, together with the possibility that they might think I was harmless because of my youth, to tell them right at the beginning of class that I'd been reappointed to their school because I'd been considered to be "dangerous." Just to be on the safe side. I didn't want them to hear it from anyone else in a way that would be beyond my control. I told them that it would be good if they were careful about the topics they discussed. What else could I do? It was impossible for me to be any more honest. If I was to be careful in my interactions with them, they needed to do the same.

The students didn't show any particular displeasure. They didn't talk about their past teachers or seem bothered by the fact that I would be teaching their class. As far as I knew, many of them already knew about me and my past. Possibly they were only curious to see what I look like. There were whisperings and a whistle when I walked into the classroom, so I realized that I was younger and more attractive than they'd expected. I said nothing and didn't even introduce myself at first. I simply glared with such ferocity at the student who'd whistled that he turned bright red, swallowing the second whistle that was on his lips. It occurred to me that I wasn't just being confronted with primitive behavior, but also an attempt at sabotage. That's why I came across so brusquely at first, so that they'd think twice about taking me lightly. However, to soften the tone of the class, I asked them how their practicums had gone and whether or not they enjoyed teaching. They were unenthusiastic, and it was clear that they didn't embrace teaching with passion. Since there were no other job prospects on the horizon, they saw it as a way to "get by." As for me, I had no desire to launch into a harangue about the meaning, importance and sanctity of teaching. There was no need to start the very first class off in a tedious way. And I was sure that they'd been treated to lengthy diatribes from their other teachers about the nobility of education.

I taught them about the Constitutional Era of the Ottoman Empire, and after laying down the historical and cultural framework, I moved on to literature; however, because the 1870s was crammed into the last week, they asked if it would be possible for me to briefly discuss Mehmet Akif because we hadn't spent much time on him. Briefly? Talk about Mehmet Akif "in brief"? Was this a conspiracy? But I consented:

If you want me to give an overview of Mehmet Akif, you need to come prepared. And we'll have to discuss the trends of thought prevalent in the Second Constitutional Era, starting with Islamism, so that we can better understand those times and be prepared to talk about his writing.

I wondered if I should tell them now or later that an interrogation had been launched against me because of Mehmet Akif? Perhaps they knew already?

Class ended without any other complications. As I was leaving the classroom, a weariness came over me. I'd forgotten that feeling; and what a sweet sensation it was! I'd missed it. The weariness of a sapling offering pollen to the wind.

The office of the chair of the department was full of people. I didn't know any of them, but I didn't bother asking who they were or why they'd come. I left my books and notes on my desk and stepped outside. Someone said: Some of our colleagues have come from the university. A sentence echoed in my thoughts. Why don't you think of yourself as being "from the university"? But I said nothing, because I don't belong there either. I decided to try to find someone to have lunch with me. I wondered if I should go to the "women's room for teachers."

They'd given me two fourth-year courses, Contemporary Turkish Literature and Theater. The classes were to be held just twice a week. Didn't that mean that it would be easier for me to go to Izmir? I could talk to the chair of the department. If I were to take off Thursday and Friday, I'd have four days in total. I could leave Izmir on Monday and be back in time for my class on Tuesday. And hadn't everyone been going on about how I could get reports and take leave? If I was given leave, then I could probably arrange for a report to be issued in Izmir. Aside from maternity leave, I hadn't taken any time off; would I be able to manage it? They said: Don't you know that there are people who've been doing that for years? So maybe I could pull it off. And I missed my children terribly. So what would I say? How about this: I've really missed my children, so can I have some time off? I despise making people pity me, but I really did miss them. If I could see them for just a few days . . . There was no need for me to get a report. I'll come back, and be here on Tuesday. What if I promise?

* * *

Akın. It was incredible. Even though I hadn't thought about him for so long, I wondered why I hadn't forgotten about him and would, in most likelihood, never see him again; even if I did, would I even be able to recognize him? But I found my thoughts turning back to him: Akın. It was him.

I ran into Burcu from the Department of Education in the teacher's room. She was getting ready to leave, so we had lunch together.

Afterward, I had no desire to go back to the "women's room for teachers." I think Burcu was feeling the pleasure of having found a close friend. She was unable to conceal her happiness at the fact that I'd come to the university, although there was no way I would be able to help dispel her loneliness. It wasn't hard for me to understand the loneliness she felt. For two years she'd never done anything that the people around her would find odd; in the full sense of the saying, she was toeing the line. But she hadn't gotten used to being here, and her sole desire was to go back to Samsun. She was younger than me, and single. There was something childish and innocent about her, and she was afraid of everything. She thought that the slightest discord would bring her down in the eyes of the other faculty members; she liked it when I spoke out against the way that men and women gather in separate rooms, but she was unable to say a word in front of the others. Her roommate was a research assistant in the School of Pharmacy. Their home was close to the school and she said that I could stay with them if I wanted; I knew that she was just being kind, but her offer made me happy. In a place like that, every little thing is important.

Since I didn't want to go back to the "women's room" after lunch, I asked Burcu if she'd like to join me for coffee in the office of the chair of the department. Was it because I'd forgotten that some people had come from the main campus, or that I figured they'd be gone by that time? The room had cleared out to a certain extent, but there were still many there who I didn't know. We took a seat in a corner. I've never liked introducing myself to people. Sitting across from me was a white-haired man and I noticed that he was staring at me. I wondered: Do I know him? I was annoyed by his staring, and as I sat there thinking that I should change seats, I realized that he'd started a conversation with the men around him and the topic was probably me. They gestured toward me with their heads, nodding. Then he stood up and began walking in my direction, smiling.

I felt like I should know him, but no one came to mind. As I held out my hand, I searched his face for familiar features, but there was nothing. All I could think was: My God, I have to remember who he is, I must somehow remember . . .

Hi. I'm Akın Özgü, from Istanbul, from the School of Education.

It was impossible. How could that man with white hair be handsome Akın? Akın from Bulancak, whose hometown I passed through on my way to Trabzon, thoughts of whom stirred up a powerful nostalgia for my student days . . . How could Akın, beloved of so many girls, who occupied Ferda's thoughts and dreams, and even brought color to my own dreams from time to time, be that man with disheveled cotton-white hair?

How could so much time have passed? I don't think I ever understood so concretely what it means to age. The only thing I could imagine was the image of "Akın" standing before me. That's what it means to get old. It's not about forgetting the past, but about not being able to find someone in their own image. He'd heard that a woman named Sibel had been reappointed from Izmir as a 1402. (In that way, I discovered that I'd become a hero of sorts and acquired a certain fame around the university.) He didn't think that it was me, although he knew that I lived in Izmir, but he did wonder: What if it really is her? That day, he'd come to our campus to see if it was me and put to rest the questions in his mind.

He said that he'd seen a woman who looked like me and was told that I'd go to the office after my class. That was me, I said, I came and dropped off my books but it was so crowded I left.

There's someone else who wants to see you, he said, but after waiting for a while, he had to leave to teach a class. He knows you as Sibel

Gökşen, and ever since he found out that you were here, he's been meaning to come see you. I think you met in Ankara. He was really impressed, and he talks about you all the time. It seems you gave quite a powerful talk.

I remember that day, but who is he?

Soon enough he'll come and see you himself. Unlike me, he knew for sure it was you.

That's true, as the Sibel that Akın knew didn't have the surname Gökşen at the time.

Akın, you know me as Sibel Ceylan, right? I asked, smiling. I was startled to realize that I was addressing him so informally. It's jolting to speak so openly with someone you haven't seen in so many years, but at the same time, being formal would be just as awkward.

That's right, and I'd always thought that your last name suited you so well. Ceylan, graceful as a gazelle.

As I struggled to decide how formally we should be speaking, his compliment seemed out of place. In an attempt to move the conversation in a different direction, I said:

The name Ceylan is gone now, along with any of the grace that went with it.

No, he said, you haven't changed a bit. The beauty of your youth has blossomed into something more lasting.

As I stood there, my mind racing to find something to say, the chair of the department came to my rescue:

I'm so glad to see the two of you. Do you know each other?

Of course, Akın replied. Sibel is an old friend of mine. I've always admired her.

Then the chair of the department launched into a eulogy of praise for Akın, just as Akın had done for me:

Akın Bey is from Trabzon. He's greatly respected around here.

Akın cut in: As is Sibel Hanım . . .

As the conversation continued, our colleagues "from the university" came up to be introduced, and I was the object of some praise as regards how, since my university days, I always stood apart, had a strong personality, and was so cultured. I was burning with curiosity to know how and when he'd found out so much about me. But I'm not accustomed to being praised; I prefer to blend in. At that point, one of the professors said that it was time for them to leave; as he turned to go, Akın said that he'd come again and that he hoped next time we'd be able to talk longer and in a more pleasant setting. As he left, the chair of the department heaped more praise on Akın, putting on airs: Did you see that? Akın Bey came here to see me.

I came to a realization: in Trabzon, it was important to have a friend like Akın. Thank you, Akın; if I'm not mistaken, you're bringing color to my image, which was shrouded in shadow.

It was disturbing to see that the chair of the department had been trying so hard to show me off as a friend of someone they held in high regard. I wondered: What prejudices do they have about me at the university that this poor man is trying to change?

I remember the gathering that Akın had talked about. At the time, we weren't yet a school. I attended a meeting organized by the Ministry of National Education about Turkish and changes in the language, and a number of people who were considered to be competent in the field were invited to join, including people from schools of higher education, select university professors and some newspaper columnists. Along with a friend of mine, I was selected as the representative of the Izmir teacher training school and we set off, fairly convinced that the government, now that it had instated martial law, had some devious plans for the language. As teachers coming from the countryside, we were stunned to see so much indifference, but we blew on the ashes with so much vigor that the flames were brought back to life.

I know the talk to which Akın's friend referred; in the beginning, everyone was reticent, defeated.

My talk began with this sentence: You have the power to shut down the Turkish Language Association; but if you do, you'll have to loudly proclaim that you're against the principles of Ataturk . . . I spoke boldly, perhaps with the courage of being unaware of the scale of the potential danger I was stirring up for myself. It all stemmed from my reaction against those who were claiming to be supporters of the ideas of Ataturk but shut down parliament and harassed the political parties, organizations, and associations that hadn't been banned yet.

At once, the atmosphere of the meeting changed. Acceptance gave way to an impassioned desire to take up the struggle anew.

The meeting lasted for three days. In the end, however, those fiery speeches merely postponed what had already been decided; a few months later, the association was closed down.

I shouldn't attribute my reappointment just to the interrogations that were carried out. Even back then at that meeting I was warned by a writer who I greatly respect:

Your talk was very good, but don't think this will go unnoticed. From now on, the threat of punishment will hang over you.

Until our school was taken under the jurisdiction of the Board of Higher Education, they didn't really do anything. Without a doubt, however, there is a star next to my name in the board's ledger of "objectionable" people.

Just one of my carnations is left. I promised that I would dry it out; but the time hasn't come yet. I just can't bring myself to place it between the pages of a book until the last drops of red have drained from its petals. Drying flowers is something like mummification. I should wait until the last vestiges of its soul have vanished; because of its defiance, it deserves to be spared any suffering.

But do those who stand up in defiance really have the right to be spared pain? And if so, who granted them that right? Does a law like that exist?

As they stand up in defiance, some suffer while others don't. Some of us see defiance as a way of being, but there are always others who are content not rising up in revolt. If the point of it all is not to resist but to be happy . . . That's how it's been, for centuries that's been the goal of humanity.

And some people think that defiance is happiness. It shouldn't be a matter of comparing, as in my case. When that which you stand up for is taken from you, a transformation occurs: you become a withered carnation, but you aren't aware of what you've become as you foolishly struggle. A kind-hearted philanthropist should step in and explain to you that your struggles are in vain, pointing out that it would be best to put an end to all your efforts and let yourself lapse into the calm waters of habit. Or maybe just wait and then show you that all your toil wouldn't even suffice to churn a bowl of salted yogurt into *ayran*. Making ayran? That's the equivalent of so much effort, nothing more.

4

We are a people of fire, clothed in flames.
—Hulki Aktunç

What's happening to me? Despite the fact that I've always believed that terms like "crisis," "panic," "tumult," and "I'm a wreck" are hollow exaggerations, generally used by people to cover up the artificial emptiness they've created inside themselves, I can find no other way to express how I feel. What am I doing here? What kind of life is this?

Did I think that I'd find a paradise here? For years I was trapped behind bars; did I think that I'd finally found an escape? And just what does "freedom" mean? Was it a matter of being unable to see that you escaped from those bars only to be shackled in other chains? Not understanding that another prison has sprung up around you? Or warming up to your chains, beginning to love them over time to the point that you're unable to live without them?

What am I seeking here?

The chirping of birds, the blue sky, the wildflowers . . . Get over it; you realized long ago that they aren't to be found.

You're a smart woman, Sibel, you know what you want. Think: what is it? To be saved from the grumblings of your mother-in-law, the griping of your husband, the clamor of your children? Sure, but then what? You wanted a new life, an immaculate, unsullied life.

But you're not immaculate! You've been used up and worn down; how could you want something unblemished? Fine, let's traverse all boundaries, and suppose that you could break your chains; but don't you see the cages out there with their doors open? All the traps and snares waiting for you . . . And then what? What are you going to do? Let's suppose that you were savvy enough to not be trapped; wouldn't that be like stepping out of an airplane into a limitless blue expanse? And you don't even have a parachute. What will you depend on? You've never stepped into such a void. You don't even know how to fall.

I should find a way to go back to Izmir. Now, so I can go back tomorrow!

My father said:

I thought that when you were appointed to a teaching position, we would move there together. By that time, I would've retired so it would be easy for me to go with you.

I knew he was insinuating that I'd gotten married too soon. But I couldn't say that it was his fault. That he left me no other means of escape except for marriage.

When he was forced to retire—even though he was just a timid civil servant who kept a scrupulous distance from politics and committed no other crime except for voting for the Republican People's Party—he was bewildered. Orhan was in Germany. Stop being so stubborn and come with me, he insisted. Soon enough I'll retire. Your older sister is still studying, so when she finishes and gets a job, we'll think about it.

After his retirement, it couldn't be put off any longer. And he couldn't bring himself to go along with Orhan's suggestion. I knew he was in difficult straits; but there was nothing I could do.

I couldn't suggest that he stay with us because of Haluk, but more than that, because of Hayriye Hanım. She once said to me: Your father's still young, and he's a decent man. At that moment, she was looking at Ozan; in those days, she was staying with us a lot, and she held the strings. Then she said: He and I can't live here together, so I'd have to move out. And that's when it all came to a halt. If she goes, how will we raise Ozan? Who will look after us?

If I'd offered, would my father have agreed to live with us? I doubt it. When I realized that he was pained by loneliness, I began to wonder if he'd want to live with me. He wasn't that old, but after my mother passed away, he didn't consider remarrying, even though we often insisted that he should. He laughed when Orhan suggested that he get married.

Son, have you lost your mind? At my age?

At the time, we didn't know that Orhan had left the country as a political refugee. When he was still in Turkey, he'd been involved in a few incidents and taken into custody, but that was it. Still, he didn't want to return to Turkey from Germany. He said that it was becoming difficult for him to stay there, but he came up with a brilliant solution, at least in his mind: marry off our father to a widow who had her own house. He'd found a woman who agreed to his proposal and all he needed to do was convince our father to go along with it.

Actually, you won't really be married, he said. It's just a formality. The marriage will just be on paper. And then you can go back to Turkey whenever you want. If you don't agree to it, then I'll have no other choice but to marry a German woman.

He knew that was our father's greatest fear, and Orhan was attacking his weakest point.

Ultimately, he gave in and went to Germany. But the widow, after having found a husband after so many years, didn't let the marriage just stay on paper.

Orhan said: Don't worry, they're happily married.

* * *

I decided tonight that I will talk to the dean. What will I say? I miss my children, and I want to take a week off. And as you know, the 23rd of April is coming up, which is Children's Day, and the best gift I could ever give them would be myself. On that day, I want to be able to make them happy. I think that you'll agree that it's a mother's right to want something like that.

Wait just a moment, Sibel Hanım! You know that you shouldn't speak so emotionally. If you truly believe what you're saying, you'll be affected by your words before the dean ever will and you'll break down in tears. Don't I know that better than you?

No, I can't let that happen; I shouldn't show my weakness, even as a mother. And if you try to put on an act that isn't even convincing for you, will the dean really believe it? The problem is that you might lose your nerve. Since the dean wouldn't expect Sibel Hanım, who'd been branded as a "1402," to change her mind so quickly and start taking pity on herself, he'd strike a negative pose at the very beginning, no matter if I didn't come across as completely headstrong, indifferent and dismissive. At the first hint of groveling, his attitude would change. What would he do? He'd think: Look how quickly we've brought you to your knees; it was as simple as that. The "rebel" of yesterday is now pleading for a week's leave. People like that are always the same. Soon enough, she'll be sniffling and scuffling, throwing herself at my feet.

I can't be sure if I'll be able to speak calmly. How can Sibel Hanım convince herself that she needs to boost her morale so that she can stand being here for a few more months? That she needs to gather

her strength so she can bear the utter loneliness of it all? If I know you, this is how it happens: you've finally been brought to your knees, hoca'nım, and the moment you start bowing down or catch a glimpse of the way we send people packing, the only thing you can do is leave, slamming the door on your way out. You'll do everything you can to avoid another encounter, as that would be even worse. There's a certain utility—for now—of not burning the bridges that will take us to unknown destinations.

* * *

The other day I came across him in the corridor—at the time, I didn't even know he was the dean—and he held out his hand:

You're Sibel Hanım, right? I wanted to welcome you to the department.

I sensed that there was a kind of complaint hidden in his words hinting that I should've introduced myself when I arrived. But what "welcome" was this, nearly two weeks in the coming?

Please step inside, he said, pointing to the department office.

What have you been up to? I haven't heard a word from you.

That was an odd question. Had they said that I tended to shout? What was the appropriate response? Of course I talk; but I guess you can't hear it from your office. I remained silent.

Seeing that the dean was in his office, a few teachers stopped in to ask some questions. Then the teachers who had classes got up to leave. I knew he had something to say to me; I waited, and it came at last:

How was your holiday?

I'm sorry? What holiday?

Did he mean my trip from Izmir to Trabzon, the fact that I was late because of my defense? He went on speaking as if I hadn't said a word:

You probably took off a few too many days for vacation.

Sensing that the conversation was taking a dangerous turn, the chair of the department drew closer.

No, sir, I replied. I think there's been a misunderstanding. Because I had to give my defense, I couldn't be here on Monday.

But you weren't here on Tuesday either, he said. Where were you on Tuesday?

I was here, sir.

The chair of the department cut in:

Sibel Hanım was here on Tuesday. She called to tell me that she'd arrived. I told her that there was no need for her to come into the office, and that she could come in the next day.

He'd said to me: You've come a long way, why don't you rest today and come into the office tomorrow? I remember thinking to myself that there truly are good people in the world. My students were still doing their practicums, so I didn't need to go to the office, and in any case I had two large suitcases with me.

The dean's response was an intonation of disbelief: Hmmm. Whether you have classes or not, we'd like you to be here at the office.

I replied in turn with a "Hmmm." Now that he'd unburdened himself of his concerns, the dean lightened up.

He turned to the chair of the department: Isn't it customary here to offer tea to your guests?

The chair of the department pressed a buzzer and tea was brought in.

I know about your school, the dean said. I've been there before.

When? I asked, but he ignored my question.

It has a nice big yard. And I know the dean.

(Oh, splendid!)

He took a large gulp of tea.

But the students are a little too intimate there, if you ask me. They walk around like this (he demonstrates) arm in arm, hanging on each other. If they had just a little less shame, they'd start kissing each other.

I was about to say: Let them kiss, it's perfectly normal. But at the moment I was sipping my tea. Based on their topics of conversation, it was clear that the two deans really were friends. My old dean often complained about how close the male and female students were.

The dean said: If you saw what goes on there, you'd be shocked.

During a lull in the conversation, I asked:

What are you going to do with me?

He turned and looked at me, as if actually seeing me for the first time, and the lines of his face softened, and he laughed:

We'll probably send you back to the Ministry of National Education.

Then he laughed again. I couldn't tell if he was just trying to lighten the atmosphere.

I'm sitting at a table which is covered end to end with a map of Turkey topped with glass. On the map there are mountains, hills, rivers, roads that would take more than a night and a day to traverse . . . The distance between Izmir and Trabzon is more than three handbreadths. How did I manage to travel so far? Thinking about my children makes my soul ache. For me to truly learn the meaning of that expression, I have to feel that ache down to the depths of my being.

In the office, people come and go, but I pay no heed to anyone, and they ignore me in turn. It's better this way. Every time I sit at this table, a jolt of pain runs through me; even when the room is empty, I come and sit down. The table probably belongs to one of the geographers, seeing as it has a map . . . But no one bothers me. I don't want my own office; but I should at least have my own desk.

When I first arrived, I was given an old oak desk by the door; in places, the veneer on the desk had bubbled up. Even in those times, no one spoke a word to me. (For some reason . . . She's lonely, an exile—keep your distance.) A silent, tolerant respect. I could never get comfortable.

Something made me see myself as a parasite, and there was the alienating feeling of being at the desk right next to the door. So to prove that I'd completely settled in, I chose for myself the desk with the map at the other end of the room. It distracts me; I estimate the distances on the map, and measuring them with my fingers, make calculations of handbreadths. Most of the time, when the door opens I look up to see who's come in, even though I'm not expecting anyone. The tea server comes to collect the empty glasses and payment for the tea. But no one lets me pay. How unsettling it is! I belong here now, I'm no longer a guest. Before anyone can say a word, I pay for my tea, indifferent to their objections: Hoca'nım, it just wouldn't be right!

That's how it is, I say. A guest is someone who stays for three days, four days, maybe five. But I've been here for fifteen days.

They exclaim: Has it been so long? Meaning that I've become one of them.

As the tea server leaves, the dean walks into the office. He rarely visits the office of the chair of the department, and even more rarely comes to our office. And when he does, it's only when the spouse or parent of a teacher has passed away. This is his second visit; until now, only one teacher's wife has died. Everyone panics; some people get to their feet while others fumble to button up their coats.

You don't ever come to my office, he says.

As I was thinking about whether or not I should stand up, some-one said to me:

He's talking to you.

To me? Who's saying what to me? I look in the direction of the door. The dean is there, staring at me, waiting for an answer.

I didn't even have time to ask: Did you say something? He repeated what he said before.

My office, I said. You never stop by for a visit.

Oh, that's great! Now I'm being summoned to his office. With typical nonchalance, I said:

My apologies. I thought you were talking to the tea server.

Did he fall silent and then tell me to come to his office, or did his face flush with anger? He closed the door and left.

Stunned, everyone in the office looked at me.

How could you say that?

I don't know. It was actually really easy.

I couldn't understand why they were so pleased with that turn of events. But I can't complain about the fact that I'd done something that no one else had ever dared. And why was he expecting me to visit him? Was it a tradition, do new teachers always visit his office? And the more I think about it, the more it disturbs me: You never come to my office. Just what is that supposed to mean? It was like summoning a tea server. It's on the tip of my tongue; but I should stop myself from thinking too much. But still . . . Couldn't I have said: I'm sorry, Mr. Dean, but do you think that I'm some kind of mistress? Which other offices have I gone to? No, I shouldn't think like that; it's repulsive! It would be in poor taste for me to insult myself like that. But there's something plainly obvious: as of now, I'll never be able to ask him for leave so that I can see my children.

Before I could savor my heroism to my heart's content, Akın came into the office. That was the second important event of the day. When he came into the room, Akın noticed that something was in the air.

What's going on? he asked.

Nothing, I said. What could possibly happen?

I brought Rahmi Bey to see you. You met him at that workshop in Ankara.

Yes, I remember Rahmi Bey. Please, have a seat. What would you like to drink?

But my thoughts were on what the dean asked me. Rahmi Bey was talking about the workshop and what we'd discussed there. What had I said? I acted as though I was listening and trying to remember, but in vain. I can't go there now, it's just not possible at the moment; Rahmi Bey must forgive me. My notes for my theater class were on my desk in front of me. Obviously aware of the fact that the conversation was proceeding awkwardly, Rahmi Bey asked:

Are you also teaching the courses on theater?

Yes, I also taught theater in Izmir, but I need to go over my lecture notes.

The way I clutched my notes betrayed my excitement about teaching again.

As he left, Akın leaned in to ask me, almost in a whisper:

Can we have lunch together tomorrow somewhere off campus?

With hardly a thought, I replied:

Sure, it would be a nice change.

Akın!

One day, a large group of us were at the cafeteria of the School of Higher Education. One of our classmates had decided to get engaged. Some people said that it was good; others were hung up on the fact that people were getting married and dropping out of school.

(I was likely among the latter.) In the corner there was a shadowy figure, wearing his usual olive-green jacket. One of the girls tittered to me: He's looking at you! At this point in the film, I tersely reply: No, what are you talking about? But I can't. I stand up and approach him. I can feel the warmth of his hands between my palms. Let them say what they will. Hand in hand, we walk out of the cafeteria into a copse of towering trees, and the grass is so deep it comes up over our ankles. And there are flowers, pink and blue wildflowers.

In those days, we watched so many films.

I know that it's a dream. But it's more like a film than a dream. I'm completely myself, and when I open my eyes, I'm unable to stop even after realizing that it's a dream. Perhaps I don't want to stop myself. I like the feeling.

I'm not married; there's no Haluk, no children, and I'm eighteen years old, at most twenty. (In those days, all the films we watched inspired thoughts of lovers coming together; that is, up until the point when they came together. Then: the end.)

In my dreams, I was usually the actress Filiz Akın, but this time I'm myself. But he's still Kartal Tibet, that charming actor. We're running, holding hands, and my hair flutters in the wind. Then he presses me up against the trunk of a tree and gently kisses me, an innocent kiss. Then we run again, and there is more fluttering of hair, more kisses . . .

In our youth, why did we always let our dreams be shaped by those silly films? We fell in love, not knowing what would happen after the film ended. That's how we got married. The films never showed what happened after the happy ending, and we always wondered about that, as if the joy of marriage would go on forever. Why did we deceive ourselves like that? Or: who deceived us?

Now that I'm in my thirties, haven't I managed to escape from the influence of those phony films? When I close my eyes, do I still dream of a lover taking me by the hand and whisking me away? My subconscious is like a lair of bedlam. Against my will, so much has gathered there.

I'm glad to see that you are happy, and that you are liked and respected here. How long has it been since we graduated? It hasn't been so difficult. In the end, this is your hometown.

Even if I don't know that it's a dream, I can imagine what happens.

I get the impression that he doesn't want to talk about this; but I don't know what else to talk about.

If it hadn't been a dream, it would've been wiser to talk about his successes.

I'd start by saying: Look, if you ask me, I don't care about these things. But go on telling me about them. Hasn't it worked out well? It's good that you got a job at a university and started your career here. I know that university professors like talking about their rise to success and their travails along the way. You should give your old friend a little praise, she's still at the bottom of the ladder, and then there is that "incident" which brought on so much despair. You are one of the few who truly know how hopeless things are. Go on and tell me about it. Tell me about your crowning moments and how you took pride in yourself, and how indebted you are to all the people who made your successes possible. (He understands that I'm mocking him. No, he doesn't.) Tell me, I'll say, let's be happy that we're both going to be unhappy. (How would he understand?)

I imagine the scenario: we're at a gas station diner on the road to Rize. I'm uneasy because I don't understand why we had to come so far and I can't help that unease from slipping into my thoughts, if not my actions. A spark of doubt has arisen within me, and it flares up every time I try to put it out, the flames spreading out. I think to myself: The weather is so nice today, we're lucky that it's not raining; if only we'd gone somewhere where we could sit outside. What's he saying? He disagrees. The Seaside Residence wouldn't do, because it's much too close. This is much better, we're out of the city. And those other places aren't suitable for women. The word "women" stabs not at my mind but at my stomach: he's afraid of being seen with me.

Why did he sit so with his back to the others in the diner?

What were we going to talk about? Our school years? All we have in common is the fact that we spent four years at the same school.

If Akın and I were to have lunch together, would there be anything to talk about? What if I don't feel like talking about our university years? Would I tell him that all of the girls were in love with him? No, why would I want him to take pride in that?

I should've thought this out before accepting his invitation. After we get in the car and I glance at him as he sits behind the wheel, would I confess to myself that he'd changed but was still handsome?

I should back out of our plans for lunch.

I'm having a change of heart. I won't be able to make him happy. Yes, at one time you were handsome; but look at you now! Your hair is like cotton, and all that remains of those old days is a pair of glimmering yet bleary green eyes. All I can see beneath that appearance of friendship is a clump of verdant sprouts, but they have begun to rot. This is not the loamy soil of Bulancak we know so well; it has been washed away.

Akın Bey, what do you think handsomeness is? Balance, harmony; (if not) then (yet again) it is the balance and harmony created between speech and behavior. Aside from your wife, you'll never have a single admirer again. And your wife . . . Long ago she forgot about your handsomeness. She cares more about the "status" you've accorded her than whether or not you love her. What else could be left in a marriage that has aged over the years? I wonder why handsome men always marry ugly women. The revenge of ugliness: cunning. Tell me, what's your ugly wife doing these days? How's Reyhan, is she doing okay?

In the imaginings of my memory, her image isn't as clear as Akın's. Out of jealousy, I remember her as being frumpy. In our senior year, news that Akın was hanging out with Reyhan spread like wildfire. All the young women turned up their noses: after all that searching, is that all he could find? They thought of themselves as the only suitable partner for Akın, and he went off and chose one of the ugliest girls at the school. Such bad taste! Reyhan hadn't changed much. The passing years leave no trace on the unattractive. Good. She also wants you. Why didn't you get together? (No, I'd shy from asking that).

He's slightly hesitant. Of course I would notice. After so many successful years, didn't our gentleman (who was so innocent and had never touched another woman) deserve a little romantic intrigue? With one of his old schoolmates . . . Somewhere far from prying eyes, somewhere like a restaurant or motel. It wouldn't cast a shadow over the sanctity of the family and home. What's the big deal; we're old friends, and what's more, she was lonely and new to town, the poor woman was in pain and lonely, pining for her children and husband. Ha!

Reyhan asked about you, asking if you'd changed or were still beautiful.

He expects the following exchange to transpire:

What did you say?

I told her that you hadn't changed. That you are still very beautiful. Even more beautiful than before.

Now he wants me to ask: Isn't your wife jealous because of me?

How he swells with joy! When women get jealous, it probably makes men feel like they're being honored. For me, it's humiliating.

Why am I so cruel? Isn't it possible that Akın thought I was tired of being in Trabzon and just wanted to break the tedium of my life here? And he'd be quite right for thinking that way. Maybe I hadn't just made my loneliness apparent; I might have even told him that I was despondent. I should stop seeing myself as a culinary delicacy that makes mouths water. This feminine suspiciousness hurts me more than it does the people I'm with. We're old schoolmates, old friends, something more than just a woman and a man. We've both been through pain and suffering.

I've been poorly educated, especially as regards male-female relationships, and I haven't been able to rise above what my grandmother taught me about women and men. I can't seem to cast off this female cat-like psychology, even when the person I'm with is someone I've known for years. My hair stands on end and my claws are sharp, and I'm always at the ready to attack, waiting in ambush. Be more civilized, pull in your claws; calm down.

Akın, forgive me, I'm a lowly person; I grew up as a small-town girl and never was able to make the transition from being a woman to just being human. You should give me a good lesson on that. Say, for example: I invited you out to lunch, but thinking that you might misunderstand my intent, I changed my mind. Tell me: I hope you didn't get the wrong idea. No, don't say that, I'd be mortified. It would be like you'd read my thoughts and were intentionally humiliating me. Please, don't be that cruel, because I can punish myself more brutally than you ever could.

A day has passed, and my fear increases as noon draws near. I'm afraid that he'll be able to tell by looking at my face what I thought about him last night. And I still haven't decided what I'll say to him or how I'll break the news. But I have to turn down his offer; after all those flights of the imagination, there's just no way I could sit down and have lunch with him as if I hadn't thought a thing.

He's late, and I'm buoyed by the hope that he won't come; but soon enough, he appears at the door. He doesn't seem to be in a hurry, which is good. I order tea under the pretense that I've just finished teaching and am tired.

The other day, I really didn't get much of a chance to talk with Rahmi Bey, I tell him. I want to say that I'm confused and talk about the incident with the dean, but I bite my tongue. There's no need to talk about it. And how well do I know Akın?

Yesterday I was a little distracted when I was talking to Rahmi Bey. I hope he didn't take it personally.

Take what personally? Rahmi Bey admires you. What you said at the meeting in Ankara made a strong impression on him. Yesterday we spoke at length about you after coming to your office. What is it about you that makes people adore you so much?

Akın, don't say such things. There's no need to fuel my imagination. Please, stop talking.

But of course I can't actually say those words. So I ask:

Do you remember Ferda? She was in our department.

But he doesn't remember her. It's unfair. For years, she worshipped him like a god, but he doesn't even remember her.

How could you forget about her? She only had eyes for you.

But he replies:

I only had eyes for you.

There you have it; my fears from last night weren't for nothing. Akın Bey, couldn't you have held your tongue?

I'd better get going, I say. I have to go back to my room. I have a lot of work to do, and we've finished our tea.

Aren't we going to have lunch? I'd thought that we might . . .

No, I don't want him to talk anymore. I can't bear the unease, and I don't want to see our friendship of so many years crumble before my eyes. I didn't like it when he said: What is it about you that makes people adore you so much? If there's a continuation of that, as I think there is, I'd rather not hear it. Maybe it won't turn out as I feared; but I can't put any faith in maybes. I shouldn't let him say another word. This faded friendship should remain as it is: faded. I don't have the strength or the desire to turn it into anything else.

He waits expectantly as I get up and start gathering up my books. But Akın doesn't understand why I'm acting like I'd forgotten that we were going to have lunch, and he never will.

But we were going to have lunch?

Thanks. Maybe another time.

I left him standing there at my desk. Forgive me, Akın. But I can't stand fools. Foolish men are even more unbearable than foolish women.

It's the weekend, and yet again I'm alone in my cell. I can't go see Metin Bey and his wife; I just visited them last week. And I can't go see the Hıncals, even though Songül had said: By all means come see us again. I can't sit by and watch as my loneliness drives people to take pity on me. Maybe I should go out and walk around town? But where would I go? I could try to find that jersey for Ozan. If I go to the market I could visit Faik's friend, the doctor. But I don't feel like doing anything. I'll get the jersey just before I go back to İzmir. I don't want to have to look at it and constantly think of my children. Here in my cell I have nothing but the pain of my experiments in self-pity. Is that really the case, or am I trying to derive pleasure from it all? I'm capable of anything. To prevent others from taking pity on me, I can take pity on myself.

Faik is so far away. Just who is he, and what does he mean to me? I realize that I'd even forgotten about the secretary with the long light brown hair, even though I swore that I'd find her. Maybe I would try to get her to talk about Faik. Woman with the long light brown hair, what do you think of Faik? He's a good person, but like all good people he's meek; we could even say cowardly, or faint-hearted. But faint-heartedness never caused anyone any harm. At least it's better than meaningless attempts at seduction. Meaningless attempts? Had I really thought of Akın? I felt relieved not because I'd been saved from Akın but because I'd been spared the torture of my doubts. I might be a wicked, malicious woman. I can come up with impossible suppositions and believe in them. I'm the source of all of my ominous expectations; they come from my flawed upbringing, from my ailing soul . . . But there is a truth that I understand in all its depths: now I must take care to not hurt myself, whatever may happen to others. That's what I need the most. Meaning that I'm not the kind of person who flings herself into lurid affairs. On that path, even the smallest possibilities are enough to drive me into madness. I should have no doubts about myself. If I lose my self-confidence, I won't have the strength to stand on my own two legs.

During these self-examinations, I feel like snakes are writhing in my mind like ropes. My temples are throbbing; my brain feels like a plastic sack sloshing with liquid. The pressure is building; I can feel it pressing against my eyes and my ears, yearning to find a way to gush forth.

If Haluk were here, he'd distract me. He'd say: Oh dear, I'm craving pasta with meat sauce, my dear. The second "dear" is for you. The first is mine.

You're so entertaining. Even in my thoughts you're entertaining.

The friendship that I struck up with Yeşim at the teacher's school has been whisked off to Istanbul, where it grows ever deeper. We both came from the same school and we're both lonely. Two people from the same big school headed off to cities that they'd never even dreamed of, so that they could continue their educations. We leaned upon each other, seeking strength and support, especially in the first semesters. As we grew accustomed to the school and our surroundings, we eventually acquired new friends and spent time with others, but we remained friends. We may not have seen each other for years, but our friendship perseveres.

It was our second year in Istanbul. We were going to meet up with some of Yeşim's friends at a patisserie, and from there we were going to an afternoon tea at the School of Economics. We felt at home.

The following week we met up again with the same group. We went to the cinema. Those group outings lasted for a few weeks, and I'm not sure how it happened, but I started spending more time with Yeşim. In those days I was wracked by the pains of a love I'd sworn to forget. For a year I tried to drive him from my thoughts but I just couldn't seem to forget Yavuz. My girlfriends knew that I was suffering, but they laughed because I promised my father that I'd forget about him. Some of them asked if I was going to ask for my father's permission if I fell in love again. Yeşim had asked the same, and said: Daughters don't tell fathers about their love lives. I replied: I didn't tell him, he found out, but the important thing is that I made him a promise.

Yavuz called the School of Higher Education a few times but I never answered. Through Yeşim he sent a letter, but I didn't read it. Then one day he came to Istanbul. It's over, I said; I won't see him.

One of the girls exclaimed: Don't you see that he really loves you? If you don't pity yourself, at least have pity on him. My answer was simple: No. I know that they secretly admired my steadfastness, but I didn't feel the same admiration for myself, and I still thought about him every night. It was around that time that I started spending time with someone from the School of Economics. I didn't feel that I was deeply in love; but he was intelligent, cultured and kind. And he was a good speaker. His name was Haluk.

That summer Haluk graduated and we got engaged. Hayriye Hanım and Gönül came to meet my family. My uncle (and my father) didn't object much. But my father did say to Haluk: She's going to finish her studies. Haluk agreed to wait until I graduated.

Haluk, my father, my uncle . . . They all live somewhere else and here I am, gnawing at my mind, running straight toward madness. I can't remember who it was, but someone once said to me: Why are you afraid of losing your mind?

You're afraid of losing your mind? I thought you weren't afraid of anything. So that means there are things you fear. That's how it usually is; those who "appear" to be fearless are afraid of the most unexpected things. "Appear" must be set off in quotation marks.

And you frighten everyone. They run from you as if you were leprous. Even your adorable friend said that. Actually there are so many people who are dying to be friends with you . . . But you've had a negative affect here. Your name and fame preceded you. Don't be angry with people who are having trouble with their reappointments, those people who are taking pains to keep a distance from you, because everyone is wondering if their contracts will be renewed in June. In a situation like that, you can't expect people to make sacrifices for you, right?

I don't expect anything from anyone. In particular I don't expect them to sacrifice themselves for my sake. A little warmth, a pinch of friendship, a dash of attention . . . Not even friendship, don't misunderstand me, I just want a little attention, nothing more. I want to hear someone say: By all means, let's get together at our place one day. Or: My wife has been wondering about you and would like to meet you sometime. Why haven't those people appeared in my life? Even Akın, who could've brought Reyhan instead of stirring up storms of doubt in my thoughts. Wasn't he my friend from the School of Higher Education? Where are those people? Did I force them to say that their wives wanted to meet me? They may not have been able to say that; but if they had, they should keep their word. Don't they know that once you give your word you have to keep it? Don't people keep their word here?

I've probably gone overboard with the cognac. But it was hard for me to find, so I feel I should give it its due.

Someone just rang the bell; who could it possibly be? It couldn't be Haluk, could it? Who would come to see me? Was it ringing all along and I didn't hear it? It could be Haluk. Maybe he missed his wife so much that he came all the way here . . . Why not?

It's Aykut Bey, the geographer.

Even before welcoming him in I ask: How did you find me here?

You told me where you lived.

Yes, I had mentioned it to him. My gaze locks on the bouquet of flowers he's holding. When he sees me staring at them, he says:

They're peonies. I brought them for you.

He says this with almost childlike shyness. At least the vase that held the faded carnations won't be empty. And now I have more flowers I can watch as they wither. So this is what peonies look like. So beautiful! Welcome, peonies, to my home of hard times.

I came to pick you up, Aykut Bey says. We have a country house up in the highlands. We decided to go today, and I thought of you. I thought that you might be bored, so I came to invite you along. The kids are waiting in the car. While you get ready I'll wait for you outside.

Get ready? Why do I need to get ready? Just save me from this nightmare. I'm tired of myself. I'm not at peace with myself.

I'm ready now, I say. What a nice surprise! Thank you.

The ego is a powerful thing! As always, I'm stunned. Even the effect of the cognac has vanished. I'm my usual self, Sibel Gökşen. Calm, confident, self-assured . . .

Do I need to bring anything with me?

No, we'll have everything we need there.

Then he tells me more about the place, insisting that I'll like it. The true pastures of the highlands, nothing like those where I'm from.

I tell him that we don't have pastures in Izmir, hoping to stave off any disappointment on his behalf.

That's how it is, he says. You know about the sea. Around here, the sea betrays us.

For some reason, I think of a poem: "To My Traitorous Husband." I still have no control over the associations that come to my mind . . .

I'm ready, so we can leave now, I say.

I get my purse and cigarettes, leaving my fear of madness behind in my room.

The country air! Indeed it is nice. Cloud-topped mountains . . . Down below everything is under the dominion of clouds and mist. The landscape is verdant. When we arrive, the women bustle about preparing food. Aykut Bey is showing me around, trying to make sure I'm enjoying myself. But there's no need! I really do like it. For me, it's an entirely new geography. A mad green covers everything in the darkest of hues. Here you don't breathe air but humidity, some kind of distilled water.

Before going to the barn, we visit some other places. Aykut Bey even shows me the areas where the straw they use as bedding for the animals grows. It has a special name: *yallık*. The people who stay there year-round are his relatives, and they look after the house, as well as the hazelnut orchards and animals. Some of their children have grown up. As for Aykut Bey, he has just one daughter (when he said that the "kids" were waiting in the car, he meant his daughter and his wife), and this year his daughter was accepted into the School of Dentistry at Istanbul University.

That's how the issue arose of "educating a daughter in Istanbul." I tried to assuage their fears: Don't worry, I studied there thirteen years ago, and nothing happened to me (if we don't count Haluk). There's nothing to be afraid of. Since the coup, there's no need for you to be worried about her getting caught up in the student movements. And Çiğdem is a levelheaded young woman. All my years of teaching have taught me this: no family ever has negative thoughts about their children. No, of course not; we have complete faith in our daughter . . . In that case, there's nothing to worry about.

Lunch was exquisite: whiting fish (had I heard of it in Izmir?) fried in a batter of cornmeal. Then there was cream, again battered in cornmeal, served as a savory side dish. Hayriye Hanım would have prepared it sweet as a dessert; I hope her ears are burning. They launch into apologies: We weren't expecting guests. But I really liked the food and found it refreshingly different.

After lunch we have tea and coffee. First there is idle chatter, and then comes the main topic: the school. What's happening? Last June, Aykut Bey was reassigned to the Board of Higher Education, but when the decision was rescinded, he was reappointed to the school like his colleagues. As would be expected, he is wondering what will happen this June. When he says, They won't keep me at this school, I wonder if he is taking some slight pride in himself . . . Or is he trying to show me that I'm not alone, to make me feel that we are together in being "objectionable"?

Toward evening we descend from the highlands. Highland roads . . . So this is what they meant by "highland roads" in our folk songs. The trees lining the road on both sides are called *karaincir*. You don't have them where you're from, they say. I don't know, I'm not very interested in trees; I'm more interested in people. But all they hear is "I don't know"; the rest is for me.

I have no choice but to ask them to drop me off at my room. It would be hard for me to get there on my own in the dark. That long road . . . But my request doesn't seem to be well-received. They object: No, you really must come with us. And I'm not even sure if I want to go back. But I don't want to be a burden on anyone, and then there's my usual obsession: I mustn't let anyone take pity on me.

Because I couldn't muster a powerful enough "No!" I find myself being whisked off to their home. Aykut Bey's mother is waiting for us and has been told that I'll be joining them. It seems that another spread is being prepared for me as their guest. The only thing that's missing is a bottle of rakı. It occurs to me that it's been ages since I've drunk it, and I'm hoping that he'll suggest it because Aykut Bey already revealed that he's a lover of rakı; but, as always, rather than expressing my desire out loud, I choose to wait. Somehow, rakı will be brought to the table and they'll offer me a glass. I realize that I've already started eating as this thought rolls through my mind: Would it be so shameful if they offered me a drink? Of course not . . . But no, there's nothing to drink but water. How much I'd love to have a glass of rakı. And what about Aykut Bey? At first I didn't notice that he kept getting up from the table, but then I caught on to his little ruse. His glass of rakı was in the refrigerator. The reason he kept getting up to get something had nothing to do with him being a good man of the house. Fine, but why was he being so circumspect? Later, Aykut Bey explained it to me: You might have noticed, but I don't drink in front of my mother. How strange! He's a full-grown man, yet still doesn't drink when his mother's around. We all know that people may do something like that out of respect for their fathers, but for their mothers? I felt a newfound respect for her. But a question lingered in my mind: if drinking is such a troublesome affair, then how did he get that red nose? I ask him: Does your mother always stay with you? Apparently so. It's astonishing! There are other mothers aside from Hayriye Hanım who offer no respite, not only for daughters-in-law but sons too.

After dinner we sit down to watch an entertainment program that was filmed in Izmir. Çiğdem has never been to Izmir. It looks like a beautiful place, she says. Aykut Bey talks about the disappointment he felt with the seaside promenade there, as he'd heard so much about it that his expectations were too high. He says: It's just a road by the sea, what's the big deal? There's nothing so special about it. I don't appreciate the way he's talking about Izmir, but I don't say anything. All I know is that I miss Izmir. Ah, Izmir, my children!

Aykut Bey's wife isn't as meek a woman as she may have seemed. When I went into the kitchen to offer to help with the dishes (of course she refused my offer and insisted that I sit down as she did them), she spoke at length, enlightening me on the topic of mothers. In fact, I was curious about this mother who held so much sway over her son, maybe because I was familiar with this phenomenon. As she spoke, her voice bore no traces of a hopeless woman's complaint. She had the decisiveness of a woman who understands the obstacles she faces and came up with her own solutions, and that pleased me. If a woman can make herself heard with an imperious mother-in-law, it's like she's acting in kind. Aykut Bey is a pleasant if somewhat eccentric man, and he seems to understand unsaid things and make profound statements as if he weren't saying anything important at all. Later I understood that he spoke ill of Izmir because he sensed that the television program could lead my thoughts down a dangerous path. After the "women's entourage" came out from the kitchen (except for his mother) to serve tea and sat down to watch television, a documentary started; it was about how animals go to great lengths to protect their offspring when danger arises. And Aykut Bey said something that would remain in my thoughts:

With animals, the motherly instinct is so powerful that it cannot be controlled.

I got the message he was trying to send, and pondered over its meaning(s). He meant that educated women can control their motherly instincts. As an educated woman, don't fall helpless before your longing for your children. In short: stay and resist. I don't know if Aykut Bey could have guessed that I'd arrive at this interpretation of what he said; it could have been a coincidence, but his timing was so good that it had to be far more than a mere casual remark.

Is the way I miss my children animalistic? In a sense, yes. Whether I agree or not, that thought put me at ease. I was slightly angry with Aykut Bey, and concealing my chagrin was no easy task; but I was indebted to him for giving me a new perspective on that truth.

Back in my room gazing at the peonies, I'm still pondering over what he said to me. And his words ring in my ears constantly, as I go to bed, as I wake up, as I get dressed and undress . . .

He might be right. Maybe the instinct for motherhood is something that needs to be brought under control. And perhaps I'm unable to see this truth because I'm trying to prove to myself, if not to anyone else, that in fact I am a good mother. Yes, maybe he's right; but he said that at the wrong time. Just as I was putting the finishing touches on my plans, why did he have to come along and stir up my thoughts? Tomorrow I was going to submit my resignation to the dean. I wouldn't launch into a speech, but just hand him the letter and say curtly: Here you are, sir.

I'd been so swept away by the thought of resigning that I was incapable of thinking beyond that point, and my thoughts circled back to imagining the expression on his face when I handed him the letter, which read:

"In order to protect the youth of the Black Sea from my 'objectionable' nature which I brought with me from the region of the Aegean Sea, I hereby submit my resignation."

It's not about missing my children or being able to bear that burden. Far from it! I proclaim that you are collaborating with the generals in charge of martial law. At your school, why have you given a job to someone who was found to be "objectionable" in a region stretching from Balıkesir all the way to Antalya? Have you vowed to sacrifice the youth of the Black Sea?

Part of me says that I'm in pursuit of some petty heroism, but I silence that voice. Still, if some people pursue great acts of heroism, then someone has to take up the smaller ones too. So that must be my lot.

What would the dean do? Maybe he'd say: That's not a proper letter of resignation, go write a real one. Or would he think: We've been expecting this, and then thank me? Or: We'll have no resignations here; just wait a little because in any case we're going to fire you.

Let him say what he likes; I'll give the Board of Higher Education a lesson and be reunited with my children!

As I think over the scenario for tomorrow, my heart lightens. I wonder what color I should wear? It should suit the color of the dean's face when he reacts to my resignation.

5

And now sadness is the greatest form of opposition.
—Hilmi Yavuz

I don't know how I succeeded in doing this, but the important thing is that I did. Before, I may have worried about the hows, but I will no longer. It's over.

First of all, I need to find a decent place to live that isn't too expensive but is in a good area. Not a crowded neighborhood, or outside town like where I live now. I'm weary of taking the bus every day. Somewhere with a view of the sea, and with two or three largish rooms. A room for each of my children. I have until summer to find a place, maybe until next winter. It's better this way, now that everything is clear-cut.

During summer vacation at the university, the Seaside Residence will fill up. They can't kick me out of here before they let me go from the department or I find another place to live; first they'll have to inform me in typical fashion that I'm being "released" from my duties as an instructor. Of course I must bear that in mind as one of the possibilities, but if they did that, they'd have to appoint me as a teacher at a high school through a reassignment or transfer, or whatever it's called . . . And it's not like I've never worked at a high school. It would be good; even better, I'd be far from all the tumult here. What if they completely forbade me from teaching? There's only a slight chance of that, but it's not impossible. I say "slight" because if that's what they wanted to do, they would have done it in the beginning. Still, it's not impossible because the board may decide, like the university, that my employment is "unnecessary." Then what? They could prevent me from getting a job at any school under their purview. Fine! Would I go hungry? No, because I'm a teacher and no matter where I go, I can teach and make a living; there are private schools, prep schools, courses . . . Let's say that doesn't work out either, because they're afraid of hiring me; in that case, I'll work as a sales clerk at a shop. Is that forbidden? It's at odds with the prestige and dignity of teaching. Accept it, then, and let's make a deal: you protect my career and I'll take care of the others.

I can't believe how easy it's been. I was hesitating too much. That decision needed to be made long ago. I idled about for too long, wasting time.

I said to Haluk: Look, I've been thinking a lot. It isn't working out between us. We're both young, and there's no need for us to create obstacles for each other. You've got a good position. If you wanted, it would be easy for you remarry. And don't worry about the children, I can look after both of them. They can finish out the school year there with you, and in any case, that's what the court would rule. When the summer holiday comes, they'll come stay with me, and then we'll figure things out from there. It's not like we're on bad terms. This is how it needs to be. I haven't been able to be a good wife for you, so I made a choice: to live life my own life. Please, don't be angry with me.

No, I didn't speak as eloquently as that. What did I say? That I didn't want to shoulder your spiritual baggage? No, I wasn't rude. I didn't say anything accusatory. I just said that I'm going to walk my own path, or something like that. He understood what I meant. But he didn't react. I was unsure if he would be combative or if an argument would break out, and I was afraid that I'd be bombarded with whys and questioned about things I couldn't even explain to myself. I don't want to be driven into a corner. What I need to do is simplify my life. It's enough that I'm a burden on Haluk; there's no way I could let him try to "bring me to my senses."

He responded with astonishing understanding. Why was he so calm and composed? Was it possible that he had the same thoughts and had come to the same conclusion? If I hadn't said anything, maybe he would've said the same to me. No, I'm dabbling in fantasy, not fact. How could I have thought that? He never imagined that I'd make such a proposal; was it so hard to suppose that he could react so coolly? Haluk is a good person. He said: If that's what you want, that's how it should be. He respected my decision. Good for you, Haluk, that's actually how I was expecting to react; you did the right thing.

It's dark, and I can't see anything outside, except when we pass through a city; but only occasionally do I glance out the window. Tomorrow I should be at the school. I didn't even get proper permission, and I think the dean only gave me one day off. I'm far more at ease than when I first arrived, and I no longer rush around trying to get everything done. Again and again I'll travel down these roads on my way to Izmir, maybe to Ankara, but each and every time I'll return to Trabzon. Watch out, Trabzon, now I'm here to stay—you won't be freed of me so easily.

The last time I made this trip, was I thinking about Haluk as we passed along this stretch of road? I think I was. All this greenery, the trees, gardens and fields, must have made me think of him and his fondness for nature. Maybe I recalled a picnic that we went on: we gathered wood for a barbecue on the beach, and he would lick his fingers after turning the meat on the grill, sipping his glass of rakı . . . I'll miss you, Haluk.

I bear no anger in my heart. Resentment, perhaps . . . The way he acted didn't suit the man I thought I knew. He shouldn't have felt a need to play trivial games with me. As a husband, he needed to understand my goals, tenacity and resolve. I cultivated in him a sense of respect, because he understood that I had to stand up for myself. But that's over now. I'm not angry because he laid traps for me; I'm sure he had his own reasons, but in the end, I was hurt.

The first thing I need to do tomorrow is rescind my resignation. I know what the dean will say: You're not leaving? Have you changed your mind? And how should I answer? There's only yes and no. I'm staying here; but I'm actually setting out on a completely different path: to learn how to be alone, to reclaim myself . . . I'm going back, but I'm not giving up. In order to succeed, I need time, and that's precisely what I have now.

Where's my letter of resignation? I take back my decision to save the youth of the Black Sea from my "objectionable" nature. You are left with me, and I revile the system.

I have to pull myself together. Yet again.

The statement I'm awaiting from the Board of Higher Education will be sent here (it's surprising that Trabzon has become "here" for me) and also to Izmir. I don't think it'll have any effect. But it's better than nothing, and maybe at the very least it will stop them, to a certain degree, from acting as though I were guilty.

What excited sense of anticipation was that? In the corridor: the lawyers were on one side, and we were on the other. People were coming and going. There was so much anticipation: a sentence of death could be handed down, or an acquittal. And there, at the main building of the board just as the decision was being made about my case, Haluk and I were talking about our divorce, as if we couldn't have talked about it anywhere else.

My trip to Ankara had been made in haste, while I was preparing to return to Izmir and making my farewells, during the course of which I even managed to visit Sumela Monastery in Trabzon. I'd called the dean to submit my resignation, but he wasn't in his office so I had to wait. I was certain about my decision. Let the dean think whatever he wants, I thought; my resignation was going through and I was going to return to Izmir on the first plane out. Intentionally I didn't tell anyone back home that I was coming, as I was dreaming of their surprise when I suddenly appeared at the door: they wouldn't believe their eyes, and Özlem would call out to Ozan, who would then call out to Aslı:

"Look, Mom's home!"

As I sat enraptured with my daydreams, Aykut Bey came into my office:

How are you, Sibel Hanım? You look happy today.

I am. I'm relieved, because at last I know what I'm going to do.

I hope that brings you some comfort.

Earlier I decided that I wouldn't tell anyone about my decision to leave; but for the sake of Aykut Bey, I broke that promise because he'd been more courageous than I ever expected and didn't hesitate to be on close terms with me. Yes, I knew I could tell him:

I'm going back to Izmir. My letter of resignation is ready, and when the dean comes back, I'm going to submit it to him.

We spoke for a while, but all I heard were his first words: Is it about Izmir, or your resignation? You were saying that . . .

Everything he said after that was a blur. Except for his last question: You should see Sumela Monastery before you go, how about a trip there?

I was about to agree, but I didn't want to miss the dean: What if he comes while we're there and I'm not able to give him my resignation?

That's easy, Aykut Bey said. We'll just find out when he's coming back.

Can we?

Sure, it'll be easy.

It turned out that the dean had gone to Akçaabat to check on the new location for the school and wouldn't be back until evening. The dean's not coming back today? How am I going to submit my resignation?

You can submit it tomorrow, Aykut Bey said. You've been here this long already, so I'm sure you can stand being here one more day.

His voice betrayed a certain hurt, as if I was slandering his hometown with my departure, but I couldn't hold back my disappointment at having to wait.

Aykut Bey said: We'll stop by on our way back, and if the dean's here, you can give him your resignation.

You can't object to everything, so I lapsed into hopeless silence. It was clear that I wouldn't have a chance to see the dean that day, and there was no point in bemoaning this fact.

As we were winding down the road from Trabzon to Maçka, rain pouring down as usual, I asked:

Are they moving the school to Akçaabat? I hadn't heard anything about it.

They've been thinking about it for a long time, but no one knows when it will happen. If all the preparations are completed, we might move there this summer.

Laughing, I said: You just said "we."

Did I? Well you never know, maybe we'll all be moving there together.

Don't harbor any hopes for me on that account, I said. You're going to have to take care of that on your own.

Until your plane takes off, there's always hope.

A few minutes earlier I'd suggested that we stop so I could buy my plane ticket, but he objected, saying that I should speak with the dean first; I didn't insist.

The plane will take off, I said. If it doesn't take off with me today, it will tomorrow.

At that moment, both of us thought of the same popular song. Aykut Bey found the cassette and put it on:

Your face, the color of rose, is freckled,
But why is your bosom so unadorned?

It seemed as if the rain might relent.

Have you ever had trout? Aykut Bey asked.

No. You keep forgetting that I'm a child of the sea, not the mountains.

That's true. You don't have trout where you're from.

Every time he said "where you're from," a jab of pain would shoot through me: a different realm, a different country—"where you're from."

There's a trout farm nearby. Since you put off your resignation until tomorrow, let me invite you to have some trout. Maybe you'll like it and come back one day.

My first thought was that it was a little early for lunch, but then I looked at the clock. We'd spent a long time talking about when the dean would return, and it was already lunchtime. It occurred to me that if I left, it wouldn't be easy for me to come back. It would be just the same as before, when I'd never been to Trabzon. But why?

Aykut Bey made another confession: That's also why I'm taking you to the monastery. You've never seen a place like it before, and you never will again, not anywhere else in the world. Maybe, as I expect may happen, it will cast its charm on you.

Why didn't I have any suspicions about Aykut Bey? No matter

what he said, no matter what compliments he lavished upon me, I didn't have a single doubt about his intentions. My thoughts turned to the trout farm; what kind of place would it be? The image of farms in my mind couldn't be reconciled with the notion of fish, but I was hesitant to ask. I didn't want to be seen as a city girl who is constantly surprised by the particularities of local life. Just be patient, I told myself, soon enough we'll see.

Soon after, we stopped in an area that was more or less devoid of buildings. A little further ahead there was a rickety structure that appeared to be on the brink of collapse, but there was no one around. Incredulous, I asked:

Is this the place?

I was thinking that we'd stopped for some other reason; maybe a problem with the car, or a tea break.

This is the place, he said.

The rickety hut up ahead was the restaurant, and further along there were ponds where they raised the trout. He said that you can pick out the one you want to eat:

And if you want, you can scoop out the fish yourself.

The fish in the ponds all seemed to be the same size, and I couldn't see much difference between them.

Any one of them will be fine, I said.

Aykut Bey pointed: This one, and that one over there.

In the beginning, I objected, saying: How are we going to eat so much fish? But in the end, we polished it all off. Despite the fact that there were pieces of wood wedged under the unbalanced legs of the table, the floor was dirt, newspapers were used to cover the tables, and countless cats kept appearing at the tableside, our lunch was truly a feast. Afterwards, I thought that we should head out to see the monastery before it started raining again.

As we went through the forest, it began drizzling. We stopped for a moment. We had to walk the rest of the way from there.

Sumela is up there, Aykut Bey said.

I looked in the direction he was pointing. Peering through the rain, I saw high up on the hillside a building that had been carved from the stone of the cliff. How can you get up there? I asked. He said that there was a path that ran along the ridge that we could climb if I wanted to see it up close. No, I said, it looks magnificent from here. I want to remember it like this.

Actually, the inside is nice, Aykut Bey said, even if it is a bit run down. The local shepherds have caused a lot of damage. Next time you come, you can see the inside.

Yes, I replied, smiling.

There were three other things that interested me just as much as Sumela Monastery. One was the vegetation covering the slopes. The dense clusters of flowers growing beneath the trees were mountain violets of stunning beauty. I considered pulling up a few by the roots and taking them with me. Even though Aykut Bey said that they wouldn't grow anywhere else, I insisted, trying to wrap them up in some papers I had in my purse, but Aykut Bey brought me a plastic bag from the trunk of his car. The second thing was the water. I couldn't decide if it was a stream, a creek or a river, but it roared with such ferocity that at times we couldn't hear each other as we spoke. The third thing was a tree growing in the middle of the rushing water. It was astonishing; indifferent to the water that rushed past, it grew straight up. It had been there for years and had no intention of giving way to the mad gush of water.

On our way back, Aykut Bey yet again rejected my suggestion that we stop at the airport so I could get my ticket:

So long as nothing extraordinary happens, you won't have any trouble finding a ticket. And I know some people who work there. You take care of your business, and when you're ready, your seat will be waiting for you on the plane. Come to our place, and we'll have some tea and rest for a while. And you can also say goodbye to my family.

Ah, those farewell visits . . .

Difficult days are ahead of me, difficult months, maybe even years. Years? Yes, from this point on I will be living my life on my own. Did I carefully think everything through? Or was it a rash decision made on a whim that one day I'll regret? I mustn't be daunted. Fine, but until now, what have I achieved without Haluk by my side? He was always there: when we moved, when I gave birth, when the children had problems, when we decided about their schools, the registration . . . If driving Haluk from my life proves to be a mistake, who will I talk to? Will I turn back? Do I really know what it means to be alone? The burden of being alone, of hopelessness?

I know. Nothing could be more difficult than what I've been through already. I was alone when I went through the most difficult times in my life. Haluk wasn't there. He hasn't been there ever since I decided to come to Trabzon.

In fact, my decision to get divorced wasn't rash. It was a longing that had been quietly waiting for a chance to be realized, a delayed desire for a home of my own that I will decorate as I like, spreading out my own rugs and tablecloths . . . One by one I will pick out what I want; I'll have my own time, my own key. My afternoons and evenings won't be whiled away in idle chatter; no, I'll choose who I want to see, who I want to host and visit. For the first time, I don't feel the weariness of the arguments that lasted for hours about whether the dishes can be washed with water from the bathtub, the drudgery of listening to prattling praise of Fitnat Hanım's daughter-in-law, the conversations about how it would've been different if my mother had raised me, the deadlock over her complaint that I was spoiling my children . . . In the first days of my marriage did I realize that what I'd longed for differed from my new life? Didn't I experience it moment by moment as Haluk was transformed from a lover into the overseer of a family? The change as subtle courtesies suddenly vanished, the shift from a kind, considerate man in love into a husband who demanded, wrested and took . . . I hadn't wanted a life with Hayriye Hanım, or a home that was under her control. But what can I do? At her age, there's no way you can try to change her, that's what she is, and you're a woman who falls in step, slinks away, goes along with everything, and bows down before her . . . Why am I trying to make myself get used to the fact that I was angry with Haluk and wanted a divorce? That's not how it is. From a distance, the tensions may appear like that. But among them there are years of compliance. That was the fallacy—all of them were false.

The last time I saw Leyla Hanım was before she went to Samsun. When we saw each other in the hallway of the court (no, I mean the Board of Higher Education building), we hugged each other. She told me about Samsun, and I spoke of Trabzon. She too was staying at the university guesthouse. I knew exactly what I wanted to say to Haluk, but I didn't tell Leyla Hanım about our impending divorce; nonetheless, I did tell her about my other decision:

I'm thinking about resigning.

But, Sibel, how could you? We set out together down this path. How could you abandon me halfway?

I tried to explain that I missed my children, and I launched into a diatribe about all the reasons that had convinced me that resigning was my only option, but she held her ground.

Indeed our situations were different. Leyla Hanım had been living alone in Izmir for years and was accustomed to solitude. She was reappointed just three months before her retirement was due, and so for her, getting through these times unscathed meant that she was guaranteed her retirement. In contrast, I had to try to bear up in a place where I knew I was unwanted and persevere knowing full well that they could fire me at any moment. But persevere against who, and how?

No matter what I said, I couldn't convince Leyla Hanım.

All she said was: No. Regardless of the justifications you give, it all amounts to the same thing: running away.

If only you could see me now. I'm not running away, Leyla Hanım; I'm going to stay and resist.

I should call tomorrow and tell her about my decision. She'll be glad to hear about it. When we saw each other, she told me that knowing I was in Trabzon comforted her. Now you can go on feeling that way, because I'm here. Tell your friend who works for the secret service that I'm not afraid and I'm not running away.

Leyla Hanım would laugh, and say: Sure, I'll tell him if I see him.

As she was getting ready to leave for Samsun, she'd had to invite a member of the secret service into her home. At the time I was rushing around getting ready and preparing my defense, so I hadn't yet heard what happened. As we stood there, Leyla Hanım explained it all. She'd received a phone call from someone who said he worked for the National Intelligence Organization:

I must speak with you face to face, he said.

Leyla Hanım replied that she couldn't meet up with him because she was leaving soon and had much to do before departing.

So what did you do? I asked.

I had no choice but to agree to see him.

He was pleased with her response and when he arrived, he explained why. He wanted to look over Leyla Hanım's bookshelves to see which "objectionable" books she had. What a polite man, I said, laughing. They didn't used to do that. But now, backed by the police department, they raid homes and haul off whatever that want because they don't like the title, author, cover or color of a book. And then you never see those books again.

Please have a look, Leyla Hanım said to him. If you want I can help you and explain what the books are about.

There's no need for that, he replied. I'm not going to take any of them, I'm just looking.

When Haluk realized that our phone had been tapped, he hauled away all the books at our home that could be deemed "objectionable." I still don't know where he took them or what he did with them. Since Leyla Hanım was by no means like Haluk, I wondered what she'd done with her books.

Nothing, my dear. They're still there, waiting.

The man took down certain books, looking at the front and back covers and shuffling through the pages, and then put them back on the shelf.

Aren't you going to make a report? Leyla Hanım asked him.

No, he replied. I've read some of these myself.

And then what happened? I asked.

He asked me what happened at the school. I told him in detail. I told him about you, about the inquiries they launched against us, about the dean and all the conspiracies. Listening intently, he stopped me occasionally to ask questions and noted down my answers. I told him that we were ready to go to where we'd been reappointed. He said that, in his opinion, it would be better if we didn't go. I insisted, but I couldn't get him to tell me why he thought it best if we didn't go. In the end, you never even asked us, I said dismissively. We're going, the both of us. You won't intimidate us so easily, and we won't give up.

What did he say to that? I asked.

He didn't say anything. He just smiled, his lips pulled into a belittling sneer.

Since he thought it was best if we didn't go, did that mean that the secret service was of the same opinion? What games are being played? We're all just pawns. Under martial law, certain restrictions about work are implemented in the region. Then the Board of Higher Education steps in and reappoints lecturers to other regions, but the secret service disagrees, and then the dean considers reappointing us to the National Board of Education, while the Grand Board of Inquiries finds no implicating evidence. What's going on?

I found the dean in his office, sitting there as if waiting for me. When I held out my letter of resignation, he asked me without opening it:

Is this about Ankara?

I didn't understand what he meant.

What do I have to do with Ankara?

When he realized that I was confused, he took another tack:

Are you requesting leave?

I was still perplexed. Did I need to request leave in order to resign? No, sir, I'm resigning without submitting any requests. Then he asked more clearly:

Is this a request for leave so that you can go to Ankara?

No, I stammered. It's my resignation.

Resignation? he asked and smiled. At this stage, you're resigning? I can't believe my ears.

I was baffled. Which stage? There are stages? I collapsed into the chair, not even noticing if he'd motioned for me to sit down.

He started to explain. The High Disciplinary Committee was going to make a ruling about my case the next day and I'd been asked to go to Ankara along with my lawyer.

So, you're going to quit before you even find out about the results? he asked.

I didn't know, I mumbled.

How could it be? I found out by coincidence. But it seems he'd known about this for days.

Both you and your lawyer must've been informed. The board is serious about these matters and there should be no slip-ups.

I wasn't told about this, I repeated.

The summons was sent to your home address and to your lawyer.

I gathered my thoughts: You mean my address in Izmir?

Of course. That's your permanent address. You're just temporarily appointed here.

But if such an important summons had been sent to my home, they would've told me. I call Izmir almost every day.

The dean sat there looking at me. What if the letter hadn't arrived?

I ask: What if I don't appear in court tomorrow with my lawyer?

Your trial will be permanently sustained.

Sustained? Meaning that I'll have no right to defend myself?

Precisely, the dean replied.

That would mean giving up at the last minute on the bitter struggle I'd undertaken for the previous year and a half. The dean rubbed his chin:

I thought you knew about this. That's why I asked about Ankara.

He held up my letter of resignation, which he still hadn't opened. My plaintive statement of resignation was a document of futility.

The dean said: I think you should reconsider resigning. I'm not going to process this yet. Let's wait for the decision to be announced in Ankara.

Sliding open the drawer of his desk, he put the letter in. Fine, I thought, let's wait for the decision; but what am I going to do now? Resign and go to Izmir, and then from there go to Ankara?

Were you going to grant me leave so I could go to Ankara?

Certainly, but that "certainly" is in the past tense; if you asked, I would have given you leave.

In that case, I'd like to request leave so that I can go to Ankara.

He was about to tell me to bring a written request, but I cut in first:

No, I don't have time. Let this be a verbal agreement, but if you really need it in writing, then I'll draw it up and sign it when I get back.

Fine, he replied.

What an odd man, I thought. It seemed like he was glad that I didn't resign. Why? Didn't he want me to leave?

When I left the dean's office, I stopped. Was I really going to Ankara? How would I get there? I rushed to the post office and called Haluk, but he wasn't in his office. Apparently he'd just left with a bid for a tender. I called my lawyer.

When he answered, I said: The Board of Higher Education sent a summons.

Yes, I know. But Haluk Bey didn't want you to know.

How could you keep silent about this? You know how important this is for me.

I know. It's very important. We should have gone.

So you're saying that it's too late?

That's how it looks. But if you'd wanted me to come, I would've gladly been there.

I knew that those last few words were said as a kind of apology. But I brushed them aside:

That's exactly what I want. We're meeting tomorrow at eleven in the morning at the main building of the Board of Higher Education.

Tomorrow? How could I possibly come? I have other trials to take care of.

What did you say just a moment ago? Postpone your trials, or have one of your partners go for you. But whatever you do, be there tomorrow at eleven o'clock.

Fine, I'll be there. I suppose I'll have to take the night bus. See you tomorrow.

Now that I knew my lawyer was coming, a feeling a relief washed over me. My next matter of business was calling Haluk to account for what he'd done. I called, but he still wasn't back, so I went outside and walked around, ruminating on all that had happened: how could Haluk do this? Hadn't we gone through so many tough times together? At this critical moment, how could he just brush my concerns aside? What does he think I'm doing here?

I went back to the post office and called again. This time he answered:

What's going on? he asked. You called so many times.

Where were you? I asked, anger in my voice, as if it really mattered where he'd been.

There's a bid in Ankara. To nail down the final price, I needed to see a few people.

In Ankara? What bid?

But that wasn't the question I wanted to ask. He started explaining that his company was taking part in a tender requested by a ministry . . .

I cut him off: When?

In a few days.

How long are you going to be there?

He paused. Had he sensed something? Or was he tongue-tied because I took such a sudden interest in his work?

Three days. The bid is on Friday.

Good. And you're going to be there too?

I think so.

In that case, ask for tomorrow off, and take the first flight to Ankara in the morning. You can rest for two days and then on Friday make the bid and go home.

He started getting angry:

What is this, some kind of game? What's wrong with you?

I paused for a moment, trying to regain my composure: Haluk Bey, it's you who is playing games. The Board of Higher Education sent a document. What was it?

Oh, that? It wasn't anything important.

What was it about?

That inquiry of yours. But like I said, it wasn't important.

I was biting my lip, and I could feel my body shaking as my heart pounded.

When did it arrive?

A week, maybe ten days ago.

Then he started mumbling about something else. I could sense that the people working in the post office had taken notice of me having an argument in the telephone booth and had stopped working to watch.

Tomorrow morning meet me in front of Gima supermarket at ten o'clock. I'm expecting you to be there.

I have a lot of work tomorrow, there's no way I can come.

I knew that, but all the same, he had to be there. Even if he didn't pick up on what I was planning to do, he must've noticed the decisiveness in my voice.

Tomorrow, ten o'clock, in front of Gima, I said and hung up, thinking: If you don't come, Haluk Bey, you'll have it coming to you.

Ok, I thought. That's been arranged, and I'll be meeting my husband and lawyer. But how am I going to get to Ankara? That's easy; I was planning on flying anyway.

Originally I'd decided to fly to Izmir with a layover in Ankara. Now all I needed to do was get off the plane in Ankara. I headed out to find Aykut Bey at the school, hoping to be able to find a seat on the morning flight. Please, I thought, it's very important.

I crossed over these shores, mountains and roads by plane. My mind was in tumult, shaken by confusion.

The captain announced that we'd be flying at 20,000 feet and the flight would last approximately one hour and forty-five minutes.

Homes look so odd from the air, as if they rest on electric wires and poles and at the slightest sense of tedium, they'll just soar away. Even at that hour, there were people working the fields. I recognized them from their striped skirts; they were all women. They were carrying pickaxes and shovels, and trundled sacks and baskets on their backs.

There were white rain clouds directly above the city. Peaks dotted with houses rose up through the clouds. The clouds were wispy, flowing between the mountains, parting like streams. We rose up into the air, and the immense mountains below stretched out into the distance. I looked back to the east, and saw nature in all its magnificence: thick clouds pierced by snow-capped peaks. And the houses were like sheep grazing in a line, spread apart here and there, and I felt like they were rising up with us.

The view from above the clouds was stunning: the sea, mottled in every hue of green, was visible between the billowing heaps of clouds, and like the strokes of a painter's brush, lighter here and darker there, there was a graceful line accentuated with a few specks of light green, and for the discerning eye, there was a pass that shaded from luscious to grass green; there were waves on the top right of the painting, and in the lower left there were white houses like fields of daises that contrasted with the waves, and great care should be taken with the shore, as every inlet and promontory must be stitched in like the edging of lace.

* * *

How long ago was it? There was that song "I'll Die Because of My Love for You," and I wonder now, in my time, how many young lovers made that their song? I never thought that I would ever say that: "in my time." But soon enough I'll have reached the halfway point in the path of my life. Which songs do the youth of today make as their own? Do people still do that? You can't dedicate your life to another person, and if you dedicate a song to someone, you're destined to separate from them. It would be more appropriate to speak about your financial standing, for example, or your ideals, or consider the fact that if someone lets you go, they'll have lost the greatest opportunity of their life and never find someone like you again . . . Those are the things of which you should speak. But no longer are people condemned to love one person for their entire life. Your freedom not to love should be powerful enough to overcome your right to love. You're not an average person who goes around falling in love with just anyone. Sadly, it's difficult to find someone who has the qualities you desire. So despise everything; it will make you a better person. Because you don't shy from taking up the courage to hate, people will have no choice but to respect you. In this way, even without being desirous of it, you'll become a well-regarded person, and also loved, because the two are inseparable. And since you aren't required to love anyone, you'll be entitled to double takings that don't have to be paid back.

How young was I? At that age, what could I have known about falling in love? I remember the well at my father's place. It was in the basement of his three-story house. I'd get the urge to shout into it: Doğan, I love you! My father would put water bottles in a basket and when food was being prepared, he'd send me downstairs to get water from the well, and I'd shout: Doğan! In a way, did I want him to hear it for himself? That his daughter wasn't as young as he thought, that if she could manage, there were things she wanted to say to him?

But because I can't remember everything clearly, I'm probably making it up. Not even Doğan ever knew that I loved him.

Now we're flying above a dazzling whiteness. The plane shudders, but I'm surprised that I don't feel an ounce of fear. Any other time I would've been terrified, and I'd visualize my children and my death; more than anything else, I'd lament my passing from this world. We're flying in the snow, but without touching a single snowflake.

Her grandmother stands in front of her uncle, blocking his way. He's in a rage.

Don't interfere, he says, pushing her aside: I've got some business to settle.

Sibel is pushed into the room that her grandmother only uses to host her wealthy relatives on holidays. What happened? What has she done this time? But Sibel knows nothing. She'd been rebuked a few times before because of Zümrüt; he said that she wasn't kind enough to her, that she didn't talk to her. Sibel didn't pay him much heed; more than being rebuked, what mattered was that she seemed important. Yet again he is angry with her, however, and the problem now seems more serious. Her uncle even shoves Orhan aside, saying: Get out of my way. Is he aware of the danger, and had he come to protect his older sister?

Then the door is shut and locked. Her uncle is like a leopard about to pounce on its victim. There was something like that in a novel that Sibel had been reading. As the curtains are pulled shut, a thought flashes through her mind: Could it be because of Doğan? Has he found out that I love Doğan? The peace of mind that came with knowing she didn't do anything wrong slowly gives way to a pounding of the heart, and she begins trembling from head to foot. She'd never even spoken with Doğan, and didn't even look him in the face; how could anyone know that she loved him?

He shoves Sibel into a chair, and then pulls a chair in front of her; placing one foot on the chair cushion, and looking down at her like he might slap her at any moment, he says:

What's going on between you two?

Who are you talking about?

Sibel wonders: Is he talking about Doğan? But that's not possible. What is he really asking about? What does he want to know? He draws nearer.

Look, don't pull this on me. Yesterday Recep saw you at the market with some guy. Who was he?

Sibel starts by saying: Uncle, I really don't know . . .

But then she tries to remember; yesterday, what time? Who? At the market? Recep said that? What exactly did he say?

She's at a loss for words; how is she supposed to defend herself?

She asks: Who did he see me with? When?

I don't know. But you were with someone. Who was it?

But Sibel knows that yesterday she left school and went home. She didn't go out again.

If you lie to me, I'll kill you. I swear, I'll tear you to pieces!

At any moment, the slap could come. If only she could understand what *he was talking about, she would explain it away, but she's at a loss. Out of desperation Sibel begins to cry. And as she realizes how hopeless the situation is, she cries even louder. She can't even apologize.*

I didn't do anything, she says, weeping hysterically. Secretly she wishes she'd done something and deserved the accusations brought against her; if only she'd done something to deserve this fury.

When her weeping begins turning into revolt, her uncle is forced to back down.

Look, he says:

You're an orphan. I don't want anything bad to happen to you. I'm the one who bears the responsibility of looking after you. Tomorrow or the next day, your father will bring me to account for anything that happens. He'll say: I put my daughter in your care, so why didn't you take care of her?

Sibel understands that, if he can, her uncle is about to apologize to her, so she falls silent. Even in her silence there is a sob of having been wrongfully accused.

The next day, her uncle will do something that he's never done before; he'll bring her one of the long novels that she'd been forbidden from reading, wrapped up as a gift by the bookseller, because Recep will explain what really happened. It will come to light that the girl he saw, wherever that was and however it happened, just resembled Sibel.

I glance around at the interior of the plane. It's the size of a regular bus; could it be a DC-9? I hadn't noticed before. There are twelve rows from front to back, with four seats in each row. I've flown in much larger planes before, so many times, from Istanbul to Izmir. When I was engaged to Haluk, after we got married . . . I had started my PhD, and as always, Haluk was so understanding. Handing me a plane ticket, he said: My wife isn't going to make that trip by bus. Then the boycotts and occupations of university campuses started, and he used them as an excuse to deter me, and in the end, I had to withdraw from the program. You're a married woman, what business do you have doing a PhD? And then the children . . . My God! How have I gotten where I am now?

We're going west, toward the light of the sun. I try to find a pen and paper, so I can work through the answers I'll give if the High Disciplinary Board asks me any questions. I find my pen which, until that day, has never leaked but the cap is full of ink so I wrap it in a napkin and put it in the front pocket of my purse. It occurs to me that people are more resilient than pens when it comes to changes in air pressure. Even though my ears are popping, I can hear a faint ringing.

The sky is a bell jar that has closed us in. Below us is a blue white-washed by puffs of cottony clouds and up above, it takes on the navy-blue of night.

It's probably summer. The teachers college is on break and Sibel is staying with her father because her uncle had a child and her grand-mother went to look after Zümrüt and the young girl. Her father sent her downstairs to get a watermelon from the well; Sibel laughs at the fact that even though he's had a refrigerator for a long time now, he still always puts watermelons in the well to keep them cool. She knew what her father would say: It keeps it at just the right temperature, not too warm and not too cold. As she pulls the basket from the well, she recalls the days when she wanted to call out Doğan's name. It's been years since they saw each other, and she wonders what happened to him. After primary school, everyone went different ways. She could have asked Birsen—she knows everything—but it never occurred to her. And now, if she wanted, she could shout a name into the well: Yavuz. But she no longer has that desire. His last letter should be right here—she peers into her bra—but it's gone. She doesn't recall taking it out. Most likely she put it somewhere else. In just a few minutes she'll be able to read it again. She wonders: Where did I put it? She thinks over what she did since the last time she read it, but then gives up; she must've slipped it into one of her books or folders.

Sibel thought little of the fact that her father hadn't spoken a word throughout dinner. Her thoughts were on Yavuz's letter, not about where she'd put it because sooner or later she'd find it. She can practically recite the entire text to herself, every single word. Yavuz had written about the plans they made for the future. In a year he was going to finish his studies and be a junior officer. He wrote: Wherever I go, will you go with me? Will you be my angel? Sibel smiles. Was that a marriage proposal? If so, what would she say? My God! They finish dinner and her father gets up.

Sibel clears the table and is about to start doing the dishes.

Leave them, he says. Let's take a walk in the park.

A walk in the park? Why? But her father seems fixed on the idea, and Sibel can't refuse.

Her father doesn't say a word as they walk. There's an unusual scent in the air. She wonders: What is this, and where is it coming from?

They walk up to the highest area of the park. It's dark there. There's no one there except for a man sitting on one of the benches; only his silhouette his visible. He turns and looks, and then gets up and starts walking toward them. Sibel doesn't recognize him until he's quite close. But when she does recognize him, she's stunned into silence. It's her uncle. He and her father weren't on good terms. Was it true that ever since the death of Sibel's mother they hadn't spoken? They wouldn't even greet each other. But now they were shaking hands.

It's good to see you, Kemal Bey.

Sibel stands in astonishment, looking at the two men. As she was told, when her mother died, her uncle blamed her father for her death. He shouted: You were the reason my sister died! And they never spoke again. So how could it be that now they were greeting each other like old friends?

Her uncle is sitting on one side of her, and her father on the other. Her uncle gets to the heart of the matter. He pulls out a folded up piece of paper and, shaking it under her nose, asks:

What's this?

Before she even unfolds it, she knows what it is: the letter from Yavuz. She wonders: How did he get it?

I found it, her father says. You dropped it on the floor.

Sibel knows that she needs to pull her thoughts together and figure out how she's going to respond. She doesn't want to just pass it off, or try to apologize. Why should she? And she knows that she can't tell them that it's none of their business. It hasn't yet become common to say things like: This is my life, and I'll do as I please.

We're going to get married, she says.

They probably weren't expecting such a response. They look at each other. Her father is more conciliatory and doesn't give her uncle the chance to vent his rage. He asks: Isn't it a little early to be making a serious decision like marriage? He reminds Sibel about her dreams, saying that he couldn't bear to see her quit her studies at the teachers college.

You always had your sights set high, he says.

And her uncle adds: Did you go to the teachers college just to find yourself a husband?

They talk for over an hour. When one of them falls silent, the other starts speaking; and when he wearies of talking, the other takes over, and in the end they convince Sibel to reconsider her decision.

You're right, Sibel says. I'm going to go through with my studies, all the way to the end. I won't bring any shame on you.

On the way back, her uncle pulls a knife from his pocket and shows it to Sibel.

Just in case you resisted, he says, smiling.

Sibel can't smile in return. She's not afraid, but she does wonder: What if I'd resisted?

For a long while now, there's been a whiteness below that looks like a plain covered in snow. Even the deep blue mountain peaks that jut up through the clouds are far below. The captain announces that we're in the area of Samsun, and says: It's partly cloudy in Ankara, and the temperature is seventeen degrees.

I begin thinking about how I'll approach Haluk and what I'll say to him. The thought that he won't come brings me no comfort; in contrast, it makes me uneasy. It shouldn't be put off, and today with the hearing, everything should be brought to a close. Above all, I have to convince him that I'm not just reacting, that my decision isn't just based on the last unfolding of events. No, it's about everything that's built up inside me, all that I've been forced to forget and suppress. That which was needed for so long, but was postponed over and over, now has to be done.

In places, the thick blanket of cottony clouds has broken apart, and I can see the slopes of mountains. Some of the clouds seem to flow like water bearing along chunks of soft ice.

There's a constant shuddering and roaring that threatens to bring on a headache. Occasionally the plane lurches to the right, and then straightens out again.

So this means that after all these years, I'm driving Haluk from my life. Can I really go through with it? Yes, I can. I'm sorry, Haluk, but this is how it has to be.

The proceedings seem unending. They didn't even give us a place to wait, so we're all gathered in the corridor. We try to rest a little by leaning against the radiators on the wall. Everyone traveled overnight to get here, and we're all tired and sleepless.

If they're not going to listen to us, they why were we summoned? Is making us wait in the corridor some form of punishment?

Was Gürcan Bey also removed from his post as a lecturer?

I ask him: What are you doing these days? But what I mean is: How are you getting by?

Hi wife Sevim had started working at a private school, but it didn't work out. The founding partners were afraid, and the director panicked. They showed her the door, saying: I'm sorry but this was the decision made under martial law, and we have to hold to it.

Gürcan Bey said: I had an interview with a company, but they said that they needed someone with experience, and rightly so. We can't do anything except teach! We teach a few private courses, and we're trying to get by with that.

At that point, I regret that I asked. But didn't I know I'd get an answer like that?

I speak with Leyla Hanım for a while. Then Huriye Hanım comes. She's exhausted. She says: Because of my blood pressure, I can't stand for a long time, and I've started shaking.

She doesn't look well.

I tell her that I'll find a chair for her; what are they trying to do, kill us? I knock on the first door I come to:

I'd like to take a chair.

Everyone in the room looks at each other. It seems they are determined to carry out this punishment.

I say: One of our friends isn't well.

I take the nearest chair, and as I thank them on my way out, they're still staring idiotically at each another.

Huriye Hanım sits down, but she isn't getting any better. Her face is flushed; if she has a heart attack, what are we going to do? She has a cousin in Ankara, so Leyla Hanım decides to take her there. She says: What's the difference? We're nothing in their eyes. They're making us wait here for nothing.

Leyla Hanım knows that she's in danger of being let go when there are just a few months left until she retires. But nothing can be done. Her lawyer is inside, and he'll tell her about the verdict.

After they leave, Haluk asks me: Why did you ask me to come here so quickly?

I've thought a lot about this, Haluk. Don't think that this was a sudden decision. I've thought long and hard about it. We've been through a lot together. But it's time for it to come to an end. I want to go through what's happening now, and what will happen in the future, on my own. I want to get divorced. I hope you can work with me on this.

Haluk doesn't react, though I sense that he's surprised. He says nothing, except: If that's what you want.

I ask: Could you take care of the trial?

Haluk lapses into silence again. It's well past noon, and we're eating sandwiches that one of our colleagues brought.

At three o'clock, our lawyers finally emerge.

Aren't they going to speak with us? Aren't we going to give our statements?

Apparently not.

Then what happened?

It's over. The final decisions have been announced. The same ruling has been made for all the cases:

There is no legitimacy for making a ruling on the case.

What's that supposed to mean?

In unison, the lawyers say: It means you've been acquitted. Exoneration. It's over. The files have been closed.

I'm still in shock. I pull my lawyer aside: Why did they say that, but not say that we were innocent?

It's the same thing, he says. It means that they didn't find anything in the file that could be punishable.

I won't ask you again if you believe it. I know that you're fed up with my suspicions. But I just can't bring myself to believe it.

People congratulate me.

It's over.

I lean my head against the window of the bus, and with every lurch my brain seems to shake in my skull. When I look out the window, all I see is myself. It is a discomforting feeling when I come across myself like that. I need some more time. What I want is just a little more time so that I can get used to myself. Then I know that it'll all be over.

I don't like this bus; I'm going back by plane.

I remember that they served pastries and cherry juice on the plane, and now they're serving tea.

Down below, wisps have begun to flit above the lower layer of thick white clouds. Thinking of my children fills me with longing.

I can see scintillating spots dancing in my field of vision. Is it the altitude? Or am I falling ill?

I could be returning home now, on another plane. The scintillating spots merge with the tingling in my mind.

It must be the altitude.

As I try to stoke a spark of joy within me, the plan for my return which I'd mapped with such zeal just a few days ago falls into tatters, and I find that inexplicable doors of darkness are heaving open.

I'm weary of battling. The war I waged against myself is now drawing to a close and I know that I can no longer bear the captivity to which I voluntarily subjected myself.

Now I know how to fly, and I'm aware that I may teeter and be on the brink of tumbling out of the sky; but that doesn't matter. If I can fly, that means I can learn how to fly even better.

I'm not returning to Izmir, Haluk, and I'm not going to return to that cage you all made for me.

Down below there is a wide river. Those are the waters where the painter washed his brush on the first leg of this journey. It is earth-colored, and green and blue.

It would be impossible to pass over without hurting yourself. And I did hurt myself, I bled; but I managed to get across, passing over and flying off.

For the first time, my grandfather's voice speaks in my thoughts more powerfully than my grandmother's, and it comes from further back in the past:

In the depths of winter the birds would seek shelter in the village coffee house. On the verge of freezing to death, they'd rush in, seeking light and warmth. When they warmed up, they'd want to fly again, but couldn't find the way out. We'd break one of the upper windows of the café. Now, we'd say, either fly out, or stay here for good.

The clusters of clouds are gone now, and down below, reddish-brown hills have begun to appear, flecked here and there with green. The plane shudders as if it struck something. Now the houses aren't so sporadic, and they appear in clumps. But up ahead there is a mountainous cloud awaiting us.

We'll pass through that too.

Tomorrow I'm going to take my resignation letter back from the dean, and I'll dry my red carnation between its pages. But if one day I can no longer fly and I plummet down, if one day I fade away, then the memory of immortality shall live on through that flower.